FOR LOVE OF GLORY

FOR LOVE OF GLORY

A Novel

by
Leslie Fish

Fireship Press
www.FireshipPress.com

FOR LOVE OF GLORY by Leslie Fish

Copyright © 2013 Leslie Fish

All rights reserved. No part of this book may be used or reproduced by any means without the written permission of the publisher except in the case of brief quotation embodied in critical articles and reviews.

ISBN-13: 978-1-61179-2271-3(Paperback)
ISBN -978-1-61179-2272-0(e-book)

BISAC Subject Headings:
FIC027050 FICTION / Romance / Historical
FIC027070 FICTION / Romance / Historical/ Regency
HIS015000 HISTORY / Europe / Great Britain

Editors: Alice Massoglia and Chris Paige
Cover Illustration by Christine Horner

Address all correspondence to:
Fireship Press, LLC
P.O. Box 68412
Tucson, AZ 85737
Or visit our website at:
www.FireshipPress.com

TABLE OF CONTENTS

                ACKNOWLEDGEMENTS

                DEDICATION

CHAPTER 1	UNCERTAIN PROSPECTS	1
CHAPTER 2	ADMIRAL KEITH PROVES OBJECTIONABLE	23
CHAPTER 3	FLORENCE	33
CHAPTER 4	TRIESTE	43
CHAPTER 5	KING TURTLE	53
CHAPTER 6	AMBASSADORS	75
CHAPTER 7	THE CAMPAIGN AT HOME	91
CHAPTER 8	CHARLES GREVILLE & LITTLE EMMA	101
CHAPTER 9	FANNY NELSON	107
CHAPTER 10	CROSS CURRENTS	115
CHAPTER 11	DRAMATIC RIVALRY	131
CHAPTER 12	TRIA JUNCTA IN UNO	145
CHAPTER 13	DAYS OF GLORY	165
CHAPTER 14	SIR WILLIAM'S END	179
CHAPTER 15	ALL AT SEA	185

CHAPTER 16	AN END TO IT	195
CHAPTER 17	WIDOW OF GLORY	201
CHAPTER 18	LOSS	213
CHAPTER 19	DISHONOR	221
CHAPTER 20	THE PRICE OF HOSPITALITY	229
CHAPTER 21	FADED GLORY	241
CHAPTER 22	REPRIEVE IN CALAIS	253
CHAPTER 23	ARREST	259
CHAPTER 24	MOTHER AND DAUGHTER	269

A WORD FROM THE PUBLISHER

At the end of *Bride of Glory*, Emma Hamilton is on her way back to England, pregnant with Horatio Nelson's child, knowing that she must face a storm of controversy and even hostility. Bradda Field meant to write a sequel, but if she did, it never materialized.

When Tom Grundner originally decided to use Fireship Press as a venue for bringing back to light out-of-print books written during and about the Napoleonic era, Bradda Field's book caught his eye. He especially liked that here was the woman's side of a famous story, and a rich, complicated adventure in its own right. But where was the sequel? Readers were left hanging at a most suspenseful cliff's edge!

Fireship commissioned the redoubtable Leslie Fish to write the missing sequel, which Alice Massoglia edited from her knowledge of Regency era style and details. *For Love of Glory* is the result. We at Fireship Press hopes it meets with your approval.

Of course, to find out about England's unsung hero of the war against Napoleon, you'll have to read Tom Grundner's series about Sir Sidney Smith.

DEDICATION

For all the readers of *Bride of Glory* who wondered, "What happened next? How did Emma Hamilton fare?" Here is the rest of her story.

And to all the descendants of Emma Hamilton, whether of blood or of spirit: may you all fare well.

Chapter 1
Uncertain Prospects

The sea was very calm; wavelets barely whispered against the hull of the *Foudroyant* and the soft night breeze scarcely stirred her new sails, pushing the ship but slowly northward through the Tyrrhenian sea, along the sunset shore of Italy. The voyage back to England would indeed be slow and long.

Emma Hamilton, standing by the rail and staring up at the huge half-moon and brilliant stars, wished it might last forever. Though her mother was safely asleep in her assigned cabin, Emma could almost hear Mrs. Cadogan's voice whispering in her ear: "Treasure this time, my gel. Live full every moment, and store it in yer memory to last ye all yer life, for life gets no sweeter nor this, and this time will not come again."

Emma drew a deep breath of the salt-scented breeze, and murmured, "I know."

Of course this time was magical; the first year of the new century, just after the defeat of the French in the Mediterranean —a defeat achieved in the main by the great Lord Nelson—and here was she, sailing home from Naples on the hero's own ship, with himself in command. In command, indeed: not only of the ship but of her heart, for he was her lover. She was mistress to the greatest hero of the age.

LOVE OF GLORY

Surely her life could hold no greater glory than this. Her years as a famed singer, as model to the world-renowned painter George Romney, as wife of England's ambassador to the kingdom of the two Sicilies, as confidante to its queen, who now sailed with them to Livorno—all of this paled in comparison to these few weeks of blissful journeying at her lover's side by day, and in his bed at night, on the way home to his rewards from a grateful nation. Indeed, she would treasure the time.

The ship rolled slightly on a swell, and Emma braced her feet on the deck. The motion made her corset pinch. She should go to her cabin and loosen it... Ah, soon enough she would have to wear it far looser, or abandon it altogether.

That was the one shadow on her contentment. She was ecstatic to be bearing the great hero's child, but how would her husband regard it? Until now Sir William had been most admiring of Lord Nelson, most agreeable to having him live in the Hamilton household, and most amiable concerning the hours Emma spent with him. How might that change when Emma told William that she was carrying a child not his own? And she must tell him soon, before her thickening waist informed him betimes. Her mother had said as much. Nelson had not known what to say, save that he loved her. No one else in the world knew of it, but her pregnancy could not remain secret much longer.

It must be now, Emma decided. If Sir William raged at her, or cast her out despite the scandal, or chose to throw her overboard, at least she would have the memory of these last few glorious days to sustain her anywhere on Earth, in Heaven or in Hell. Squaring her shoulders, she turned and paced toward the fore-cabin door.

Sir William lay drowsing in his bed near the cabin windows, his linen nightshirt sodden, whether with sea-spray or perspiration she could not tell, its damp cloth revealing how his torso had lost flesh in this past year. He looked so thin and old and ill; Emma was struck with pity for him. In the light from the overhead lamp, which doubtless Mrs. Cadogan or Miss Knight had lit before departing, Emma found the basin and ewer in the washing-cabinet. The ewer was partly filled with cool, fresh water, and Mrs. Cadogan had thoughtfully placed some kerchiefs beside it.

Sir William roused as Emma wiped his forehead with a dampened kerchief, and he smiled at her care. "Still a comfort," he murmured. "I'm grateful, Em, that you've still such fondness for such a withering gaffer."

"Say not so, Will'um," Emma responded, her eyes brimming with tears. "Not withering at all. Surely you shall recover your strength, and be hale for many years yet."

"My dear," he said, gripping her hand gently, "I am past three-score-and-ten, and cannot expect many years more. I am but pleased that I am to spend them companioned with such beauty." A sly look crept over his gaunt face. "I recall how shocked Greville was when I chose to wed you. My silly nephew never guessed what a treasure he lost, thinking he'd handed off his mistress in exchange for becoming my heir. He never guessed that I'd the best of the bargain."

"Please, my dear husband..." Oh, he was making this difficult! "I swear, I have been utterly content as your wife, these dozen years and more."

"Even though..." His smile faded. "I've not properly treated you as my wife this past year or so."

Emma felt the tears spilling over, and could think of nothing to say. She had no doubt that Sir William knew, and had known for long, that she hadn't slept alone all those nights, nor had Nelson.

"Come, Emma," he said gently, "why this weeping? Pray tell me."

"I am with child," she whispered.

LOVE OF GLORY

Silence stretched long between them, broken only by the faint susurrus of the quiet sea. Sir William continued to hold her hand, his grip unchanged.

"Ah, 'tis Nelson's, is it?" he said at last.

Emma could only nod her head, scattering tears on the pillow.

William heaved a vast sigh. "I should have expected nothing less," he murmured. "Venus was ever drawn to Mars, the beautiful to the brave. But I shall not be so spiteful as old Vulcan, knowing my work to have been the greater; I have forged kingdoms rather than thunderbolts, and done my part to turn the tide of the Jacobins. I am content with my role."

"You are not angry?" Emma whispered.

"No, no..." William smiled again. "Besides, even the jockey who can no longer ride may take joy in observing the breeding of his best mare to the finest stallion. Indeed, I wish to see that foal. With two such parents, I doubt not that he will accomplish great things."

"Oh, dear William!" Emma pressed his hand to her lips and kissed it many times over. "Surely you are the truest of gentlemen!"

"We'd best travel gently, all the way to England," he noted, "for all our sakes."

*****

The fair weather held, and next morning Sir William felt strong enough to dress and come out on the deck. He made a slow promenade around the ship, Emma at his right hand and Nelson at his left, while the sailors and officers kept respectful silence and distance. He noted the presence of seagulls, remarked at finding them so far from land, quoted some lines from the *Odyssey* concerning the glassy smoothness of the sea, and complimented Emma on the appropriateness of her classic Grecian-styled gown of white muslin.

Nelson, bemused, commented that the ancient vessels had one advantage over the great modern ships of the line, in that they had banks of oars to drive them when the wind failed. "Oh, but were not such oars often manned by poor galley slaves?" Emma countered. "Far more honorable are we of England, whose sails can make use of any wind, and whose crews are all free men. The vilest of the slanders made by the Jacobins was to claim that possessing a king made every Briton a slave."

"Just so," Nelson agreed curtly. "It is the very rights of Englishmen, and the duty incumbent upon them, that makes ours the finest navy in the world."

"The rights of man..." Sir William pondered. "I'd be interested to see what manner of navy England's scions produce. Know you aught of that American sailor, John Paul Jones? I'd heard that he was sent to Russia as advisor to the navy there."

"I regret that I never encountered him," Nelson admitted. "From what I've been able to gather, he was indeed a fine captain, perhaps especially so since his ships were nothing to compare with ours today. I've also heard that, in Russia, his every attempt to improve their navy was opposed by jealous princes and entangled in court politics."

"Ah, that sounds much like our experiences in Italy," Sir William laughed. "I have not the slightest doubt that only your firmness of purpose whipped those squabbling factions into line and saved Naples from the French."

"I could hardly have done it without your excellent help," Nelson demurred. "The French are not the most superior of soldiers, but that Bonaparte fellow is the exception. He is quite competent as a commander, at a time when so few are. And no, I shall say nothing further about the Austrians."

LOVE OF GLORY

Whatever Sir William would have replied was lost in a sudden burst of coughing. The spasm shook his aging frame until, at Emma's insistence, he returned to his cabin and his bed. He chuckled indulgently at Emma's fussing, bade her bring him a book and promised that he'd rest until dinnertime. "Oh, go on," he swept his hands toward the door. "You need not abort your enjoyment of the good weather to wait upon me. Mrs. Cadogan will provide, if I need any service—or Miss Knight, if she is not too busy with the Queen's party."

Emma's mother nodded agreement, then cast a significant glance to the doorway. Needing no further encouragement, Emma retreated back to the deck.

Nelson was there, waiting for her. He took her arm in his and resumed their stroll down the ship's length to its bowsprit.

"I told him about the child," she ventured to say. "He was not at all upset."

Startled, Nelson turned his good eye toward her.

"Indeed," Emma went on, "he said that he was eager to see the offspring of Venus and Mars."

Nelson halted for a moment, pondering that statement, then shook his head and marched on. "I must endeavor to meet Sir William's expectations," he muttered. "You know I do greatly admire the man. I'd not for the world cause him hurt."

"Nor I." Emma drew a deep breath. "My dearest love, though I cannot bear the thought of being parted from you, yet I will not divorce my good Will'um and leave him alone in his old age."

"And I would not ask it." Nelson squared his shoulders. "If I am to remain with you, we must continue as a...*tria juncta in uno*, as Sir William puts it."

Emma pressed a hand to her belly. "Or *quatre*, considering the child."

"A peculiar family, at any rate, one blessed by the ancient gods of Rome."

LESLIE FISH

"But not by the God of the English church," Emma considered. "You shall have a hero's welcome at home, but what greeting shall be mine?"

"We shall be discreet," Nelson said firmly. "You will be protected as the ambassador's wife, and if any doubt that a man of his years could sire a child, well, I believe there is a Biblical quotation concerning a man's virility in age."

"I shall find it, and have it ready to hand," Emma promised.

With that assurance, she turned away from thoughts of the distant future and concentrated on her present happiness. The sea was a deep green-blue, complimenting the perfect blue of the almost clear sky, and the light breeze was faintly scented with the distant pines and flowers of Italy. The ship moved gently as a rocking cradle, and the sun poured golden light like a blessing on all below. And her true love, the great hero who was surely Mars incarnate, paced lovingly by her side. Surely this voyage was as much of Heaven as any mortal could know while still walking the Earth.

Then a shadow slid across the deck as a wisp of cloud crossed the sun, hinting at possible storms ahead.

*****

The storm came early that evening, sudden and blustery. In the aft cabin, Emma and Queen Carolina and her daughters gave up all attempts at their game of draughts, and took to their beds simply to keep from being tossed against the walls. The Queen herself hugged Emma close and moaned about the chance of being drowned before any of them could reach Vienna. Emma tried to reassure her, but the combination of rough seas and pregnancy were upsetting her belly miserably. She was already regretting her dinner, and bitterly envied the princesses their cast-iron stomachs.

LOVE OF GLORY

The girls, treating the movements of the ship as a marvelous adventure, shrieked with excitement at every heave and drop of the deck. Emma only gritted her teeth and pressed a hand to her belly.

Perhaps it was the princesses' screeches that drew him, for the cabin door opened to reveal Nelson himself, looking a bit ragged but confident. "I assure you, miladies," he said, "there is nothing to fear. The ship is sound and tight, we are heading into the wind, and the waves are quite reasonably low. 'Tis an uncomfortable ride, but not a dangerous one—"

At that point the ship bucked like a horse, tossing the women a good six inches in their beds. The lamps in their chains swung wildly. Nelson turned white as a sheet, muttered "Excuse me," turned and hastened back out.

"We are surely doomed!" wailed Queen Carolina, clutching the bedclothes.

"We are surely nauseated," groaned Emma, rolling over on the bed to reach for the bucket stowed handily below. Only the giggling of the princesses gave her the strength to grit her teeth and keep her stomach under control.

She wondered briefly how Sir William, Mrs. Cadogan and Miss Knight were faring, not to mention the Queen's servants below-decks in the much smaller cabins. She was not truly concerned for Nelson, despite his pale look; surely he'd dealt with much worse dangers at sea. Oh, and were the waves tossing the ship a little more gently now?

Yes, surely: long rolling swells instead of sudden sharp impacts. The storm must be moving on, and all she need do was endure for another hour.

By the time the sea quieted it was full night, and even the boisterous princesses were growing sleepy. Queen Carolina was weary and much calmer, enough so that Emma could afford to leave her and go out on deck.

Once out in the fresh air, Emma felt far better. Yes, she decided, once they reached shore she would take her mother's advice to eat cheese and drink milk as often as possible, so as to forestall morning-sickness. Meanwhile she should see how the others fared, and a brief walk along the deck would do her good.

She found Nelson leaning on the rail near the bowsprit, looking ahead into the still-clouded sky and dark sea. He turned to give her an apologetic look as she approached.

"So, Emma," he grimaced, "you've learnt my guilty secret."

"I see no reason for you to be guilty," she said, taking his arm.

"Only one," he laughed. "Would you believe that I, commander and victor of ever so many sea-battles, suffer from...sea-sickness?"

"What?" Emma puzzled. "It has surely not affected your skills, nor cost you any victories."

"Only because no one can fight at sea in the midst of a tossing storm," he grinned. "God has been good to me on that score."

"Might I recommend my mother's physic?" Emma smiled. "Ingest much of cheese and milk, for such tend to anchor the stomach."

"I shall try it indeed, for your mother is a very clever woman." He frowned briefly. "I'd not say as much of Miss Cornelia Knight, though. From what little I've seen of her, she is naught but a terrible gossip."

"Ah, well, I suppose she has little else to do," Emma shrugged. "Since her mother died, she has had no one to turn to but Sir William and me. I have trained her to assist me as Sir William's secretary, but she seems to think the work a bit beneath her."

LOVE OF GLORY

"I," said Nelson, gazing grimly out to sea, "am very tired of those whose social pretensions make them scorn the work that keeps them alive. I've seen entirely too many of that sort."

Emma said nothing, but could make some guesses as to whom he meant.

"This I will say for Queen Carolina's husband," he went on, "old Ferdinand was a boor and more than a little of a fool, but he did not scorn to go among the ordinary folk. Indeed, I've heard he would amuse himself by going out with the fishermen of Naples, hauling on the nets as readily as any of them, and even selling his catch in the streets like a common fishmonger."

"Indeed," Emma remembered, "far from losing respect for his rank, his people adored him for that."

"As my men respect me all the more for my willingness to seize a line or pull an oar at need." He frowned again. "Yet how many naval officers have bothered to follow my example?"

"Any with sense, I should imagine."

"Then there are far too few officers with sense in His Majesty's navy. Too many place social conventions foremost, and efficiency in battle close to last. That, my dear, is what makes me fear for England's future."

Emma clutched his arm fiercely. "Then we must teach them otherwise," she said, "by example, if by nothing else."

*****

At length the *Foudroyant* pulled into the Medici Port at Livorno just at sunset. Sir William observed the HMS *Alexander* at the dock and frowned at what he saw. "I believe Lord Admiral Keith has arrived before us," he commented to Nelson.

"No doubt to scold me for being tardy at obeying his orders," Nelson noted gloomily. "The fact that I won battles thereby will little impress him."

LESLIE FISH

"Then let us put off the confrontation until we've had time to formulate a strategy," said Sir William, putting his spyglass away. "Let off Queen Carolina and her suite first; surely that will take hours by itself, and no doubt she will also seek Keith out to upbraid him for not letting us take her by the sea-route to Vienna, and that will take hours more. That should give us sufficient time."

Nelson laughed shortly, and went to do as Sir William suggested.

Indeed, docking the *Foudroyant* and disembarking the Queen's party took all the next day, giving Nelson and the Hamilton party the advantage of another night on board ship. Lord Keith, Nelson considered, must be fuming like a kettle on the hearth.

"Let him steam," commented Sir William. "The Queen's arrival shall alert the city fathers of Livorno that the famed Lord Nelson is here, and they will give you such a welcome as even Lord Keith must respect."

And so it proved, for on the next morning the entire waterfront was crowded with celebrants. A band of musicians played hymns of welcome with great verve, crowds cheered and threw flowers, and banners proclaimed the adoration of Nelson, Lord of the Sea. One quickly sketched portrait, held up above the crowd, showed him as Neptune, complete with trident.

"Am I to be Neptune or Mars?" Nelson chuckled as he prepared to descend to the dock.

"Whatever the Livornese imagine, make use of it," cautioned Sir William, a few steps behind him. "The last news I read told of French troops uncomfortably close to the city. If your reputation can encourage the Livorno soldiery to oppose them well, then by all means harness and employ it."

"Surely all of Italy loves our gallant commander," Emma breathed, delighting in the scene. She wondered for a moment if there would be an opportunity for her to sing and play

LOVE OF GLORY

harpsichord, or perhaps perform her Attitudes... Ah, but no. Not only would her theatrical poses be considered a bit below the dignity of an English ambassador's wife, but—she glanced ruefully at her belly—her form was no longer slyph-like but rather Junoesque.

"I am a sea-commander," Nelson grumbled, though smiling for the appreciative crowd. "What good would I do in a land-battle?"

"You could rally and order the kingdom's generals, on the force of your character and reputation," Sir William suggested. "One thing I have learned, during all my years in Naples, is that in Italy political influence is everything, and Reason nothing. Smile, my good sir. Smile."

The trio descended the gangplank amid a hailstorm of flower-petals and a thunder of cheers. As they set foot on the dock they were encircled by handsomely-liveried guards and met by a flurry of the splendidly-dressed Livornese nobility, though there was still no sign of Queen Carolina or Lord Keith. Emma and Sir William stepped forward to flank Nelson, effectively insulating him, and enabling them to meet his effusive hosts as his translators. In short order the welcomed trio was bundled into a fine Italian-style state carriage pulled by two splendid, if aging, white horses, and driven up the Via Grande. Their guide, a swarthy little fellow named Guido di Montenegro, who spoke excellent English, happily pointed out the town's landmarks: the Old Fortress, the New Fortress, and the canals and towers designed by the famed architect Bernardo Buontalenti two centuries earlier. Up the road they went at an easy pace, surrounded by cheering crowds.

While di Montenegro momentarily focused his attention on Nelson, Sir William leaned close enough to Emma to whisper to her: "France has prohibited Livorno from trade with England, and by all accounts the city's purse has suffered greatly as a result. I daresay the Grand Duke is eager to show us off to the populace, as an assurance that Livorno will soon be free once again to trade as before."

"We shall not disappoint them, then," Emma pledged.

The ride ended at the Palazzo del Governatore, where the three were assigned sumptuous rooms but given little time to rest, for a grand state dinner had been planned to welcome them, and the Livornese dined early.

Dinner was a lavish affair of ten courses, most of them seafood in various forms. Seating was formally arranged to alternate men with women, so Emma found herself ensconced between Sir William and Nelson, with no opportunity to translate. The mayor's wife, in embroidered green velvet and three ropes of pearls, sat on Nelson's other side and did her best to beguile him with her stiff and limited English. The noise of so many diners made it hard to hear beyond one's neighbor, although Emma tried.

While addressing herself to the steamed prawns in wine sauce, Emma caught mention of Queen Carolina of Naples, and pricked up her ears like a hound.

Her reaction was not lost on Sir William, who leaned closer to his neighbor, a plump woman in orange taffeta, bedecked with emeralds, and questioned her further. When he returned his attention to Emma, his expression was grim. "It seems that Queen Carolina has encountered difficulty," he said quietly. "Far from assisting her on her way to Austria, the Livornese have confined her in the Dogana palace, just across the street."

"What?!" Emma almost dropped her fork. "What possible complaint can the Livornese have against Queen Carolina? She is as staunch an anti-Jacobin as can be found in this world! Do they not know that she swore vengeance for the beheading of her sister, nor that she was instrumental in organizing the defense of Naples? You must tell them, Sir William!"

LOVE OF GLORY

"It is not any transgression of the Queen's that matters," Sir William grimaced. "They hold her in hopes of forcing Lord Nelson to lead them against the French."

"This is intolerable! As if he needed any such prompting to battle the Jacobins! Oh please, Will'um, let us go to the Dogana at once and free Carolina!"

"That, I think, will be easily done." Sir William smiled slyly. "You need but convey the facts to Nelson—ah, but wait until the dinner is ended; he'd want to go immediately, which the Livornese nobility might consider rude. Let us choose the proper moment, my dear."

Emma bided impatiently through the rest of the dinner, scarcely noticing the food she tasted, excellent though it was. At length Nelson noticed, and bent close to ask what troubled her.

"Later, my dear," she whispered, near blushing. "I must wait for Sir William's signal."

Nelson raised an eyebrow at that, but questioned no further. Instead he paid attention to the mayor's wife, who was asking for details on the battle of the Nile, which she dutifully passed on to her husband. Emma caught herself counting the seconds until the slow and sumptuous feast should end.

At length the last dessert dishes were cleared away, and the mayor stood up to make an elaborate toast to Nelson, who accepted it with his usual good grace. The moment he resumed his seat, Sir William lifted his glass and rose to his feet. "Now, Emma," he murmured to his wife.

Emma turned immediately to Nelson and clutched his arm, gaining his instant attention. "I have something to tell you," she whispered. Then, as Sir William solemnly announced his news and intentions in Italian, Emma translated for Nelson. "We've heard that Queen Carolina is here, imprisoned in the Dogana just across the street, held by the Lazzaroni. They hope by this means to compel you to lead them in battle against the French troops. Fear not, love!" she said hurriedly at his darkening frown. "We intend to go there and free her the moment Sir William finishes his speech."

"We shall, indeed!" growled Nelson, flinging down his napkin. He pushed back his chair and rose to his feet just as Sir William was setting down his glass.

"We go!" announced Emma, rising beside him.

The Livornese watched in eager silence as the three turned and marched toward the door. A handful of the city's guards, after a quick signal from the mayor, hurried ahead of them to take up torches and clear their path. The younger men attendant at the feast hastened to follow, and a ferocious buzz of conversation rose behind them.

Once out the main door and into the open air, Emma felt revived and doubly eager. The Dogana across the broad street looked ill-lit and forbidding, but she cared nothing for that. Without realizing that she had done so, Emma took the lead, with Nelson and William falling in behind her. She reached the closed double doors, lifted the bronze ring on the left side one and slammed it imperiously into the wood.

"Open!" she shouted in Italian, "We have come for Queen Carolina!"

Movement in the upper windows made the building seem to blink in surprise. After a brief pause, the door creaked cautiously open. A gaunt man in threadbare shirt and trousers, with a Turkish sword in a scabbard at his waist, peered out. "We shall yield her only to Lord Nelson," he grated.

"And Lord Nelson is here!" Emma retorted.

She turned and pointed to Nelson, who was drawing himself up to his full height with an angry gleam in his good eye. Grasping the situation, he thundered, "I do not make war upon women, and I do not need anyone's urging to battle the French."

Emma translated loudly and clearly, eyes full of adoration.

LOVE OF GLORY

"Well said," Sir William murmured in appreciation. "What excellent opera this would make."

The expression on the scruffy doorman's face showed that he appreciated the scene too. The stirring at the windows revealed that the other Lazzaroni did as well.

"I will, of course, direct the armies of Livorno against the French invaders," Nelson roared on. "Now let us come in to see Queen Carolina, or bring her out here to us. I will see that lady safe, and her family also, before I go against the French. Bring her here, I say!"

Emma could hear eager shouts from beyond the portal, and a moment later the doors were flung wide. The ragged army of the Lazzaroni cheered wildly, and then quickly stepped aside. Down the aisle thus opened, Queen Carolina paced slowly forward. Her satin gown was limp and rumpled, and she looked inexpressibly weary. "Oh, Miledi," she almost whimpered, upon seeing Emma, "is't truly you?"

"It is indeed!" called Emma, spreading her arms wide in welcome. Carolina hastened the last few steps and all but fell against Emma, weeping in relief. As Emma embraced her, the crowd gave a great cheer.

"We shall return to the Palazzo del Governatore," Sir William announced as the Lazzaroni paused to draw breath, "where we shall begin planning immediately the rout of the French troops."

The crowd cheered again, echoed by the smaller crowd of Livornese crowding the doorway, as Emma drew Queen Carolina out onto the porch and down the stairs. Behind her, her daughters and servants, dutifully dragging the party's luggage, hastened out the door behind her. The cheering continued as the whole party returned to the Palazzo, where they were met by louder cheers from the guests at the feast. Queen Carolina managed to draw herself up for a moment and give a queenly courtesy to the assembled nobility, but she whispered to Emma, "Oh quickly, take me to whatever room the mayor has given you, for I am so overcome as to feel faint."

Emma dutifully half-led, half-supported the Queen up the stairs to her bedchamber, while other household servants quickly steered the princesses and their retinue to other guest-rooms. Nelson and Sir William proceeded onward to the banquet hall, already making plans for the attack upon the French. Emma, leaving such details to the men, helped the Queen into her chamber and closed the door. She gave quick orders to the waiting chambermaid and assisted Carolina onto the bed.

Relieved of duty and alone with her friend, Carolina burst into tears. "Oh, Emma!" she wept. "I feared I'd never see freedom again. How could they treat me so, when God knows I've done all in my power to oppose the French? Indeed, I came here in hopes to proceed to Vienna and enlist more aid from my kinsmen. Instead I was seized by low ruffians who dare claim that they oppose the French. Oh, is there no justice in this world?"

"There is indeed," Emma soothed, dampening a kerchief from a nearby ewer. "All they wished was to entreat Nelson, and knew not how little such entreaty was needed."

"Nor, it would seem, how to treat a lady in delicate health," Carolina sniffled. "I must go on to Austria now, Miledi, though I am sick at heart, sick unto death, for I've heard worse news."

"What could that be, pray?"

"Why, that Napoleon is on the march in Italy again, and but yesterday he defeated the Austrians at Marengo. Oh, how shall I go on? I am too weak, too close to the grave, to go about the eastern Empires imploring them to lay down their petty quarrels and unite against France. Oh, would to God that there were someone who could do it for me!"

LOVE OF GLORY

"There, now." Emma pressed the damp kerchief to the Queen's forehead. "You are safe, and among friends. We will come with you, and shall not let your mission fail."

"Dearest Emma," Carolina murmured, and almost instantly fell asleep.

Emma sighed and sat down on the bed, took one of the aging Queen's hands in hers and patted it comfortingly. She might have to sit with Carolina until late, and no doubt Nelson and Sir William would be ensconced with the Livornese nobles that long. Yet she must stay awake long enough to give Nelson and Sir William the news about Marengo. There would be no chance to lie in her beloved Nelson's bed tonight. But then, she had accomplished a bold rescue. No doubt the Livornese would sing of it for generations to come, linking her name to Nelson's glory. For this, if nothing else, she would be dearly remembered.

*****

Queen Carolina required a day's rest to recover, during which time Emma made certain that the Livornese provided her with sufficient guards. While the Queen regained her strength, Emma informed Sir William of what she'd learned. Meanwhile Nelson took his flag and baggage off the *Foudroyant*. Emma learned from palace sources that Admiral Keith had ordered Nelson back out to sea to join the fleet, but that Nelson had remained in the city at Sir William's behest and that of Queen Carolina. Admiral Keith, not impressed by a mere ambassador and a foreign queen, threatened to come ashore and demand an explanation. Meanwhile, Sir William had Nelson attending various meetings with the rulers of Livorno. When not closeted with generals and the nobility, Nelson took refuge in Emma's rooms. Sir William, when not engaged as

Nelson's translator, made an effort to study the art abounding in Livorno.

In the sweltering afternoon of the third day, Nelson lay on the divan in Emma's chamber, stripped to his smallclothes, continually wiping his face with a dampened kerchief, but smiling despite his discomfort. "All's well, truly," he explained. "Livorno already had sufficient ships to keep its own waters safe, and sufficient troops—especially stiffened with all those enthusiastic volunteers from the Lazzarone—and competent enough officers to proceed against the French. All they needed was someone to take them in hand, order them to give up their petty political squabbles for the nonce, and make them all move in the same direction. They needed me for that, simply because —being an outsider and not inclined to any of their factions—I could be trusted to give equal treatment to all of them. I was but a figurehead, in truth. I swear, Emma, I don't know how Sir William has so patiently endured Italian politics all these years."

"He says it gives him insights into the workings of the ancient court of Byzantium," Emma laughed, taking the kerchief from him. "Truly, experience as the ambassador's wife has made me appreciate the straightforward nature of England's politics."

"Straightforward only in comparison to Italy, which is no recommendation," Nelson grimaced. "How fares Queen Carolina?"

"Much recovered," said Emma, wetting the kerchief afresh. "She plans to proceed on to Vienna in another day or two, and begs us to accompany her."

"What does she intend in Austria?" Nelson asked, taking the freshened kerchief from her.

"To confer with her royal kinfolk on strategies to contain France, and," Emma admitted, "arrange suitable marriages for the last of her children. She might also look to securing a safe retreat for the Italian Royals in Vienna, should the French take all of Italy."

"Yes," Nelson sighed, "We cannot discount that possibility. Bonaparte's star is rising, and heaven only knows how far it will take him."

"I must ask, Horatio," Emma dared, "could we join her in her mission, and go overland to Vienna? Surely Sir William's work is more important than your returning to the fleet."

"It is quite certainly so, and Keith must be made to admit to it." Nelson rubbed his forehead, then favored Emma with a keen look. "Sir William has much chatting to do with crowned heads in Austria, and Prussia, and Saxony, and as many of the small states in the west as possible."

Emma smiled in understanding. The more states Sir William visited, with his pretty wife and showpiece hero in tow, the longer the journey home would take. She considered how much her pregnancy would show by the time they reached England, and mentally catalogued her gowns accordingly. The new neo-Grecian fashion would conceal a middle-term pregnancy nicely enough.

"One thing, I confess, I do not understand." Nelson fanned his face with the damp kerchief, hoping to stir the air a little. "Given the French propensity for lopping off any crowned head they find, one would think that every such head in Europe would be united firmly against France. Yet they squabble and jockey among themselves, forsaking unity for the sake of an inch of gain over the nearest neighbor. I feel that I am watching fools who will brawl in a burning house rather than form a bucket-line to put the fire out. I am but a simple sailor, yet even I have a better sense of perspective than that."

"Simple sailor, indeed!" Emma laughed, trailing a teasing fingertip across his chest. "You are the hero of the age, my love, and don't forget it."

"How can I, when you remind me so well?" Nelson smiled and caught her hand. "Or when Sir William parades me, like a caparisoned war-horse, before all those addled crowned heads. He uses me, I know, as a showpiece to strengthen his argument. Indeed, I'm happy to be so used, if it gains England the alliance he seeks."

For a moment Emma caught a fleeting glimpse of Sir William's plan, saw how Nelson figured as a game-piece in it, and even how she might be a game-piece herself, used to keep Nelson close and biddable. For an instant she wondered if even Sir William's absence from her bed these two years past had been calculated... But then she indignantly cast the thought aside. No, Sir William's lack of passion was surely no more than the natural failure of age; he was, after all, nearly seventy.

But Nelson was speaking again. "Aye," he said, "Sir William, with Carolina's help, will surely persuade Keith. We shall go on to Vienna, and then wherever else Sir William may wish: the sea-hero and the lovely flower of England. Whether as warrior and secretary or as showpieces to bedazzle crowned fools, we shall yet do our part."

He closed his eyes, and for a moment Emma thought he was asleep. But as she stretched out beside him he opened his good eye and gave a roguish grin. "Choose your gowns to best bedazzle, my lovely, and train your sweet voice, and practice your art poses..."

"I call them Attitudes," she reminded him.

But his eye had closed, and he slid surely into sleep.

Chapter 2
Admiral Keith Proves Objectionable

It was Emma's mother who first saw Admiral Keith's jollyboat coming toward shore, for she had gotten into the habit of watching the harbor with a spyglass in the event of just such a situation. She wasted no time hunting down Emma, who was in the garden having tea with Lord Nelson.

"Emma, my dear," Mrs. Cadogan said, dropping a quick curtsy to Nelson, "you and the good captain here must hurry to the side of Sir William and Queen Carolina, for I've espied the Admiral Lord Keith a-rowing to shore."

Nelson gave Mrs. Cadogan a respectfully raised eyebrow, then turned to Emma. "Just so, my love. 'Tis best we meet him all together, and present a united front."

Thus when the admiral came marching into the Palazzo a quarter-hour later, demanding shortly to see Lord Nelson, he was directed to the privy chamber. On opening the door he was flummoxed to see not just Nelson, or even Nelson and Emma, but the two of them accompanied by Sir William and Queen Carolina. He was obliged to bite back the sharp complaint on his lips; one could not call Lady Hamilton a whore in front of her husband—not to mention the Queen of Naples and Sicily—

especially as that husband was the Crown's ambassador to Naples. He restrained himself to only posing the somewhat cold question: "Sir, why have you not returned to the fleet, as I commanded?"

"Because," Nelson replied smoothly, "that order was overridden by other orders from a superior officer—to whit, the ambassador." He turned to look at Sir William, who only smiled and nodded.

Lord Keith opened his mouth, shut it again, and grew red about the jowls. "And just what orders are those, sir?" he finally managed, turning to Sir William.

"Why, to conduct our ally, Queen Carolina"—he turned to the Queen, who inclined her head—"safely upon her mission to Vienna by way of Florence, then Ancona, then Trieste, and then to accompany me northward to Prague,"—Sir William counted off on his fingers as he continued—"Dresden, Dessau, and then Hamburg, whence we shall take sail for England."

Lord Keith, in Emma's estimation, was swelling up like a bullfrog. She almost feared he would burst from the excess of blood darkening his cheeks.

"And for what possible purpose," the Admiral grated, "do you take a naval officer away from his proper place at sea to accompany you and…and…"—he caught himself at the last minute—"to go overland on this grand tour across Europe, swanking it at every fashionable waterhole, rather than attending to his naval duties?"

Nelson scarcely raised an eyebrow. "My orders from the Crown were simply to return home," he said. "No mention was made of what route I should take."

"And my intention," added Sir William, hardening his voice, "is to make use of the gallant commander's presence and reputation to stiffen the resolve of our allies, for some of them have wavered lamentably in their opposition to France. I daresay, when they see Lord Nelson himself, the only man who has ever defeated Napoleon, and hear from his own lips his accounts of defeating the French Navy in diverse battles, they will be both more heartened in their resistance and more reliable in their unity. Achieving that unity, sir, is my mission—and I need Lord Nelson's presence to accomplish it." His tone brooked no argument.

Lord Keith tried another tactic. "Are you aware," he said, "that Napoleon is abroad in Italy? That he defeated the Austrians but two days ago, and now threatens the road to the port of Ancona? How do you intend to get past his troops safely?"

There Queen Carolina spoke up. "The overland journey would not have been necessary," she said tartly, "if you had kept to England's agreement with us. You should have taken us—and indeed the ambassador's party—safely to the port of Vienna upon an English ship, such as Lord Nelson's."

"By our alliance," Sir William added, "the Queen must be conducted safely."

Lord Keith turned from one to the other, like a bull being baited by dogs. "I have no such orders!" was the best he could manage. "If you are fixed on this course, you must go overland—and Nelson must give over his flag!"

"I beg your pardon?" said Nelson, raising an eyebrow.

"On land, you are no naval commander!" Keith snapped, stamping his foot. "Remove your baggage from the *Foudroyant*, sir, and yield your flag to me!"

Right there, Emma saw what was happening. Keith could not drag Nelson away from Sir William—and her—so he soothed his pride by making certain he could claim, as could no other commander in the world, that he had made Nelson strike his colors. Another effect of this was to deprive Nelson of his emblem of office, and thus prevent him from commandeering any British ship he might come across and doing yet more daring deeds. It was a petty insult, not an injury.

LOVE OF GLORY

Unless, of course, Keith actually hoped that Nelson—and the Hamiltons, and even Queen Carolina—would meet with Napoleon's troops on the way to Trieste. Should Nelson be captured or killed, Keith would conveniently and easily be rid of a troublesome rival.

Then again, it was possible that Sir William, Nelson and Queen Carolina among them could raise enough troops here in Tuscany to defeat Napoleon's army. What might that add to Nelson's military reputation? She thought that perhaps Keith's plans were a bit shortsighted, and could play well to her lover's advantage.

With this in mind, she stroked Nelson's hand soothingly, and he was not slow to take her meaning.

"So be it," he shrugged. "I've already brought my gear ashore and my aide as well. I shall send the mayor's guard to deliver the pennant at once."

"The mayor's guard?!" huffed Keith, "No! I cannot allow that some Italian soldier should touch an insignia of the English navy!"

"What of an Italian Queen?" said Carolina, leaning forward as if she would rise from her chair. "Lord Nelson, pray give me the banner, and I shall hand it to this good Admiral myself."

Keith seemed on the verge of apoplexy, but succeeded in holding his tongue. Nelson took pity on him. "Don't trouble yourself, your majesty," he said, rising. "I have the pennant in my own apartments—"

Keith flinched visibly.

"—and shall fetch it myself at once. If you will excuse me, Sir William?"

"Of course," murmured the ambassador, keenly studying Admiral Keith.

Nelson departed, leaving Keith alone with the ambassador and the two women.

"What complaint have you," Sir William promptly pounced, "concerning Lord Nelson's bringing his flag with him? Certainly such is allowed under naval law, as I have had occasion to see."

"It is not commonly done," Keith murmured, shooting a glance of pure hatred at Emma.

Emma had a sudden vision of Lord Nelson personally taking the pennant to the *Alexander*, Lord Keith's men seizing him the moment he set foot on board the ship, and Keith dragging Nelson back to England in chains. Had Nelson, or Sir William, guessed that some such intrigue might happen?

And now Queen Carolina spoke up, addressing herself to the ambassador. "By your leave, sir," she smiled sweetly, "I shall call for my servants to pack my suite and your own upon sufficient carriages. I assure you, they shall be wonderfully swift. We have, after all, often performed this maneuver before."

Upon his nod of assent she lifted the tiny bell off Sir William's desk and rang it. The door opened instantly, and a liveried Livornese servant was revealed—standing between a pair of tall, muscular and well-armed city guards. Queen Carolina gave her orders quickly and clearly, in Italian. The man bobbed assent and closed the door again. Admiral Keith looked as if he'd bitten into an unripe lemon.

Emma, understanding the message conveyed by the small byplay, was hard put not to laugh. Yes, Nelson, Queen Carolina and Sir William had, among the three of them, thought of everything.

Lord Keith glowered, but said nothing further.

Before Carolina had quite returned to her chair, Nelson returned with the pennant, rolled and cased, in his arms. He held it out to the admiral, who had no choice but to take it. "Here you are, then," Nelson smiled. "No doubt we we shall meet again, in London."

"In London," Keith promised, rising to his feet.

LOVE OF GLORY

Queen Carolina stepped forward and brazenly took Nelson's arm. "Shall we go, then?" she purred. "There is somewhat that I would say to the good folk of Livorno, and your presence would greatly assist me."

Nelson gave her a wink, and escorted her out the door. Admiral Keith looked at Sir William, glared at Emma, then hastily followed the other two out the door as if unwilling to let Nelson out of his sight.

"That was neatly done," said Sir William, as the door closed behind the others. "My dear Emma, you must understand that you have a determined enemy in that man."

"I am aware of it," Emma replied.

"And so, of course, does Nelson. Lord Keith has already spread slanders about the two of you through the Admiralty—which is, no doubt, why he was promoted over Nelson when Jervis departed. He will surely do more when he returns to England before us."

"What is to be our counter-strategy, then?"

"Our surest strategy," Sir William smiled, "is to return to England covered with glory. Being without a ship at the moment, Nelson's best hope for achieving that is to assist in my campaign through Europe. When he comes home with such a victory on land to supplement his victories at sea, Keith will be able to do naught but gnash his teeth in frustration, for Nelson will be unassailable."

"Let us hope that it will indeed be such a victory as you foresee, Sir William," Emma frowned, "for I do know, as just one example, that the Danish merchants dislike our prevention of their trade with France."

"Alliances never hold for long," Sir William sighed, "but I expect to make one that will last long enough to give us eventual triumph. And now, my dear, we should make haste to proceed overland to Florence before Keith can come up with new tricks."

LESLIE FISH

*****

On the 12th of July, Queen Carolina and her suite departed for Florence. Her retinue included 14 coaches, 4 baggage-wagons, a company of the Tuscan army and a countless number of Lazzarone, armed with anything they could find and spoiling for a fight.

The Nelson-Hamilton household quietly followed the caravan the next day: Sir William, Emma, and Nelson riding in a fine coach, with Mrs. Cadogan and Miss Knight. Nelson's aide, Tom Allen, followed in a covered wagon, which carried the baggage and was guarded by yet another detachment of the Tuscan army. It was, Emma considered, as if the army was using the Queen's and the Ambassador's parties as the excuse to scout their route for the French.

The road from Livorno to Florence was well kept, but the wind still was dust-laden, so the coach windows had to be kept closed, despite the stifling July heat. At one point the captain of their Tuscan guard reported that French patrols had been sighted within a mile, and Nelson perked up in hope of some excitement, but the battle never materialized and the overland journey went swiftly.

Emma pulled back the window curtains to admire the passing scenery of beautifully cultivated farmland. Mrs. Cadogan kept busy with her embroidery hoop, and Miss Knight with her journal. Sir William regaled Nelson with analyses of the political obstacles that they might soon encounter.

"The trouble with the whole Empire," he gloomed, "is that the Habsburg line is woefully inbred. Even marrying into the Lorraine dynasty hasn't helped, for the Lorraines are little better. To our advantage they have no love for the Jacobins and happily oppose France, but they've become weak and indecisive —and often terribly stupid. They leave much of the business of

LOVE OF GLORY

ruling to their courtiers, who are a contentious self-serving lot, and to their generals. Fortunately, their generals do seem to have good sense about the business of fighting wars, and the courtiers are frightened enough of the Jacobins—and Bonaparte—to let the generals have their way. Thus, it is the generals above all whom we must persuade, and there, my dear Nelson, you shall be invaluable."

Emma roused from her contemplation of the landscape to note: "The Bourbon dynasty of France married far and wide, yet t'was the French royal house that fell to revolution, thereby causing us all this trouble."

"King Log, King Turtle and King Heron," Sir William chuckled. "Have you never heard that fable?"

"I have," said Nelson. "According to Aesop, there was once a pond-full of frogs who wanted a king, so the gods indulgently tossed them a log—which, of course, did nothing but float about the pond, providing a convenient bench."

"A Wooden Idle!" Sir William laughed at his own pun.

"Of course, the log did nothing to protect the frogs from being eaten by the occasional water-snake, so the frogs petitioned the gods again," Nelson continued. "This time the gods tossed them a turtle. The turtle did well at driving away the snakes, but otherwise he did nothing, and the frogs deemed him a dull and stupid fellow, so they petitioned the gods again. By now the gods were annoyed at the pesky frogs, so they brought in a heron—who promptly proceeded to eat the frogs. But how does this relate to the royal dynasties of Europe, Sir William?"

"Why, in that the attenuated line of the Lorraine-Hapsburgs are King Turtle," the ambassador smiled. "They are generally dull and stupid fellows, but—let us hope—they are good enough at defending their folk from various snakes. For that very reason they don't offend their own people, and therefore the populace is content under their rule. Ah, but the Bourbons are a fierce and vigorous lot, ever grasping for more power, for more control of every aspect of their land and people, and as such they prey upon their own subjects—thus, King Heron. The French populace rebelled first out of desperation, then for vengeance, and now for ambition. Had the Jacobins remained within their own borders, I daresay none would have raised a hand against them. But now, with Bonaparte at their head, they go out to seize all of Europe; now the turtle-kings have no choice but to rouse and unite."

"I believe I can persuade the turtles to snap," Nelson smiled. "How long yet to Florence?"

"We should be there tomorrow," Mrs. Cadogan spoke up. "We 'shall spend yet another night at an inn."

"The rustic comforts of Tuscan inns are quite sufficient," Emma smiled, thinking of the night to come.

"Let us but hope," Sir William murmured, "that the Lorraine-Hapsburgs of Austria are still King Turtle, and haven't backslid to being King Log."

Chapter 3
Florence

Queen Carolina's party reached Florence safely and gave word of Nelson's coming, alerting the crowds to turn out to welcome his caravan. The only difference between this welcoming party and the Livornese version was that the Florentine crowd was dressed in a slightly more militant style, and the cheers were harsher. Sir William noted it too.

"Florence has more history of independence than Livorno," he explained, "and more pride, being the capital of all Tuscany. Florence has been a free republic more than once. They endured the rule of the Medicis solely because of the wealth and glory they brought. When the Medicis died out, the Florentines grudgingly accepted the rule of the dynasty of Lorraine; they had been mollified by the marriage of the Lord Lorraine to the Empress Maria Theresa of Austria, last of the Habsburgs, which effectively made him co-ruler of the Empire. They are stalwart in their opposition to France. We need fear no lack of support for our cause here."

"Pull back the curtains, milord Nelson," said Emma, "and open the windows. Let the loyal crowd see you."

LOVE OF GLORY

Nelson obliged, leaning out the right-hand window, and Emma leaned out the other, blowing kisses. She had dressed lightly for the July heat, in a short-sleeved muslin Empire gown, and only a few jingling gold bracelets adorned her arms. The Florentines cheered more loudly.

As their coach passed within the great city walls the crowds thickened, slowing the progress of the caravan. This gave the Hamilton party time to observe the splendid architecture and abundant public statuary of the city, at which Emma gasped in admiration. Even Nelson was impressed. Sir William smiled at their reaction.

"Were you not aware," he said, "that Florence is the source of the Italian Renaissance? Or that it is one of the most beautiful cities in the world? Look there..." As he went on to describe the monuments and arts of Florence, Emma smiled indulgently. Lord Hamilton was in his element, and she knew that if he had his way, not a few *objets d'art* would find their way into his keeping before they departed Florence.

As they proceeded up the broad avenue, the guards and driver moving them readily to their destination, Sir William pointed out one splendid landmark after another: elegant piazzas, palazzos, fountains and churches, the River Arno and its magnificent bridges, and finally—when the leading guard drew them to a halt—the famed Piazza della Signoria, where a row of bejeweled officials stood waiting to greet them.

As the coach stopped, Sir William surveyed the welcoming party with a practiced eye. "My dear Nelson," he said, "pray do you step out first, take two steps forward and bow to the officials. Then wait as Emma and I step out after you. We shall then approach the assembly in our usual formation."

Nelson complied, being well used to such formal theatrics by now, and the trio marched gravely into the effusive welcome of the city fathers. The speeches, which Sir William translated with commentary, were mercifully short and mostly expressions of enthusiasm for the victories of England. Nelson bowed solemnly, then quietly asked Sir William, "How shall I reply?"

"You may discourse upon the flowers of Canterbury, if you wish," smiled William. "Only pause after each sentence, so that I appear to translate whilst I make my appeal for solid alliance."

Nelson grinned, and began reciting the list of his commands, ships and battles. Sir William solemnly recited, in the Tuscan dialect of Italian, his set piece about the importance of the civilized peoples of Europe standing united against barbarous France and its upstart leader, Bonaparte. Emma turned her most dazzling smile on the company around, and observed the adoring expressions of the audience.

At length the ceremony concluded to the thunderous cheers of the assembled Florentines, and an under-official stepped forward, offering to guide them to their lodgings. Nelson and the Hamiltons returned to their carriage and let the guide and their guardsmen conduct them away. Much to Sir William's delight they were escorted to nothing less than the huge Palazzo Pitti, former residence of the Medicis. Queen Carolina was there to greet them, and soon was gossiping happily with Emma.

Once accompanied to their elegant suite of rooms, the party was left alone to rest. "This shall be a longer respite than the Livornese gave us," Sir William noted, "but only because we shall be expected to attend a grand formal banquet tomorrow. From what I have heard of Florentine custom, we may expect it to last all the afternoon and well into the night. I would strongly recommend that we eat but lightly in our rooms this evening, fast next morning, and visit the privy just before we go to dinner."

Emma couldn't help it: she sank onto a velvet-covered divan and brayed with laughter. "Oh, Will'um," she panted between gusts, "I'd best fast between all banquets hereafter, lest I grow fat as an elephant on formal hospitality."

"And I had best hunt out my most generously cut vest and breeches for tomorrow," Nelson smiled. "Hmmm, and I should lay out all my decorations, lest I look drab as a crow compared to these fine birds."

"Certainly," said Sir William, looking fondly around at the carved walls and artfully painted ceiling. "Begging your pardon, but I simply must take advantage of our situation to study the artistic treasures of the palace, for 'tis said to be a fine-art museum and gallery all in itself, and I cannot wait to view its collection."

With that, he went to the door of the suite, opened it and requested the assistance of the footman waiting outside. As he left, Mrs. Cadogan turned from the task of unpacking the party's trunks and went to Emma. "We shall be busy indeed settling your gear in here for a time, lovey," she said. "Best that you and milord retire to one of the sleeping-chambers." She kept her face properly expressionless, with never so much as a wink. Miss Knight promptly carried an armload of gowns into Emma's and Sir William's bedchamber, and didn't glance behind her.

Nelson and Emma looked at each other, clasped hands and wordlessly proceeded to the inner room. The door closed behind them, and Mrs. Cadogan could clearly hear the key as it turned in the lock.

"Aye, be happy whilst you can, my dears," she whispered. "Enjoy your time."

*****

The Florentine formal banquet the next day was every bit as elaborate and artistic as one might expect from such a city. It began with a reception, where Queen Carolina, Sir William,

Emma and Nelson stood and shook hands with what seemed to be hundreds of the gentry, all of whom attempted at least a few words of English to Nelson. Then there was the parade into the dining hall and the arrangement of seating. Queen Carolina sat between the mayor and Nelson and happily translated their conversation, with Emma to assist. There were no less than a dozen courses, each accompanied by a toast from a different official, and almost as many wines and cordials. The dishes were exquisite, of course, but by now neither Emma nor Nelson needed to be warned to taste only a little of each. The dinner was accompanied by music from a highly accomplished string quartet seated in a classic minstrel's gallery at the second-floor level. The meal dragged on for hours, and by the dessert course —a beautifully decorated lemon torte—Emma was very grateful for Sir William's warnings.

At last, with the dining ended, the mayor stood to make a last brief speech, and the assembly departed, first for the Necessary Rooms, as the Florentines quaintly called them, and then for the elaborately decorated concert hall, where a comic opera was given its maiden performance. Except for the physical comedy, Nelson understood little of it, despite the Queen's and Emma's rapid *sotto-voce* translations. He did, however, enjoy the music, and applauded as hard as any at the conclusion.

After that the company moved to the gambling tables, where the real business of political gossip would take place. Emma remained at Nelson's side, taking care to wager but little, and slowly, while Sir William sauntered from table to table, speaking with various nobles, as did Carolina. A gray-whiskered gentleman in the full dress of a Tuscan admiral made a point to sit in at Nelson's table. He barely glanced at his cards before beginning a friendly barrage of technical questions—relayed through Emma to Nelson—concerning his battles. Nelson was delighted to answer in the same vein, and Emma was often

LOVE OF GLORY

hard-pressed to find translations for the English naval terms. At length, Nelson gave up his card game entirely, and used the cards to represent ships as he illustrated various maneuvers on the tablecloth, much to the amusement of the assorted onlookers.

Eventually, an elaborately-dressed herald announced a spectacle to be viewed from the rear balcony, and the company rose and moved there. The view from the balcony included a splendid formal garden, at the rear of which was erected a long platform, and on it stood models of full-rigged ships bearing French and English flags, mounted like puppets on a field of blue cloth. After a brief trumpet-blast, fireworks shot up from behind the platform, and the model ships began jigging toward each other.

"Not precisely an accurate rendition," Nelson murmured, "but prettily done."

The fireworks, ever more complex and gorgeously colored, upstaged the puppet-show on the platform, where French-flagged ships one by one descended behind the blue cloth. The crescendo was a sky-full of fire-flowers, at which point all but one of the remaining model ships—that one bearing the English flag—disappeared. As darkness and natural stars reclaimed the sky, the audience applauded enthusiastically and the string quartet struck up an ornamented version of "God Save the King."

"Not the most politic of tunes, given the state of our king," Sir William muttered, "but 'twill serve, 'twill serve."

The mayor and his wife departed with due ceremony, signaling an end to the festivities, and the other guests prepared to leave as well. The Carolina/Hamilton party, in its usual formation, moved out slowly enough to accept last-minute greetings and messages.

It was well past midnight by the time they returned to their apartments in the Palazzo Pitti. Queen Carolina hastened off to speak with her daughters, who were much annoyed at not having been invited to the banquet, for all that their mother had promised that their formal Coming Out would be in Vienna. Sir William made haste to get out of his shoes and clothing, and sent Mrs. Cadogan for a basin of warm salt water to soothe his feet. "Many more such amusements, and I am undone," he groaned.

"I scarcely would have thought," Nelson agreed, shrugging out of his coat with Emma's help, "that a day of feasting would be as strenuous as a day at sea, but now I've observed it with my own eyes—and my own stomach."

"It is as if Florence vies with Livorno to celebrate our hero to the greater extreme," said Emma, unfastening the bodice-ribbon of her gown. "Still, I should count the day successful for the knowledge conducted both ways, if naught else."

"True enough," said Sir William, rubbing his foot. "The Tuscans are eager to fight Bonaparte's troops, and indeed they glower at the timidity of the Austrians. There is even a faction that supports the Bourbon-Parma dynasty, and who would cast out the Lorraine-Habsburgs and pursue a fiercer course against France. I cannot swear that the Bourbon-Parmas would make better rulers, but perhaps the threat of them might bestir the Austrian crown to stronger action. In any case, I must send dispatches as swiftly as possible."

At that moment Mrs. Cadogan returned with a steaming basin and some towels.

"Ah, put it there, under my writing-desk," directed Sir William. "I must write some letters quickly, and would rather do so in comfort. As for you two—" he waved a brief hand at Nelson and Emma, "—be off, and get what rest you can. I expect there shall be more work tomorrow."

He hobbled over to the writing-desk, where Mrs. Cadogan had thoughtfully placed the basin, and did not so much as

LOVE OF GLORY

glance in their direction as Nelson and Emma quietly padded off into the same bedchamber.

*****

The party took two more days to finish with Florence, visiting galleries and churches, piazzas and palaces by day, attending formal entertainments by night. Sir William took the lead in these excursions, discussing far more than art and architecture with his assorted hosts, while Nelson trailed behind him with Emma on his arm. Nelson was content to follow the ambassador's lead, indulging in the beauties of the city by day, and in Emma's arms by night. Mrs. Cadogan warned Emma that her waist was thickening, and not just with her advancing pregnancy, so Emma took care to eat nothing but fruit outside of the formal dinners the trio attended.

At length Sir William announced that it was time that they move on to Trieste, and they left the city in the same formation as that in which they had arrived: Queen Carolina and her guards first, the Hamilton party following. They left the city by way of the northeastern road in two swift coaches, accompanied by the fond farewells of the Florentine gentry and a large company of Florentine guards, but this time the journey was not as easy.

The mountain air of the Apennines was much less dusty, but the roads were in serious disrepair. A hard lurch into a rut overturned the Hamiltons' coach, which was universally disturbing, but in the end no one suffered worse than bruises. The accompanying troops soon set the coach upright again, but its wheels now rattled ominously, and it at last broke down completely—fortunately near an inn—at Arezzo. By now Sir William was fretting at the time lost, and the amount by which Queen Carolina's party had outdistanced theirs. He commandeered their second coach for his immediate party,

LESLIE FISH

leaving Mrs. Cadogan and Miss Knight with the broken coach in the town, arranged for its repair and bade the two women follow to Ancona as soon as they might. He did supply them with a sufficient purse to speed them on their way, but this mollified Miss Knight only a little. Sir William, Nelson and his aide, and Emma pressed on, along with the majority of the loaned troops, as fast as they could.

During the first few days of the long journey Sir William buried his attention in a book, being distracted only by his worry that the Queen might have sailed for Trieste without them. As the party descended from the central mountains into the long flat northern farmlands, Emma noticed that he grew ever more notably agitated. She was concerned by this, even as she pointed out to Nelson the beauties of the legendary vineyards and olive groves they passed and the towering snow-peaks of the Alps in the far northern distance. Still, she kept a respectful silence with Sir William, knowing that he would unburden himself when he thought the time was right, and not before.

At length, while staying in a well-appointed inn on the night before they would reach Ancona, Sir William drew the both of them into his private chamber and gave them his warnings.

"Despite all we have done, and will do yet, in Trieste," he said, "I fear that Italy shall yet fall to the French. The Tuscan states produce fierce fighters, but its generals are still promoted by favoritism rather than merit. Bonaparte is ambitious, ruthless, and most dangerously competent. At best, Italy can but slow his advance while the empire in Austria prepares to receive him. The best that we can do is to hasten Austria's preparations, for if Austria cannot contain him, the burden shall fall upon Russia—and I have no idea what the czar will do. At present, he maintains the Armed Neutrality, which benefits the French. England's part must be to harry Napoleon's ships at sea—every sea that we can reach—for if we can block its trade,

LOVE OF GLORY

France cannot maintain an army of conquest. This will be a long hard war of attrition, and we must hearten our allies to endure it. I need hardly add, you must mention nothing of this in Trieste."

"France has threatened all of Europe for more than ten years," Emma protested. "Surely it cannot continue at such a pace for many years more."

"With the booty of Spain, and then Italy, I fear that it can," Sir William predicted gloomily. "It may indeed take ten more years, or even fifteen, before the threat of France is abated. I only pray I may live long enough to see that, and do my best to hasten it."

"In this half of the world, there is no navy the equal of England's," Nelson frowned. "We can indeed restrict France's trade and conquest to the land. As for England's army, I have little knowledge—and that is not encouraging."

"Altering that must be the work of other men," Sir William sighed. "I have my own task to perform, and shall do it to the best of my ability. Now go, my dears, and leave me to my rest. I shall need all of my strength on the morrow."

Nelson nodded acquiescence, rose and departed. Emma lingered a moment longer to cast a fond look at Sir William before following.

Chapter 4
Trieste

By the next afternoon their coach and guards came rattling down the road into Ancona, where they found to their delight that Queen Carolina and her party awaited them.

"No, I've not sailed yet," she explained over a sumptuous meal at the mayor's own house. "There was an Austrian ship ready to receive us, but I had word that her crew had mutinied just a short time before, so I was unwilling to trust them. I have word that a pair of Russian frigates will dock here shortly, and we can proceed to Trieste upon those."

"Russian ships?" Nelson pricked up his ears like a hound. "Indeed, I'd like to inspect them. Can you trade upon my reputation for that, Sir William?"

"Indeed," chuckled the ambassador, "but I shall need someone to translate the Russian for me."

"Have no fear," said Queen Carolina. "I've a secretary from Poland whom you may borrow."

"You have such a remarkable number of translators," said Emma, knowing it never hurt to flatter the Queen.

LOVE OF GLORY

"It is rather necessary," Carolina sighed. "You would not believe the number of tongues spoken in the empire alone, not to mention its neighbors."

"I see we shall have to stay closer to your majesty until we reach Vienna," Sir William noted.

The Russian frigates arrived three days later, by which time Sir William had been obliged to quietly compensate the mayor of Ancona for the expense of feeding the Queen and her party. Mrs. Cadogan and Miss Knight had arrived in the repaired carriage. Miss Knight had complained bitterly of the hardships of traveling all night, about which Mrs. Cadogan merely shrugged. Nelson, with Sir William and the Queen's Polish secretary, went to examine the Russian ships, whose captains were delighted to meet with The Great Sea-Conqueror.

Nelson returned from the visit, looking somber. "The American admiral's attempts at improvements did not spread far among the Russian ships," he commented. "I badly wish I could have kept the *Foudroyant*; we'd all have found the voyage much safer and more comfortable than in those Russian hulks. Still, 'tis only a short jaunt, and needs must when the devil drives. And I believe we can borrow enough Tuscan troops to guard our cabins while we sleep."

"As bad as that?" Sir William shook his head sadly. "Then England must rely on her own navy, and persuade the czar to commit land-troops if we are ever to defeat Bonaparte."

*****

The sea was calm and the wind favorable, and they crossed to Trieste quickly, which was just as well, since both Sir William and the Queen were troubled by annoying head-colds. In the soft light of sunset the city lay revealed ahead of them, its pale walls climbing from the sea to the heights of the Kras Plateau. There were many more buildings than in Florence; indeed, as the Queen explained, this was by population the fourth largest city in the Austro-Hungarian Empire. Its wide and busy waterfront was illuminated, filled with crowds crying, "Viva Nelson!" and carrying banners that celebrated the second anniversary of the Battle of the Nile. Several ships were docked there, bearing flags of many nations—thankfully, none of them French.

"It is a most cosmopolitan city," Queen Carolina expounded as they pulled into the dock, "being not only the most important and active port of the empire, but also the place where the Latin, Germanic and Slavic peoples meet. It has been so since Roman times, and thus possesses a marvelously vigorous culture. It was occupied by the French just three years ago, and Austrian troops liberated it with much difficulty. Though a free port within the empire, Trieste no longer welcomes French ships—most understandably, for the Triestines are a proud people. I think we shall have no difficulty pressing our mission here."

The city had been fully forewarned of their coming, and a band of officials and guards in parade dress awaited them, happy to cheer for the only man ever to defeat Napoleon. The Tuscan guards handed off their charge to the Triestines in a nice bit of close-order drill, and the officials stepped forward to welcome the visitors. Queen Carolina descended the gangplank first, followed by her daughters, then Sir William and Emma, followed by Nelson, and they took their usual formation to the cheers of the assembled populace. Nelson, by now accustomed to the formalities, smiled and nodded and replied politely to the translated compliments.

To Emma's surprise, some of the officials spoke German— which Sir William could translate, although Emma could not. She recalled his earlier statement about the city being a cultural crossroads, and hoped that nobody would expect them to converse in Slovenian. She also wondered whether there might

LOVE OF GLORY

be some tensions between the different peoples, and if so, how this would affect the city's resistance to France.

Eventually the ceremony ended, and the party was conducted through the well paved streets to what Sir William referred to as the historic castle of San Giusto. "A most remarkable piece of architecture," he enthused. "Built on late Roman ruins, it was constructed over a period of two centuries, and finally completed in 1630."

"Let us hope the amenities have been kept up to date," Emma worried, as the imposing pile came into view.

"I suppose we can assume that we shall have the same arrangements as in Florence, eh?" said Nelson, idly patting Emma's hand. "And the same duties, as well?"

"Just so," agreed Sir William, "only somewhat complicated by the myriad of languages. Still, I expect that none of the servants in the castle may be expected to speak or understand English, so at least we shall have sufficient privacy."

The castle was drafty, but that proved to be a blessing in the August heat. While Sir William expounded upon the changeable weather of the city and the variable Bora wind that swept in from the sea, Mrs. Cadogan, Miss Knight and Tom Allen arrived with the baggage and settled the party's gear in the suite of elaborate rooms. There was sufficient time for everyone to wash lightly and change for dinner.

Their first dinner at Trieste was a small affair in the castle, hosted by the castellan, an elderly gentleman named Sir Rugio di Palma, who spoke impeccable Italian. He was understandably deferent to Queen Carolina, but was fascinated by Nelson, and questioned him constantly about his opinion of Trieste's defensibility, even spreading detailed maps on the dinner table to facilitate the discusion.

Nelson reluctantly concluded, to his host's visible dismay, that the best defense from the sea would require enough ships to blockade most of the Gulf of Trieste. The mood brightened when Nelson recommended that the defense fleet should be a host of small, fast, maneuverable ships, carrying few cannon but low to the water, which could slip in under the guns of the French and shoot the hulls at the waterline.

"A host of small craft would be manageable," Sir Rugio explained. "We could choose whole crews that speak Slovenian, Friulian, Hungarian or whatever, so there would be no confusion of orders or petty divisions of loyalty."

Nelson and Sir William exchanged a worried glance.

"But surely," Emma cut in quickly, "Triestines of whatever tongue would unite against the French. Surely they would do whatever is required to keep their city from being occupied again."

"Indeed, yes!" pronounced Sir Rugio, thudding a determined fist down on the map.

After dinner Queen Carolina returned to her apartment. Nelson and Emma retired on the excuse of wishing to bathe, and Sir William and Sir Rugio withdrew to the study to talk further.

The bath-chamber, which they located with the help of a maid's halting Italian, was better appointed than Emma had expected of a castle completed in 1630. Hypocausts heated a small sunken pool, benches of cedar-wood lined the walls, and a large laundry-basket stood near the door. The bath-maid provided jars of sweet-scented soap, whole sea-sponges, a pile of warmed drying-cloths, robes and rope sandals, and then discreetly withdrew.

Emma gratefully stripped to her skin, tossing her clothes willy-nilly into the basket, and stepped cautiously into the water, which she pronounced delightfully warm. Nelson undressed more slowly, not taking his eyes off her. Finally naked, he paused a moment as if unsure. The light of numerous lamps hung about the walls revealed his muscular build, but also his every scar, the stump of his amputated arm and the dull

LOVE OF GLORY

smeared color of his ruined eye. Understanding perfectly, Emma raised her arms to beckon him toward the water, and whispered "Come, my hero."

"Ah, surely you are one of those sea-sprites," he smiled, stepping toward her, "luring unwary sailors into the water, to become servants of the sea-god forever after."

"Ah, and would that be so terrible?" Emma pured. "Think: we should be together forevermore, in the element which you have made your own, to sport among the waves like merry dolphins..."

Nelson slid into the pool and stepped boldly into Emma's arms. She quivered at the feel of his bare flesh touching hers, and pressed him tighter against her. He kissed her fiercely, and slipped his arm lower to grasp her hip. They paused for a long moment, feeling their pulses beat together through the skin, like waves under a steady keel.

*****

When they returned to their suite, thoroughly dry and wrapped in the warm robes, they found Sir William awaiting them in the parlor. He waved them distractedly toward two chairs and consulted a page in his notebook.

"As you apprehended, Sir Horatio," he explained, "our mission here shall have but mixed success. The Triestines are united in their detestation of Bonaparte, divided by languages and regional customs, united again by eagerness for abundant trade—most especially with other cities of the empire. The chief obstacle is the defensibility of the city. There is an excellent shipyard—which our host wishes to see expanded, by the by—and I daresay that the city could build and staff such a fleet as you suggested within so little as a year. Still, the Gulf of Trieste is very wide, and there is no way to guarantee that a well-manned ship could not sneak past any blockade during the night. The land itself creates difficulties for defense, since even the heights of Kras are readily passable by cavalry and gun-carriages. Trieste has a large population, but unless every man —aye, and every woman—were pressed into service, she would still lack the troops needed to guard her every approach. In brief, without great numbers of troops and ships from the empire, I doubt if Trieste could hold for long against a determined attack by Bonaparte."

"Then what can we do?" Nelson asked.

"The best we can," sighed Sir William. "We can urge the city fathers of Trieste to build the ships you spoke of, and cannons aplenty, and to expand their guards and train all the populace as militia, but then we must press on quickly. The salvation of Trieste will lie with the imperial court of Vienna, and it is they whom we must persuade."

"Then we have our marching orders," said Emma. "I expect we shall face the usual festivities tomorrow, and in days afterward."

"So we shall; we are expected for a banquet in Nelson's honor..." He trailed off, glancing from one to the other, and smiled. "I see the castle has excellent bathing facilities, so I shall go and avail myself of them. Go to rest, my dears; we have much work to perform tomorrow."

With that, he pulled himself to his feet and tottered out the door, leaving Nelson and Emma looking fondly at each other.

*****

Old hands, by now, at the art of formal state banquets, Sir William, Emma and Nelson formed their triad, below Queen Carolina, near the head of the table. The mayor was full of effusive flatteries, which the Queen faithfully translated. Nelson responded pleasantly, being by now accustomed to the toasts and pronouncements.

LOVE OF GLORY

Emma, finding herself with little to do, studied the faces of the guests across the table. Sir Rugio, she noted, was placed a dozen seats further down the table than was Sir William; he was talking animatedly to a Slavic-looking gentleman just beyond the lady to his left. The French Empire style of clothing, she saw, had made only a few inroads into the fashions of Trieste; women's gowns had a classical Greek look and cut, but were far from plain or austere. Men seemed to have adopted the English fashion of long tight trousers, but still wore frill-fronted shirts and cutaway jackets that revealed elaborate waistcoats. Everyone wore ostentatious jewelry, as if to prove the wealth of their houses against any challenge. More than a few glances met hers: the men openly admiring, the women calculating or envious. Emma smiled genially at all of them.

"—yes, most definitely, small quick ships," Nelson was saying. "Oh, you may keep a few of the great wallowing hundred-gunners to defend specific positions, but the quick-boats shall be foremost in attack—like a pack of hounds upon a bear, or like the dread mosquitoes of the Nile, which are more to be feared than all the asps of Egypt." He paused to let the Queen convey the gist of his speech to the mayor.

At that moment Sir William patted Emma's arm to gain her attention. "My dear," he asked quietly, "I confess I need your womanly perspective upon this subject. The Slovenes, whose lands surround Trieste, feel some resentment toward the city for its wealth and political influence, from which they feel shut out. How shall we secure the loyalty of such?"

Emma thought briefly of the well-tended farmlands she'd seen on the journey, and had a ready answer. "Assist them to improve their crops," she said, "and to market the same for good prices, selling them through the port to all lands bordering the Mediterranean, and beyond. Good wine and sweet olive oil is prized in England, as I recall. Increased wealth tends to improve the temper—and the loyalty."

Sir William barked a short delighted laugh, then turned to relay the message—in German—to a bejeweled elderly lady beside him. The lady gave Emma a look of frank admiration, and passed on the message in turn to the equally gemmed elderly gentleman at her other side.

"A fine answer, my girl," Sir William beamed at Emma. "When we reach England, I will endeavour to win you some fitting reward for your services to the crown."

For an instant Emma felt a shadow of future time darkening her present happiness. Sir William was more than thirty years her elder; in time he would die and leave her widowed. What would she do then? Nelson loved her, but he was married. Sir William might leave her some estate, but his primary heir was Greville. Greville, having provided for her daughter, clearly felt that all his obligations to Emma were thoroughly discharged. Queen Carolina was fond of her, but the aging Queen was beset by countless troubles and could not guarantee her own future, let alone a friend's. A glance at her thickening waist showed Emma that she would never again be the sylph who had so fascinated the painter Romney, and her singing voice was no longer so pure as to win her a career in opera. What indeed would she do?

Well, there was time yet to consider that, and Sir William had just promised to win her some gratitude from his majesty's government. She would worry about it later.

"—for the land defenses," Nelson was saying, "Trieste simply must have more cannon and more troops. I would go so far as to say that the city must arm and train the entire populace to serve, at need, as militia. No, I don't believe there is time to build fortifications. Bonaparte might attack next year, and what good are walls in any case without good riflemen to defend them?"

The Queen duly turned to repeat his comments to the mayor, and Emma felt her old mood of elation descend on her

LOVE OF GLORY

like a soft blanket. Here she sat, among nobility and even royalty, at the center of wealth and power and a storm of great deeds; at the fulcrum of history. Whatever her future fortune, she would have glory enough for a dozen queens.

Chapter 5
King Turtle

Within the week, the party set out for Vienna. The Triestines sent them off in two grand carriages, two coaches and several baggage-wains, with a fine troop of cavalry for escort. Emma wondered if this was meant to impress the Viennese. There was, after all, talk that the Habsburg royal family intended to make Vienna the capital of the Austrian Empire, and the officials of Trieste must wish to remind the Emperor of the importance of his best seaport.

As they traveled up the wide road, the countryside grew ever lovelier, with smooth cultivated fields yielding to splendid old forests, and the blue snow-peaks of the Alps ever closer in the background. Everywhere that Emma looked the people appeared healthy and prosperous, and the road was filled with wagons of produce and lumber, yet theirs was the only troop of soldiers to be seen. "King Turtle rules well," she noted.

"Quite well," Sir William agreed. "Heaven knows, the successive rulers of Austria have enough history to guide them. Vienna itself was founded by an early Celtic tribe, and then became a Roman frontier city. Germanic kings have ruled it ever since, and quite successfully. When the Mongols and then

LOVE OF GLORY

the Turks invaded the eastern part of Europe, they were stopped at the gates of Vienna. The only invader to strike it severely was the Black Plague, in 1679, from which the city has long since recovered. I believe its population is some 270,000 today."

"Amazing," said Nelson. "I couldn't swear that London boasts the same."

"The Habsburgs have ruled here for nearly four centuries," Sir William went on, "and they have striven to make the city beautiful as well as prosperous; it has become a great center of the arts, particularly music. I anticipate a pleasant stay there, at any rate."

"And let us pray," Nelson said pensively, "that King Turtle does indeed rule here, and not King Log."

Everywhere they were anticipated and welcomed. Where the road passed through Laibach in Slovenia, the party was entertained by a remarkably good municipal philharmonic orchestra performing a work called *La Virtu Britannica*, composed especially for the occasion. As they rode through the mountain passes to Klagenfurt, they were met by a colorful troop of local guards, complete with military band, which accompanied them all the way to Graz, in Austria, where another decorated guard took over, trumpeting to clear the way.

Finally the road bent to run alongside the great river, and the travelers saw the array of boats, small and large, plying their way along the Danube. Emma could have sworn she heard distant strains of jaunty music.

And ahead of them lay the city, sprawling colorfully through the wide basin at the end of the easternmost Alps. It seemed to glisten like a jewel in the late summer sun under the warm sweet wind.

"Oh, it is so lovely!" Emma breathed.

LESLIE FISH

"In truth," Sir William admitted, "not even Paris at its height could match Vienna." He leaned out the carriage window and called something to the guardsmen in German.

The guards and the carriage driver plied their whips lightly and the horses broke into a smart trot. The well sprung carriage rocked at the pace, but didn't bounce, and the ornamental brass pendants on carriage and harnesses jingled merrily. To the music of trotting hooves and ringing brasses, the ambassadorial coach rolled into the city.

The welcoming committee this time was smaller, more artful, and more calculatedly beautiful. While a military band played, a small but colorfully dressed troop of mounted Viennese guards formally took charge of the party from the Graz guard with astounding precision; even the white horses pranced. A group of exquisitely dressed little girls danced beside the carriage, tossing flower petals in the cleared path from its door to the dais where the officials waited. A chorus of women in neo-Greek gowns sang in harmony as Queen Carolina got out and curtseyed, followed by her daughters. Then Sir William descended, bowed formally, and led Emma and Nelson after the Queen toward the dais. The cheers that greeted Nelson sounded smooth and practiced.

Emma, knowing theatrics when she saw them, whispered to Nelson: "Follow my lead," and paced slowly, with all the dignity she could manage, after Sir William. The officials saluted together, Sir William bowed deeply, Nelson did likewise and Emma gave a deep curtsy. Sir William led them up the steps to the dais and, with a practiced eye, picked out the Emperor's personal envoy to greet first. The envoy gave a short speech in German, the choir sang something brief, and Sir William moved down the receiving line of imperial and city officials.

For Emma, who spoke no German except for the formal greeting Sir William had taught her the night before, the formalities were an interminable bore. Lord Nelson looked as if

LOVE OF GLORY

his polite smile was plastered onto his face. Nonetheless, knowing their duty, they made their stately passage down the line.

Near to the end, Nelson gasped in pleasure and seized the hand of a middle-aged gentleman in formal dress. "Sir Gilbert, is it truly you?" he marveled. "Here, of all places! Ah, Emma, this is my old friend, Sir Gilbert Elliot."

"Lord Minto now," the man smiled, "and British ambassador to the imperial court. Allow me to present my wife, who will doubtless wish to dine with you at your earliest convenience." He introduced a buxom woman with a wide smile and a keen eye.

At last the final hand had been shaken, the last greeting suitably made, and the ambassadorial party was ushered into the imperial palace of the Hofburg and to their rooms. Mrs. Cadogan was already there, with a steaming basin ready for Sir William's feet, and glasses of cordial on the sideboard. The trio sank gratefully onto the divans, and Emma's mother set about making them comfortable. "The butler speaks very good English," she revealed, "and he knew exactly how to get the wagon brought around and unloaded. The housekeeper speaks English too, though not as well. I imagine that they are even now scouring the palace for English-speaking maids to attend us."

"No doubt," Sir William said dryly, pulling off his shoes.

"They are certainly doing their best for our comfort," Mrs. Cadogan went on, as she brought around the cordials and a note in a cream-colored envelope. "This was left for you, sir."

Sir William opened the envelope and scanned the note. "It is an invitation for me," he said, "to dine privately tonight, with no less than the Emperor Francis himself. I expect that there will be the usual state banquet tomorrow, but for tonight, my dears, you must dine here, in our quite satisfactory quarters. I'm quite certain the excellent Mrs. Cadogan can manage for you—while keeping prying palace servants at bay."

"That I can," Emma's mother smiled grimly.

For a moment Emma wondered how much of her present good fortune—indeed, how much of the good fortune of her life—had been managed by her clever and practical mother. Following that came the disturbing recognition that Mrs. Cadogan was elderly, and couldn't last many years longer, and how would Emma manage without her? The thought was painful, and Emma pushed it away.

Dinner that night was small and intimate: just herself and Nelson, with a repast of roasted gamecock with assorted fruits and a light pale wine. The dishes were excellent, but Emma scarcely noticed them. Her attention was fixed upon Nelson, and how splendid her battered warrior looked by lamplight. He, in turn, couldn't seem to look away from her.

"You know," he said presently, "I don't protest being dragged from one reception to another, being a part of Sir William's scheme to strengthen the alliance; 'tis my duty, and I would do it in any case. But I will say, Emma my heart, that even were this tour unneeded for any politics, I would do it solely for the delight of being with you."

"And I with you," Emma replied breathlessly. "Surely you know that."

Nelson smiled slowly, and then—with the decisiveness that had won him so many battles—set down his glass and rose, extending a hand to her. Emma rose likewise, and clasped his fingers in hers. With no further word spoken, they proceeded to his bedchamber.

*****

Nelson, as was his military habit, awoke first. Used to his ways by now, Emma scarcely roused as she felt him leave the

LOVE OF GLORY

bed. After a few moments more of sleep she was wakened by his insistent tugging at her shoulder. "Up, my love," he said quietly. "Sir William has some news for both of us."

Arrayed in her dressing-robe, Emma went out to the parlor and found Nelson and Sir William there, gloomily devouring the eggs and ham. She worried to see their long faces. "What now, Will'um?" she asked, settling at the table. "Was the emperor unwilling to commit more troops against Bonaparte?"

"Oh, on the contrary," the ambassador sighed. "Emperor Francis despises the French, their revolution, and certainly The Little Corsican. He is quite willing to draft and train and send out more soldiers, should he have to drain the empire to do it. It is not his willingness that concerns me."

"What, then?"

"His...competence." Sir William cast an automatic glance around the room, leaned a little closer to the table and lowered his voice. "I've never met a ruler less able, and I knew Marie Antoinette when she was a flighty girl. His primary concern is for the sanctity of his own person, his second for the preservation of his own power and dignity, and only third comes the welfare of his own realm. Under his pretty manners, he is fiercely suspicious and fearfully reactionary. I've heard that he served adequately with an army regiment in Hungary, but that was before the entire unpleasantness with France. The man has not an original thought in his head, nor has he retained any brilliance from his studies. It is just as well that he handed over command of his armies to his brother, the Archduke Charles. I can only pray that he likewise hands off all the other necessities of government and war to ministers and generals of proven ability. Insuring that is what I shall try to accomplish during our time here."

"How can we help?" Nelson asked.

"By playing a pretty bit of theater. You must make the rounds of social and artistic engagements, ever looking the part of the gallant warrior and—" Sir William gave Emma a fond look, "—his beautiful companion. The good Lord and Lady Minto from the embassy will act as your translators when I cannot be with you. After Florence and Trieste, I daresay you know your lines by heart. Only impress the Austrians with your valor, beauty, ready wit and solid tactical sense, while I do my scheming behind doors. I trust you can manage that?"

Nelson gave him a bemused look for a long moment, and then laughed. "I daresay I can tread the boards as well as I once trod a deck. With Emma's keen wit to guide me, I believe we can perform an adequate strolling play."

"A *Commedia del Arte* indeed," the ambassador sighed. "Now, since we are invited to the inevitable state banquet this evening, let us spend the day preparing for our roles."

*****

Lord and Lady Minto arrived soon after breakfast, and while Lord Minto engaged Sir William and Nelson, Lady Minto conferred with Emma. She spoke fluent German, all dialects, and her quick-moving eye convinced Emma that hers was a wit to be reckoned with. The two women drew aside to one corner of the suite's parlor and quickly reviewed the plan for their entrance and seating.

"Once we are seated," Lady Minto directed, "simply be charming, eat daintily, drink even more daintily, and smile at everyone. I daresay all questions to you will be relayed through Sir William, whilst I play shield for Lord Nelson. Still, do not speak too freely, for many in the court understand English. Ah, and may I add, that Grecian gown of yours is a superb choice."

"I thank you. Should I wear more vivid jewelry?"

"Oh, no. The simplicity of the diamonds is a perfect touch. Hmmm, one more thing: be charming, but not overly fond, toward Lord Nelson. Rumors have preceded you."

LOVE OF GLORY

"I see," Emma sighed. Yes, at a formal state banquet one did not flaunt one's indiscretions. "I shall be cautious. Afterward, you must tell me the extent of these rumors."

"At present," Lady Minto smiled, "no more than that you are his mistress—and his inspiration. So long as his achievements are impressive, you shall be admired for it."

"Excellent," Emma murmured. So, no word of her pregnancy had yet spread. Very good.

At that moment a footman came to announce the imminent dinner, and the co-conspirators rose to greet the challenge.

The walk through the wide corridors turned into a promenade so formal it became almost dreamlike. The footman led, followed by Queen Carolina, then her daughters, then Emma on Sir William's arm, then Lord Nelson escorting Lady Minto. Various ladies and courtiers dawdling in the hallway stepped back against the decorated walls and bowed extravagantly as they passed, then closed behind them like a ship-plowed sea to whisper and mutter in their wake. Touches of gold were everywhere, gilding the elaborate moldings, the frames of ever-larger paintings, and the glass-topped sconces on the walls. Plush, figured carpets rustled under their feet, and distant strains of delicate music sounded from somewhere ahead. Even Nelson seemed subdued amid all this elaborate finery.

At length they came to the great double doors of the receiving hall, which were hastily pulled open by two more liveried servants to reveal a huge and sumptuous room filled with elegantly dressed nobles. The footmen announced them, Queen Carolina first, to a light applause of bowed heads and fluttering fans. Next came her daughters, then Sir William and Emma, and then Lord Nelson and Lady Minto to a surprising chorus of cheers and elaborate curtseys, soon followed by some stirring music played by the string quartet in the gallery. Nelson only raised an eyebrow, smiled, and nodded briefly. He was back in his element, and understood it well.

Though there was no apparent receiving-line, Sir William steered Emma unerringly from one knot of aristocrats to another, smiling and speaking briefly in German. Emma had only to smile and nod, and note that behind her Lady Minto and Lord Nelson were performing the same act—save that numerous questions were aimed at Nelson, whilst very few were being directed toward her. Such queries as she did receive were easy inanities about how she found Vienna, had she seen or heard the work of this artist or that musician, and did she know that the current fashion for revived- Greek clothing styles owed far more to herself and her famed artistic Attitudes than to anything from France. Emma could have replied in her sleep, and indeed felt again that she was half-dreaming as she floated from cluster to cluster, towed on Sir William's arm. The only sign of their serious purpose was the length of time that the ambassador spent conversing quietly with various hard-faced older gentlemen of military aspect.

Sir William and his party had worked their way almost to the far end of the hall when the even larger double doors there were opened to display the banquet-room, and a butler with a large gilded staff-of-office formally invited the party within. The guests followed him; a slow-moving river of velvet and satin, with the Hamilton party near its head.

After an interminable period of settling, Emma found herself near the head of the enormous banquet table, again between Nelson and Sir William, with Queen Carolina and her younger daughters across from her. Beyond Sir William sat the Empress Maria Theresa of Naples, second wife of Emperor Francis and daughter of Queen Carolina. Emma was both delighted and dismayed to see her old friend's daughter again; Maria looked utterly elegant, composed and well cared for, yet also worn and aged beyond her years. That, Emma considered,

LOVE OF GLORY

might be a result of bearing seven children in the ten years since her marriage. Throughout the meal much intense commentary passed between Carolina and her Empress daughter, in German.

Fortunately Maria Theresa had forgotten none of her Italian, and when she turned to speak with Sir William and Emma she chatted brightly about events that had occurred in Sicily and Naples since she had last been there. She was especially fascinated by the story of how her mother had been rescued in Livorno, by Emma herself.

"Lazzaroni, those wretched beasts!" Maria Theresa snarled, reaching for her wine goblet. "Nearly a generation now, raised on the shocking insolence of the French and their revolution. Oh, if only we could be rid of the lot of them."

"Then where would Naples and Sicily find labor quickly, when they need it?" Sir William smiled. "The country peasants cannot be spared from farming, nor soldiers from the army. No, I fear we are entering an age when great numbers of laborers must always be kept in readiness, regardless of the inconvenience."

"One would do better to summon demons, as did the legendary Doctor Faustus," the empress sighed. "At least, those can be dismissed from this world when their task is done."

Sir William laughed appreciatively, as did Emma. At that moment the emperor leaned toward Maria Theresa and commandeered her attention for a brief exchange in German, letting Emma have a long look at him.

Holy Roman Emperor Francis II, King of Bohemia, Hungary, Croatia and Germany, was nothing much to look at. He was slender without being muscular, flabby without being fat, with fair receding hair, pale watery eyes, and a long thin face with the characteristic Habsburg jaw. His speech was peremptory and halting, proceeding in bursts. His expression was slightly sour, as if the mind behind it remembered and treasured every slight and insult, but had learned nothing from them but resentment. No doubt he was still stinging over his defeat three years previously, and over the lands he had lost to France with the treaty of Campo Formio. Of a certainty, he would proceed against France again, as soon as he had rebuilt his army sufficiently. The question, Emma considered, was whether he would pursue his next campaign any more intelligently than he had the last one.

The problem, as she also understood, was to choose the best generals to lead the strategies against Bonaparte, and then persuade Francis to let them do their work unhindered. That was Sir William's mission, and she could support it best by being charming and ornamental. It had not escaped her notice that Emperor Francis's eye strayed often in her direction, just as often as it flickered toward Nelson beside her.

The food was exquisite, the music enchanting and the company dazzling, but Emma felt time weighing upon her like heavy chains.

After the interminable dinner there was a return to the reception hall for a mercifully brief concert, after which the company moved to another lavishly-appointed room for dice and cards. For once Emma had no stomach for such amusements, and Nelson drank enough of the champagne that his aide had to warn him that another glass might make him sick. When Lady Minto tactfully suggested that they depart Emma and Nelson gladly agreed. Only Sir William stayed on, moving through the crowd to speak at length with various gentlemen. Emma marveled at his indefatigability. She and Nelson returned through the gilded corridors, accompanied by Lady Minto, who artfully fended off assorted questioners.

Once in their apartments, Emma dropped gratefully onto a settee, while Nelson went to visit the necessary room. "Oh, Lady Minto," she sighed, loosening her gown, "I had thought that nothing could be more exciting than to banquet with the

LOVE OF GLORY

emperor, but now that I've done it, I swear I'd take more pleasure simply strolling the beaches of Sicily."

"I've heard the emperor's children confess the same," Lady Minto chuckled, thoughtfully helping Emma out of her gloves. "Still, if one can understand the language and enjoys the intricate games of politics, state banquets can be most intriguing. You did quite well, you know."

"I but smiled much, and spoke a bit with Maria Theresa," Emma demurred.

"And do you not think that rescuing the empress' mother from a mob is a notable adventure?" Lady Edith winked at her. "You may be sure, Maria Theresa will repeat every detail to her husband. You and Nelson made a fine picture: a pair of heroes, brave and beautiful, seated between your translators. Neither I nor Sir William wasted the opportunity, I assure you."

"Ah, but what then is to be the fruit of all our labors?" Emma wondered, rubbing her back. "I know the emperor will take the field against Bonaparte again, but... Please tell me: what do you think of his chances?"

Lady Minto twined her fingers together slowly. "To be blunt, milady, they are poor. Surely you've heard that Napoleon is proceeding unchecked through Italy, and will soon enough turn his attentions north again. Bonaparte is not a great general, merely a very competent one, but his opponents here in the East are... worse. The one advantage the empire has—and Russia, too—is sheer numbers. So long as your beloved Nelson can best Bonaparte at sea, the empire can, in time, wear him down, simply because it has more land and troops than France. If England can produce a good general too, our eventual victory is assured. The question is, how long will it take?"

Emma shivered, and toed off her shoes. "Then is all Sir William's work for naught?"

"Oh no!" Lady Minto assured her. "If he can arrange to emplace the best officers the empire has against the French, then... well, a half-competent general is better than a total incompetent. They can slow Bonaparte's advance and wear him down the faster. We can accomplish that much."

"And the sooner the war ends, the sooner Horatio will be safe," Emma concluded, rolling down her stockings.

At that point Nelson returned, carrying his jacket over his shoulder and looking as if he wished to peel away more. Lady Minto gave an understanding smile, rose and excused herself. Nelson tossed his jacket carelessly onto the settee and turned to Emma.

"'Tis a lovely night," he said, "and the view from the balcony is excellent. Would you like to see it...with me?"

Smiling, Emma rose and took his arm, and padded after him in her bare feet.

*****

The next morning they encountered Sir William at the breakfast table, where he studied a small mound of letters while demolishing a dish of bacon and eggs. "You have your work cut out for you," he informed Emma and Nelson as they sat down. "I have here a most remarkable number of invitations for you, requesting your presence at gallery showings, concerts, balls—oh, and you must attend the mass at St. Stephen's cathedral this Sunday, where the city's finest composer, a fellow named Haydn, will be leading the choir and orchestra in his latest work, the *Missa in Angustiis*. 'Tis said he is dedicating the work to you, my man: a most signal honor."

"And no one is concerned, I suppose," Nelson sighed, buttering a delicate bread roll, "that I am not a Catholic."

"Not in the least," Sir William smiled. "It is the artistry that matters. Here in Vienna, art is everything."

"I shall pick out our clothes for the event," Emma agreed, reaching for the invitations. "Indeed, if we are to be here long,

LOVE OF GLORY

we 'are going to need more. Have we enough funds for a good tailor and seamstress?"

"Unnecessary!" Sir William barked with laughter. "My dear, don't you realize that all the dressmakers of the city are panting to provide for you, *gratis*, in the hope that you will wear their creations to these most fashionable events? A single wearing will make a tailor's fortune for decades after, you know. Such is fame. And besides, should any such tradesman be so crass as to ask for monetary payment, be assured, the empress would straighten it all out in good time. Have no fears on that score, dearest, but study your invitations and make your plans."

"We shall," said Emma, casting a swift smile at Nelson. "Come, Horatio: we must study our scripts and plan our costumes, for our roles need to be played to perfection."

"The crown's mountebank," Nelson laughed, reaching for the pot of excellent Viennese coffee. "I confess, 'tis an amusing change of work. Hmm, far better fed, anyway, than that of an admiral at sea."

"At least at sea you have fresh fish," Emma murmured, puzzling over Sir William's translation of the topmost letter.

"Oh, not at all," said Nelson, over the rim of his coffee cup. "English sailors won't eat fish, for they think that fish feed on the bodies of drowned sailors. No, they'd rather eat stinking salt beef, months in the barrel, and weevily biscuit, hard as stone, then stoop to dining on fish."

"What a remarkable superstition," Sir William marveled. "Italian sailors have no such compunctions, which might account for their good health despite all other conditions."

"True." Nelson paused to wolf down his roll. "At least we've persuaded our sailors to take a daily ration of lime juice for their health, but even so, it needed rum to persuade them. The good Vice-Admiral Edward Vernon—a most notable seaman, and the victor at Porto Bello—took to mixing the juice in the crew's daily rum-and-water ration, which made it palatable to them. He had been nicknamed 'Old Grog' because he habitually wore a sturdy grogham coat, so the drink was dubbed 'grog' in his honor."

"What heroic admiral would be required," Emma pondered, "to persuade sailors to eat fresh fish?"

"I shall see what influence I can exert in that quarter," Nelson promised, smiling at her.

"With Lady Minto's good help, see if you can persuade our good Austrian nobles to provide adequate foodstuffs to their armies," said Sir William, pushing back his chair. "I find it astounding that it took Bonaparte, of all people, to recognize the importance of sufficient food and supply-trains to an army. Too many of our allies cling to the ancient notion that an army can feed itself by looting the countryside it passes through—a most disastrous idea, which I am doing my best to discourage.

"Now, with good Mrs. Cadogan's help, I shall array myself to go out and persuade more of the aristocratic idiots to our side. *Buon giorno*, my friends; let us meet here at four to plan for dinner."

As he plodded off to his dressing-room, Emma's hand snaked across the table to clasp Nelson's. "As a political comedy or a subtle campaign," she said softly, "I enjoy every moment of it with you."

"You have taught me the joys of such subtleties," he whispered back, making her blush.

*****

That afternoon Lady Minto brought the dressmakers for fittings, and the evening was spent at a ball given by the emperor's brother, the Archduke Charles—who also happened to be the commander of the emperor's army. Emma was wonderfully grateful that the cunning Lady Minto had taught both her and Nelson the Viennese waltz, for most of the dances

LOVE OF GLORY

were just that. She and Nelson twirled across the polished floor while Sir William sat in a corner talking with the Archduke. Emma knew that she and Nelson were drawing all eyes, and took care to hold their attention. The waltz was considered a daring, if not shocking, dance—not only because the couples held each other so closely, but because the twirling, if done strenuously, would cause the lady's skirt to rise up. More than once she felt the light draft of air on her knees, and heard the gasps and whispers from the filled chairs at the sidelines. No one, she felt assured, was looking at Sir William and the Archduke Charles.

Once, as she sat out a more stately dance, she heard two young ladies whispering behind their fans in Italian—girls too silly to realize that she knew the tongue.

"Shocking," the black-haired one was whispering. "Did you see her knees?"

"Her knees," the redhead—perhaps all of sixteen—agreed, "and an inch or two of bare thigh beyond."

Emma smirked and fluttered her fan, knowing that she had perfectly good knees—and thighs.

"It is simply outrageous," the black-haired girl went on, scratching at a spot on her jaw which could be nothing but a pimple. "Why, she must be all of thirty-five years old!"

So I am, Emma remembered, jarred.

"Old enough to be my mother," the redhead concurred, "or your grandmother."

Only if the women in your family married at twelve, thought Emma, nettled.

"Oh, it is so unfair!" the younger girl hissed in frustration. "She has no business looking like that, or dancing like that, at her age!"

"Let alone winning the affections of great heroes," the redhead whispered venomously. "Oh, what will be left for us?

Lubberly boys and cackling old lechers! Did you see that wretched old stick my mama invited for luncheon yesterday?"

"Worse, I swear, is that young lout my aunt is pushing at me..."

Emma smiled to herself, recognizing hopeless jealousy when she heard it. She turned her attention back to Nelson, who, with Lady Minto's unobtrusive help, was discussing something about tactics of supply with an iron-bearded Saxon gentleman. She heard him say, "For every man in the field there are ten behind him, providing supply and support, in a chain reaching back to the nearest city capable of providing them. Bonaparte knows that, and so do I. But who else does, sir? Who else?"

Emma smiled again, drained her slender goblet of champagne and held it out to a passing waiter, who deftly replaced it with a full one that sported a cut strawberry in its pale-gold depths. Yes, Sir William was in his element, and Nelson in his—and she, in her way, in hers. State banquets in Vienna might be interminably boring, but she wished that this ball would last forever.

It ended, in fact, shortly after midnight, whereupon the ambassador's party promenaded to their carriage amid a crowd of well-wishers, and rode back to the Hofburg under a starlit sky. "Well, sir," Nelson ventured to ask, "was the ball satisfactory?"

"Oh, yes indeed," grinned Sir William. "I believe I have convinced the archduke to place only his best officers in the regiments which will actually engage Bonaparte. The rest shall be occupied with guarding and maintaining supplies—with regard to which, by the by, I do thank you for your timely comments, good Horatio. And you, my dear," he turned to Emma, "I thank for providing such excellent, ah, I believe the term is 'covering fire'."

LOVE OF GLORY

"Most well done," Lady Minto agreed. "Indeed, perhaps you and Lord Nelson should practice the more dramatic figures of the waltz."

"Ah, but will it be enough?" Nelson sighed. "Will all this capering and conniving be enough?"

"And cannot Queen Carolina be of help?" Emma asked.

"The Queen is absorbed in her own concerns," said Lady Minto, soberly. "She is engaged in arranging suitable marriages for her last two daughters, and a plan of safe retirement for herself, for as Bonaparte advances through Italy, she dare not depend upon a return to Naples. No, I fear that from here onward we are cast on our own resources."

The others looked at each other, understanding very well what she meant.

"If the czar will commit himself—" Emma began.

"If the empire can hold for but five more years—" Sir William verbally collided with her.

"If England can build up a good enough army, under a good enough general," Nelson finished for them. "Well, we shall do our part to buy her the needed time."

"We certainly shall do our best," said Emma, capturing his hand.

"Our best," Nelson concurred, smiling at her.

No more was said until they reached their apartments at the Hofburg.

*****

Next day Lady Minto came early, and soon the tailors and dressmakers arrived, displaying three sets each of Royal Navy blue and snowy white uniforms for Nelson, and a small rainbow of gowns for Emma. Miss Knight and Tom Allen scurried about like mice, arms loaded with new clothes, hastening to find room for them in the clothes-presses. Mrs. Cadogan clucked her tongue at the display, impressed. "They must have had every seamstress in the city working all day and night to finish these so lively," she commented.

"I believe there is, indeed, an army of seamstresses and tailors in the city," Sir William noted. "'It is a trade most commonly available to the poor, the better to keep them out of mischief. Ah, and here are two perfectly sober suits for myself, as well. We shall all be properly arrayed for battle."

"Not aforetime," Lady Minto noted. "I believe you have an invitation to luncheon with one of the Saxon princes this noon, and I am promised to teach our hero some fanciful turns of the waltz before tonight's concert at the Hungarian ambassador's residence."

"Ah, such labor," Sir William sighed. "Well, let us prepare. Mrs. Cadogan, please take charge of our new finery—save for this suit, with which I shall need your assistance."

"To the dancing lessons, then," Nelson smiled at Emma. "I swear, I'm coming to enjoy this more than a battle at sea."

"Glory enough, either way," Emma beamed back at him.

*****

The round of social engagements whirled them on until Sunday morning arrived, when the party dressed simply—or as simply as they could withNelson arrayed in one of the white uniforms with its elaborate gold trim—and proceeded to St. Stephen's cathedral. The building was elegant and elaborate, as indeed most of Vienna seemed to be, and the interior was breathtaking. It was all Emma could do to keep from exclaiming aloud at the wealth of splendid statues and paintings displayed amid fine carvings and gilding. Save for the altar and Rose Window, this could have been a superb art gallery rather than a place of worship. A large crowd was already seated, making a visible effort to be silent as the

LOVE OF GLORY

ambassadorial party entered, and with all eyes—obviously or not—fixed upon Nelson. Sir William led them with smooth expertise to the places appointed for them in the first pew, and no sooner had they taken their seats than the ceremony began.

It began not with words but with music, exquisite music from a small orchestra and choir concealed in the loft above. Forgetting propriety, Emma turned her head to look, lips parted with delight, and Nelson did likewise. Only peremptory tapping on their arms from Sir William and Lady Minto made them resume their proper position. Emma wondered fleetingly if the crowd, which had surely seen them turn, admired their appreciation or found them rude.

Then out came the formal procession, led by no less than a bishop, and the formalities began in earnest. Emma had attended a polite number of Catholic masses in Naples, and the procedure was enough like the Church of England ritual for Nelson to follow, so they committed no further lapses in protocol.

Still, they kept being distracted by the beauty of the music. The winding strains intertwined with the spoken parts of the mass—surely this had been rehearsed with the officiating bishop—to create a seamless whole. Not only was Emma enchanted, but Nelson too; his rapt expression could not be mistaken.

During the shuffling of worshippers down to the communion rail, Sir William took the opportunity to whisper to them that he expected the musical piece would hereafter be referred to as the *Nelson Mass*, a concept at which both of them were amazed.

Emma smiled toward the great rose window, feeling as if she were floating. Surely this was the crown of glory, to sit in one of the grandest cathedrals in the world, hearing such magnificent music played for her and her lover, knowing that it would bear her lover's name forever after. Surely there could be nothing greater than this.

*****

The waking dream continued for long days afterward, as Lady Minto duly led Emma and Nelson through the lovely city, from art gallery to banquet, from concert to ball, while Sir William worked quietly behind the scenes. Sir William had primed Emma and Nelson on what to say, but most days it was enough for them simply to be present and be seen. They learned and displayed the intricacies of the waltz, and twice Emma was invited to show her 'Attitudes' to the sound of splendid music, for the appreciation of nobles and princes. They were lionized throughout the city, and saw nothing but beauty wherever they cast their eyes.

The enchanted time lasted a full six weeks before Sir William informed them that it was time to leave. Mrs. Cadogan saw to the packing, and set the loosest gowns at the top of her trunk with a warning comment that Emma would need them soon enough. Queen Carolina bid them an emotional farewell, which included shamelessly embracing Emma and presenting her with a bouquet of late roses. The emperor provided them with a magnificent coach and honor guard and heralded their departure with a splendid fanfare, after which the ambassadorial party trotted away on the warm winds of the last week of August, heading up the road to Prague.

For the first hour of the ride nobody spoke, everyone content to bask in the warm sunlight and watch the beautifully cultivated landscape slide by. Eventually Emma was moved to remark: "It is lovely. All of the empire that we've seen is so beautiful, so...civilized, and it seems so prosperous." She gestured out to window to where some farmers were busy mowing hay. "Even the peasants are well fed and well dressed."

LOVE OF GLORY

"Oh yes," Sir William sighed, frowning. "All the empire is elegant, prosperous...and stupid! God, how stupid! I only pray it can hold against Bonaparte for another five years, though I have my doubts. Good Lord, the Holy Roman Empire was founded by Charlemagne nearly a thousand years ago, and I fear it cannot last another hundred. I pray that my counterparts in St. Petersburg have had better luck than I, that the czar's generals have more practical sense than the emperor's, and that Russia will give up its dangerous neutrality quickly. I fear, though, that most of the burden shall fall upon England, and I pray that we shall be strong enough to bear it."

"The empire and the czar have at least the advantage of numbers," Nelson soothed, "and I daresay England has the benefit of clever officers. Bonaparte cannot stand against them all forever."

"No, not forever," Sir William agreed. "But for how long? And how much damage can he do in the meantime?"

Hoping to lighten his sour mood, Emma asked, "What shall we be doing in Prague, then?"

"More of the same," Sir William shrugged. "I have sent letters ahead, and we shall be met by able translators. Fortunately, those to whom I must speak most candidly also speak German. We shall spend but a few days there, my colleagues, and then on to Dresden, Dessau and Hamburg. Play the game well, my dears, while I search for nobles and officers with the good tactical sense to turn Bonaparte. *Tria juncta in uno*, we must play well."

Chapter 6
Ambassadors of Goodwill

They reached Prague in the first week of September, as the weather was just beginning to turn cool, presenting the capital of Bohemia at its best. Sir William discoursed happily on its marvelous Baroque architecture as they rolled across the historic Charles Bridge into the Old Town, and he noted how the city had prospered with various new inventions that had improved trade. He added, "My chief labor, I think, will be to persuade the Bohemians to fight alongside the Prussians, for they've not yet forgiven them the bombardment of the city in 1757. Still, the old Emperor Joseph II seemed to have persuaded the current generation to let bygones be bygones. Let us hope that the current emperor can maintain that accord in the face of Bonaparte."

Their welcoming party awaited them at the gates of the enormous Prague Castle, where the ceremony was lovely, elegant, and mercifully brief. The translators awaited them there, a gray-haired couple named Esterhazy. The elderly gentleman, who spoke German but no English, attached himself to Sir William. His frail wife, speaking a stilted but passable English, introduced herself to Emma, gushed over

LOVE OF GLORY

Nelson, then hurried to deal with Mrs. Cadogan and their baggage. In short order, the ambassador's party was safely ensconced in a suite of rooms in the renovated part of the castle. Nelson and Emma, with the ease of practice, settled themselves at a table in the parlor and sipped a cherry-flavored cordial until the bustling servants finished their work and retired.

"Ah, at last," said Sir William, settling in a chair beside them. "Good Mrs. Cadogan, can you prepare a foot-basin in my chamber? Thank you. Now, my dears, it being late in the day, we are expected for only an intimate dinner with the mayor, his wife and no more than a dozen officials. The formal banquet will be tomorrow evening, after our required presence at a concert in the gardens—the last of the season, I believe, so wear white with dark trim and all your decorations. I believe there is also a celebration planned, my dear fellow, for your birthday."

"My 42nd," Nelson grimaced. "Truthfully, I'd never expected to live this long."

"Given the translation problems," Sir William hurried on, "I don't expect that you will be called upon to speak overmuch. Your roles in this act of the play should be quite easy. Now I shall be off to my chambers for some rest before facing the lions. Be well, my dears." And he departed, leaving Nelson and Emma looking at each other.

"It won't take me long to change gowns," she almost whispered.

"Nor myself to change breeches and shirt," he smiled, taking her hand. "Shall we make good use of our time?"

Emma laughed softly, and they both rose and proceeded into Nelson's rooms.

*****

LESLIE FISH

The 'intimate' dinner' of no more than twenty people provided Emma with another surprise; one of the guests, Sir Czcesinski, a representative from a coalition of merchant houses, spoke excellent Italian. With his help and that of Mrs. Esterhazy, Emma fielded questions to Nelson with relative ease. Most such questions concerned Nelson's now-famous battles, and he replied with special emphasis placed on strategy and tactics. Emma wondered how much good this advice would do in landlocked Bohemia, but reminded herself that such knowledge was never wasted among allies. The dinner progressed quickly, though the food was heavy and Emma felt obliged to pick lightly at it. Afterward there was chocolate and a few songs by reasonably good singers with excellent accompaniment. The host stood and formally ended the proceedings well before ten o'clock.

As they paced back to their rooms, Sir William seemed far more cheerful than he had been in days. "Excellent progress," he announced, as soon as they were alone. "It seems that there are a few good officers in the Bohemian army, and the local merchants well understand the importance of adequate supply. I daresay I shall be speaking with a number of them tomorrow morning, whilst you two let good Lady Esterhazy guide you through the preparations for the concert. Good work, my dears. And now I'm off for some well-earned rest. Good night, then, and don't stay up too late."

He paced off to his own chamber, leaving Nelson alone with Emma.

This time, Nelson was a little slower to depart for his rooms. "I know little of...women's matters," he fumbled. "Is the child paining you in any way?"

"Oh no," Emma smiled, pressing a hand to her abdomen. "I've not even been sick of a morning, thanks to my mother's nostrum of drinking milk and eating much cheese, which hasn't been difficult these past few weeks."

LOVE OF GLORY

"And you hardly look any...rounder," Nelson fairly blushed. "I simply wish to know how long we can, ah, go on as we have."

"Another two months, certainly," Emma reassured him. "I shall have ample warning when we must stop."

"Let us not waste this time, then," he said, taking her hand and sliding to his feet.

"Not at all," she agreed, rising to meet him.

Only later, lying warm amid the blankets with the sleeping Nelson's good arm around her, did Emma think to worry about the future. Another two months and they should be in England, and who knew what would happen then?

*****

The next week they set out in river barges, on the Elbe, bound for Dresden, capital of Saxony and the royal residence of the Saxon kings and electors. Nelson was pleased with the easy river-travel, and Emma also found it delightful. Sir William's party was welcomed with a modest ceremony into the royal Dresden Castle. That evening, while soaking his feet, Sir William discoursed on their plan of action.

"The King's own household will provide you two with a translator," he promised. "At the state banquet tomorrow, proceed as you so well know how to do. Before or after that, I daresay, you will be invited to a tour of the superb art collection in the Zwinger Palace just across the road, whilst I go about speaking more privately with various officials. I have high hopes of assuring cooperation here, since the Saxons have a long history of war-craft. Indeed, 'twas a branch of the Saxon tribe that invaded England over a millennium ago, where they provided the basis of our common tongue. It should not be difficult to persuade them to join with us in common cause against Bonaparte."

They took supper privately in their suite, made use of the excellent baths, and then retired to their rooms in fine spirits. Nelson and Emma spoke no more about the future beyond their immediate mission, by mutual consent letting the problem of England wait until they reached it.

The next day, as Sir William had predicted, a deferential little man named Herr Frankel, in the livery of the royal house of Saxony, accompanied Nelson and Emma to the Zwinger Palace. There they strolled from room to room, listening politely to Herr Frankel's monologue on the various paintings and sculptures, while being observed by a remarkable number of Dresden's nobles. Only a few of the observers—always those wearing assorted military decorations—ventured to speak to Nelson, by way of Herr Frankel. Their comments were the usual congratulations on his assorted victories, then a few detailed questions about strategy. Nelson played his assigned role well, and Emma could see that he was enjoying himself.

At the banquet that night, where Emma found the food oddly spiced and heavy, Nelson was seated next to a bejeweled Lady Von Karten, who spoke stilted English but managed to convey various questions adequately. Emma noticed that Sir William, at her other side, seemed thoughtful and preoccupied even as he conversed at length with an elderly but impressive lady beside him.

Afterward, once alone again in their suite, Sir William voiced his misgivings. "They don't seem to understand their situation," he worried. "I swear, the Saxon nobles are more concerned about their battle with Frederick of Prussia, forty years ago, than with their upcoming conflict with Bonaparte. Surely they will serve their commanders from the empire well enough, so long as they are not situated anywhere near Prussian troops, but...ah...I cannot name the cause, but I have a sense of foreboding."

LOVE OF GLORY

"Do you think, then," Nelson pondered, "that the Saxon states are the weakest part of the empire?"

"Beyond doubt, they are," Sir William gloomed. "So many, so small and so scattered... Yet, if they will unite against the French they can, at least, slow Bonaparte's advance and whittle away his forces. Ah, well, let us see how things stand when we reach Dessau, for that shall be a harder nut to crack."

*****

They reached Dessau, capital of the state of Anhalt-Dessau, a week later as the nights were beginning to grow chill, and were welcomed to the impressive Georgium Castle with formal pomp and ceremony. The next morning they were invited to ride in an elegant open carriage through the immense Dessau-Worlitz Gardens, accompanied by no less than Duke Frederick Franz Leopold III of Anhalt-Dessau himself.

The Duke at sixty years of age was still an impressive figure, and spoke excellent English. As they rode through the splendid garden, laid out in the English style, he discoursed of his admiration for England and for the English Enlightenment, and he merrily named a conical flower-planted mound "the Nelsonburg." Sir William took care to flatter the Duke on his excellent reforms in education, public health and industry, noting how these had made Anhalt-Dessau one of the most prosperous of the German states in the empire. The Duke was delighted at the flattery.

On the subject of war with France, though, he was less enthusiastic. "You must know, sir," he said carefully, "that in my youth I served in the Prussian army and fought in the Battle of Kolin. I've been told that I made an honorable accounting for myself, but in truth my primary memories are of the hideous, stupid waste of war. I soon afterward resigned from the army and declared Anhalt-Dessau neutral, which did not please the

Prussians. Indeed, I was tried before the Furstenbund—the League of Princes—for refusing to stand with Prussia against the advances of Austria."

"I believe the Furstenbund was dissolved ten years ago," Sir William ventured.

"Even so, I have maintained the neutrality of Anhalt-Dessau these forty years and more, and seen my policy repaid by my duchy's progress and prosperity. I see no cause to change that policy now."

"But do you think Bonaparte will respect that neutrality and leave you in peace?" Nelson countered. "Will he not gobble up Anhalt-Dessau on his way to devouring the empire? Would you not do better to join with the rest of the empire in resisting him?"

"With what should we resist?" The old Duke smiled sadly and shook his head. "In all my duchy, I doubt if there are seventy-thousand souls in total. Its army consists of a few old officers who command the militia, all the men between the ages of 16 and 60 who can fit into a uniform and drill upon the city greens of a Sunday. Why do you think I joined the army of Prussia in my youth to gain military experience? The army of Anhalt-Dessau it is scarcely fit to chase bandits. What use would such be against the army of France?"

"What then will you do when the French army approaches?" Emma asked, genuinely worried.

"Ah, we have our strategy well planned." The old duke gave her a sly smile. "We shall welcome the army with cheers and flowers, and with endless bottles of our tasty but powerful local cordial and a mountainous supply of our famed pastries—some of which you will doubtless sample at the banquet tonight. With flattery and compliance, with endless reassurances and soft living, we shall fatten them like capons—and corrupt their skills and discipline until they can scarce remember how to march in straight lines. The best way that we can break our enemy's sword is to rust it in the sheath. That, I daresay, is a stratagem for which Bonaparte is unprepared."

"Good Lord," Nelson muttered, clearly recalling unpleasant memories, "I can see how that might succeed! Of course, once you have softened your enemy past redemption, some other army must come and finish him, but... Good Lord!"

"I can see possibilities there," Sir William murmured, looking impressed.

Emma thought it best to smile and say nothing.

At the formal banquet that night, she discovered what Duke Leopold had meant by fattening the enemy like capons. There were several meat courses—including fish, lamb, chicken, pork and beef—served roasted, fried, baked in pastry and poached in cordial, each with its own thick and savory sauce, each accompanied by its own color and flavor of wine. The vegetable dishes—assorted roots, squash and cabbage—were garnished with slivered nuts and drenched in butter or cheese sauces. There was a thick soup swirled with sour cream, fruits honey-glazed or served with sugar and whipped sweet cream, and a dessert of assorted chocolate and cream tarts. At every course, there was wine and more wine, and Emma was obliged to ask for water to "clear the palate," at which the servants looked askance. After dinner there were speeches, accompanied by brandies and cordials. Sir William took care to speak slowly and thoughtfully, and even Nelson looked a bit weathered.

When they finally escaped back to their apartments, Sir William was groaning softly at every step. "Dear God," he exclaimed, sinking gratefully into the nearest chair while Mrs. Cadogan went to fetch his foot-basin, "I can see how the Duke's strategy would affect the French! For two centuries France has prided itself upon its cooks; they could not resist sampling, and criticizing, the Duke's dishes—or his wines, or that cordial he so kindly warned us about. He, of course, would rise to the challenge by offering them more and ever more elaborate dishes, which they would likewise sample. In short order, the French commanders would be reduced to fattened and drunken hogs, unable to govern so much as a farmstead, while the Duke's subjects would go on about their business untaxed and unmolested."

"An excellent strategy for preserving his own folk," Emma agreed, unfastening the belt of her gown, "but not of much help to the rest of the empire, or England."

"Attrition," Nelson muttered, pulling off his shoes. "If the empire can whittle away Bonaparte's forces, by whatever means, that leaves Old Boney with less to oppose England."

"Yes, attrition," Sir William agreed. "I scarcely know how to calculate just what degree of attrition the entire empire can inflict on the French. Perhaps I shall have a clearer picture when we reach Hamburg...

"Ah, here comes the good Mrs. Cadogan. I am off to my chamber, then. Hmmm, and I should caution both of you to protect yourselves from the Duke's...strategy...by eating as lightly as possible until our next state banquet."

"Oh, indeed." Nelson rubbed ruefully at his distended stomach as Sir William plodded away, and turned an apologetic glance to Emma. "Another effect of the Duke's strategy is that I'm in no condition for any, ah, strenuous activity tonight."

"Nor I," Emma grinned back. "Well, there will always be the morning."

Nelson laughed, and laboriously peeled off his waistcoat.

*****

From Dessau, the ambassador's party took a state barge down the Elbe to Hamburg. As the brisk days of October slid past, Nelson spent most of his time on deck, studying the river and observing the passing boat traffic, often accompanied by Emma. "An excellent river," he commented, noting a large

LOVE OF GLORY

pleasure yacht sweeping past. "With its depth, wind and current, I daresay I could bring a small fleet of light cutters up it, as far as Dessau at least. Their cannon would be limited, but they could make the French unsafe on land."

"Leaving the French to console themselves with the Duke's cooks," Emma laughed. "We shall defeat Bonaparte in the end. Never doubt it."

"I don't." Nelson paused to drop a quick kiss on Emma's hair. Then he caught himself, looked around to see if he'd been observed, and frowned thoughtfully. "When we reach England," he said quietly, "we can no longer be so free. We shall live in separate houses, if not in separate towns. Our moments together shall be hasty, and stolen."

"All the sweeter for that," Emma whispered. "You will come to see me, won't you?"

"Of course." He gripped her shoulder. "You and Sir William, and... our child."

"Yes," said Emma. "I shall name him for you: Horatio."

"And if it should be a girl?" he smiled.

"Horatia, then."

"A child of my name and my blood." Nelson turned to stare out at the rolling water, his expression grim. "More than Fanny ever gave me."

Emma bit her lip, but couldn't help saying, "I should not, before God, hate a woman whom I've never met."

"And I," Nelson muttered, "should not feel so embittered toward a woman who has taken such good care of my aging father."

"Your father?" Emma asked, confused.

"Oh yes." A bleak look came into his eye. "They get along famously. She has established and maintained our household for his every comfort, and teaches her son to call him Grandpapa—or, more often, just Papa."

A shocking suspicion darted to the forefront of Emma's mind, but she had the sense not to voice it.

"I suppose," Nelson went on, "that their affection is only natural, seeing that Reverend Edmund stays home, whilst I am ever away at sea. Still, betimes I feel outnumbered by landsmen in my own home. And that is not even to speak of my assorted siblings." He cracked a bitter smile. "I've long since learned that the best way to keep them from begging me for money is to beg of them, first."

Emma feared that if she bit her lip any harder it would surely bleed.

"No," said Nelson, straightening and looking out at the sinking sun, "for all that I'm an Englishman, my home is at sea. I'm never happier than in a good vessel, on the water…" he turned again toward Emma, "…or with you. This little river voyage is the best of both worlds, indeed—for here, I'm not even plagued by seasickness."

Emma laughed softly in pure delight, and stretched out a hand to him. He took it, and kissed it without a single glance around him. Emma clutched his fingers, knowing that she must never speak to him of what she now knew: that Nelson's family made him so miserable that he fled to sea to escape them.

*****

Whatever the Dukes and Princes of Saxony might think of him, the populace was fascinated by Nelson. As the ambassadorial party made its leisurely way down the Elbe, crowds gathered on the riverbanks to cheer as the barge passed, and Nelson took to standing at the prow, waving his hat at the passing locals.

When they reached Magdeburg, the curious crowds pressed so thickly around the King of Prussia Inn, where they had stopped briefly, that Nelson asked for the doors and windows to

LOVE OF GLORY

be opened, and ordered cups of wine and cakes to be handed out to the crowd. He answered questions, as their accompanying barge captain was pleased to note, from people of every standing—always urging them to fight the French. Emma likewise smiled charmingly on everyone and answered what questions were relayed to her. Sir William was kept busy with translation.

Still further down the river, one boat full of eager observers came too close and was rammed by the barge. The little boat promptly overturned, dumping its passengers into the water. Nelson, not even jarred off his feet, shouted directions for the rescue of the passengers, which were duly relayed by Sir William and promptly obeyed by the barge's crew. When the dripping sightseers were deposited safe on land, everyone on the riverbank cheered and shouted Nelson's name.

Not everyone was quite so pleased with him, though. The ship's quartermaster repeatedly failed to provide food and drink for the party while on the barge, and Sir William, after privately describing the man as a "jackal", had quiet words with the captain.

Also, the weather was growing colder.

They reached the Imperial Free City of Hamburg in the latter part of October, when the days as well as the nights had become chilly, and Emma was obliged to wear her warmer clothing. This caused her some concern since, even with a long-sleeved Empire cut, heavy wool showed the growing bulge of her belly. Fortunately, the weather also excused the wearing of artfully draped shawls and cloaks, which Emma knew how to use to perfection.

The town's mayor, bishop and merchant-guild masters were lined up along the riverbank to welcome the ambassadorial party, and enough of them spoke passable English that there was no need for a translator. After the expected ceremonies, Sir William, Emma and Nelson were conducted to the Imperial

Gasthaus: a handsome but unremarkable building done in the Renaissance style, with a fine view of the splendid St. Michaelis Church. Once left alone in their suite, the party relaxed and settled in to plan their next move.

Sir William had expected a British naval frigate to be waiting for them to take them back to England, but there was no sign of it. Nelson wrote a letter, and sent it out on the regular mail-packet ship, requesting the navy to send a frigate for the ambassador and his party, but admitted that he had no idea when he'd receive an answer—or a ship.

"Then let us make use of our time here to further our goal," Sir William pronounced. "The best we can expect from Hamburg is for it to build numerous warships for the empire and her allies, for it cannot create its own navy nor fight the French itself—save, perhaps, in the manner of Dessau."

"Why ever not?" Emma asked, indignant.

"My dear, did you not look carefully at the maps during our journey? The city sprawls across the confluence of the rivers Elbe, Alster and Bille, and is cut through with numerous canals. It has more bridges than Venice, if you please! There is nothing to prevent enemy ships from sailing up the rivers and bombarding the whole city. Likewise, the surrounding land is low and flat, and there is nowhere to place effective walls. To be blunt, Hamburg is indefensible."

"Cannot even a sufficient navy...?"

"No," Nelson sighed, "not until heaven grants us the wisdom to make cannon that can shoot for miles, rather than merely tens of yards."

"Hamburg has survived this long," Sir William went on, "upon sheer economic leverage. It has been one of the major seaports of Europe since the 12th century, and indeed was the core of the Hanseatic League of trading cities; its usefulness as a port makes it too valuable to destroy or even damage, and the sheer extent of its waterways makes it impossible to close."

LOVE OF GLORY

"A smuggler's heaven," Nelson added, smiling ruefully.

"Thus, unless our combined navies can keep the entire French fleet away from all approaches to the port, Hamburg needs must accept any French ship that lands—and if such ships carry troops, the city could not stop them. Thus, though nominally part of the Holy Roman Empire, Hamburg must perforce remain neutral."

"That would still allow it to give us certain...assistance."

"Precisely," Sir William grinned cunningly. "And it is precisely such assistance that I must go and assure. Play your parts well, my dears."

With by now practiced ease, Nelson and Emma prepared for their roles. The formal banquet, held in the town hall, found Emma in a wine-colored heavy silk gown, draped cleverly with a jacquard-silk shawl. Sir William wore his formal black with his modest ambassadorial badges. Nelson was in full dress uniform, glittering and jingling with badges of rank and his many awards. The mayor and burghers seemed suitably impressed.

While presented with such exotic dishes as green beans cooked with pears and bacon, fried forcemeat and several varieties of fish, Emma and Nelson fielded questions from their neighboring diners, most of whom spoke passable English. Most of their questions concerned the effect of the war upon trade. Emma slanted her answers to give the strong impression that French rule was ruinous for trade, giving sad examples from her experiences in Italy. Nelson told of his adventures accompanying merchant convoys and fighting off raiders. Sir William conversed at length with the mayor, in German.

The dinner ended with an entertainment performed by assorted singers, then a slow departure while exchanging brief conversations with small knots of admirers. It was a good hour before the Hamilton party reached their lodgings again.

"There is much that I will need to calculate," said Sir William, hurrying off to his own rooms. "On the morrow, I recommend that you accept the invitation to the boat tour."

Emma retired with Nelson to his bedchamber, where she undressed slowly under Nelson's scrutiny. Both of them could see how far her pregnancy was showing.

"When?" Nelson asked softly.

"January, I think," Emma replied, wincing as she felt the child kick.

Nelson stroked her bulging belly as if touching a fine vase of fragile glass. "Then…once we reach England, we cannot be together until after the child is born," he sighed. "Our time grows short, my love."

"Then let us make good use of it while we can," said Emma, gliding into his grasp.

Ever so carefully, Nelson lay back on the pillows and gently pulled her down on top of him.

*****

The boat-tour was delightful for both of them, a leisurely progress along the rivers and canals in a boat little bigger than a gondola, conveyed by two unobtrusive oarsmen and conducted by an English-speaking guide named Herr Gluck. He waxed poetic in his descriptions of the various churches, theaters, gardens and monuments, while politely ignoring the number of boats that trailed theirs, filled with goggling Hamburgers jostling each other for a glimpse of Nelson and Emma.

Nelson was, of course, particularly fascinated by the immense riverside warehouses, the numerous docks and the ships anchored there. He managed to persuade Herr Gluck to steer the little canal-boat as close as he dared to the working shipyards. Afterward, their guide was curious to know what

LOVE OF GLORY

Nelson thought of the yards, and the conversation wandered off into the technical.

They returned from the ride wind-burned, a bit chilled, and thoroughly pleased. Nelson, happy to find Sir William there awaiting them, took him off to the parlor to discuss what he'd observed.

Emma wandered into her dressing room, pulled off her outer gown and reclined on a settee, where she promptly fell into a reverie. The enchanted time was coming to an end, and she knew that she must prepare for the next stage of the journey. She must plan how to conduct herself in England. Surely that sour Lord Keith had already reached London months ago, and was doubtless spreading jealous tales about Nelson and herself. She would have to plot with Sir William as to how to counter them. Of course she and Nelson must behave with absolute propriety in public...

But her best weapon had always been her beauty, and she must take care of it.

Slowly Emma got up, studied herself in a mirror, glanced at her collection of cosmetics and thoughtfully unfastened her hair.

Chapter 7
The Campaign at Home

In preparation for their return home, Emma, on Miss Knight's advice, arranged to buy some elegant lace trimming, suitable for a court gown, as a formal present for Nelson's wife. She also sent formal letters, with Sir William's help, for her spelling was awkward, to associates in England whom the Hamiltons had met in Italy. Meanwhile, they waited for the frigate.

As October wore on, with still no ship having arrived, Sir William announced that they would need to make their own way to England. On the last day of October, therefore, they took ship on the mail-packet *King George* heading for the English port of Great Yarmouth. As a returning Crown Ambassador, Sir William had no difficulty securing the best cabins for himself, his wife, her mother and their maid, and of course the famed Lord Nelson, along with his aide. Indeed, the captain of the sturdy brig nearly fell over his own feet in his eagerness to welcome the great sea-hero, and the crewmen clambered into all manner of vantage-points to get a look at him. Nelson smiled and took care to be gracious, even strolling around the deck—while artfully keeping out of the working sailors' way—to let them all look their fill.

Emma, draped almost completely in a hooded cloak, paced daintily close to Sir William, who went straight to his cabin. Mrs. Cadogan followed, watching keenly over the loading of the party's baggage, and had everyone efficiently settled in by a good two hours before sailing time.

Knowing full well that their cabins were among the largest on the ship, Emma still felt cramped and stifled by their narrow confines. Despite her earlier resolve to be as inconspicuous as possible on the ship, she yearned to go back up on deck and pace around it with Nelson, and let the sailors gossip as they might. When Mrs. Cadogan brought the basin to tend to Sir William, Emma compromised by withdrawing to her mother's cabin.

Once safely alone, she studied herself critically in the small pier-glass mirror. Did the skin of her throat seem to sag the slightest bit? Were those the tiniest of lines at the corners of her eyes? She knew that Nelson found her beautiful, but how would her enemies see her? She must give them cause for jealousy, not for scorn. Emma went to the nearer of the sea-chests, opened it, and pulled out the alabaster jar of rendered wool-fat and olive oil. This she opened, and smeared a good-sized dab of the ointment on her face, throat, and each hand.

She was still rubbing the ointment into her skin when her mother entered, saw what she was about, and sat down on the second bed. "Eh, dear," Mrs. Cadogan smiled knowingly, "preparing for battle, are ye?"

"I must," Emma murmured, studying the effect of her work in the mirror. "Lord Keith has doubtless spread slanders about us, and they will have had time to fester."

Her mother nodded sad agreement. "Ye must walk and speak, dress and conduct yourself as every inch the lady, then. Be most utterly proper. Ne'er be seen in public except upon your husband's arm, and ne'er speak a word but in the calmest and sweetest voice. Let no man nor woman look at you and dare to call you a whore."

Emma bit her lip at the hard words, knowing well that they were true. How to paint and powder her face, then? It would have to be subtle: just enough smoothing and color to show her beauty to best advantage, not anywhere near to garish. "I have a few days yet to practice," she muttered.

"Plan well your entrance into Yarmouth," Mrs. Cadogan went on, "for 'tis very good chance that Nelson's wife shall be there."

Emma shivered. "I've never met the woman," she said. "I wouldn't know her on sight. How, then, shall I prepare to deal with her?"

"By being every inch the ambassador's proper wife."

"And this?" Emma pulled the cloth tight across her belly, showing its undeniable swell.

"Older men than he have gotten children upon pretty young wives." Mrs. Cadogan shrugged. "Cling close to Sir William, for none shall dare question whose child it is before his face."

"So I must be utterly proper—and utterly beautiful," murmured Emma, peering into the mirror again. "and I may as well start with tonight's dinner, at the captain's table."

With that, she picked up her cosmetics box and began experimenting with subtle applications.

*****

At dinner that night, the ambassadorial party played their roles to perfection. Nelson sat next to the captain, then Emma, then Sir William, then Mrs. Cadogan, while Miss Knight and Tom Allen sat below them. The ship's officers lined along the other side of the table, and the captain at its head, took their eyes off Nelson only long enough to goggle at Emma. The conversation was desultory, since the captain and his officers frequently lost track of what they were saying. Nelson kindly covered for their lapses by telling tales of his battles.

Emma smiled politely while judging her effect on her audience. She knew how well her long-sleeved blue wool Empire-cut dress flattered her, especially with the addition of her red and silver brocade draped shawl, and it seemed that the studied subtlety of her face-paint and powder made the proper impression too. Though entering her seventh month of pregnancy, she was still beautiful enough to turn heads. The food was indifferent—fresh chicken and less-than-fresh greens—but it hardly mattered. Her experiment was a success.

She would well hold her own in England.

After dinner Sir William and the others retired to their cabins, and Nelson artfully offered to accompany Emma in a constitutional stroll around the deck. They had little privacy, of course; first the sailors and then the ship's officers found a wealth of excuses to be somewhere on deck within watching distance. Only by brief whispers and the unseen pressure of fingers upon arms could they express anything of their feelings. The air was chill, with clouds to muffle the moon, and after only a single turn around the deck the two of them were more than ready to retreat indoors.

Seeing no one in the passageway to note their destinations, Emma paused in front of Nelson's door and gave him an intense look. Her returned it for a long moment, then sadly stroked the bulge of her abdomen, shook his head, and led her on to her own cabin's door. Once within, Emma sank down on her bed with a sigh.

Her mother sat on the other bed, waiting for her. "Well done, my gel," she said quietly. "Well done indeed. I ne'er saw a prettier showing."

"Oh, speak not to me of 'showing'," Emma grumbled, stroking her protuberant belly. "I can't wait for these last months to be done."

"'Tis always thus," he mother chuckled, gently tugging away Emma's cloak and hanging it on a peg. "Ye'll have excuse aplenty to retire from all social engagements when we reach home."

"Home?" Emma murmured. "These past 15 years and more we have lived in sunny Italy. England's chill fogs and rains seem alien to me now. And..." She felt tears start. "How shall my love come to me with all eyes watching?"

"Eh, dear," her mother soothed, "he could do nothing with ye in any case, not 'til the babe's come. 'Tis just as well ye retire from public view as soon as might be, and leave cruel gossip to die for lack of fuel. Dazzle the crowds once, at the banquet upon our return, and flit away like a will o' the wisp."

Emma raised her head and peered suspiciously at Mrs. Cadogan. "Have you been plotting with Sir William?" she guessed.

"Oh, but surely," her mother grinned back. "And some right clever plotting he has done, too, as ye'll see. But heed our warnings, my dear, and all will be well."

"I pray so," said Emma, letting herself sink back onto the pillows. Only to herself did she wonder how she would endure three months without her beloved.

*****

On November 6th the packet ship pulled into the harbor at the mouth of the River Yare, and drew up to the long quay on the west side of Great Yarmouth. An enormous crowd was waiting there under the stormy sky, waving small flags and cheering as the ship drew to its anchorage.

LOVE OF GLORY

Nelson, who had been fully expecting this, marched out on deck in his best dark blue dress uniform with all his decorations, strode up to the bow and struck a well-rehearsed pose. The crowd went mad, roaring like a wind-lashed sea, throwing flowers and waving banners. Nelson smiled and raised his arm in an all-purpose salute. A great groaning sigh went through the crowd as everyone saw the black patch over his blind eye and the empty sleeve where his right arm had been, and then the sound shifted to a rhythmic chant of: "Nelson! Nelson!"

The packet's crew made the ship fast at fore and aft, and set out the gangplank. On shore a band with many drums and horns struck up "Rule, Britannia" in cadence with the crowd's chanting. As Nelson set foot on the gangplank, the clouds parted enough to let a fortuitous shaft of sunlight brighten the quay and gleam from the band's brass horns. It also lit Nelson and made the medals on his uniform shine blindingly. The noise redoubled as Nelson marched slowly down the gangplank, with Sir William and Emma only a few steps behind.

"God favors us," Sir William breathed in Emma's ear. "That is a splendid bit of stage lighting."

"Dr. Graham himself could not have managed better," Emma agreed, remembering her days performing as a Hygeia, the goddess of Heath, in Dr. Graham's shows. "Now you must tell me who are the notables among this crowd."

"None but the mayor and his cabinet," Sir William noted, watching a group of be-wigged and be-ribboned officials come marching up to Nelson. "Ah, let us take a few steps closer, my dear, so as to be included in the formalities, for we are but Nelson's adjuncts now."

Nelson, after the practice he'd received in the various cities of the Holy Roman Empire, handled the pomp and ceremony well. His speech was brief and pithy, and at just the right moment he introduced "the recent ambassador to Naples, Lord

William Hamilton and his wife, Lady Emma," and the magistrates bowed with just the right amount of civility before turning their attention back to Nelson. Among other profuse expressions of admiration and gratitude, the mayor presented a well-worn bible to swear in Nelson as "a freeman of the borough." As Nelson placed his hand on the book the town clerk thoughtlessly said, "Right hand, please"—then blushed almost purple as his eyes took in Nelson's empty sleeve. "You will have to be content with this one," Nelson smiled, and took the oath to the crowd's thunderous applause.

"That makes him officially a subject of Great Yarmouth," Sir William whispered at Emma's enquiring look. "He has legal residence here, and can vote here if ever he happens to be in the district during a Parliamentary election."

"I thought he held residence in London," Emma puzzled.

"Oh, indeed," William chuckled, "and a few other places as well. He might vote a dozen times in the same election, could he but gallop across the country fast enough."

As so many times before, Nelson and the ambassadorial party were escorted to a low-backed carriage and paraded through the streets, where more crowds lined the roads and leaned out of windows to cheer them. Emma noted that Mrs. Cadogan had readily arranged transport for their luggage, and was following with Miss Knight and Tom in a closed coach some 50 yards behind. The procession went first to the Norfolk church, where the organ played "See the Conquering Hero Comes." The parade ended at the mayor's mansion, where the three were settled into smaller and plainer apartments than they were accustomed to, and promised entertainment the next day and a formal banquet the next evening. Emma's mother arrived soon after, and chivied the servants into fetching and unpacking the party's luggage. That done, she arranged for refreshments and for Sir William's foot-bath.

LOVE OF GLORY

"Ah, excellent," Sir William sighed, the moment they were alone. "I expect, good Horatio, that you will be greeted with similar hero's welcomes all across England. Pray tell me, where does duty require you to appear next?"

"I've received an invitation from my wife," Nelson replied, flat-voiced, "to bring my 'friends' with me to Roundwood, our new house near Ipswich. Since the welcoming party took care to read the invitation aloud, I daresay half of Norfolk will want to accompany us there."

"So there is to be no evading it," Sir William sympathized. "Well, soon after, we must all return to London and make our reports—you to the admiralty, and I to my ministry. Doubtless we will be called upon to attend court, as well. I see no reason why we should not travel together that far."

Under his stoic mask, Nelson looked infinitely relieved.

"As for lodgings," Sir William went on, "I've arranged in advance for the loan of a house, from an old friend, in Grosvenor Square, and it should be ready in a few days. Of course you are welcome there at any time, my dear fellow."

There was a long pause before Nelson replied. "I'm most grateful for the offer, Sir William," he said carefully. "Please do keep a guest-room available."

Sir William only inclined his head in acknowledgement. Emma said nothing, understanding what was implied here.

*****

Next morning the party set out, in an open carriage and a discreetly following coach, for Ipswich. Nothing else about the cavalcade was discreet. A cavalry detachment of the Norfolk Volunteers accompanied them to the Suffolk border, where an enthusiastic crowd was waiting and cheering. At Ipswich, the admirers detached the horses from the carriage and pulled it themselves through the town and up the road to Roundwood, intending to witness and cheer the reunion between Nelson and his wife. Nelson, in the seat of honor at the rear, sat alone and waved his hat, wearing his best formal dark uniform and a stern but dutiful look. Emma and Sir William, in the front seat facing him, wore subdued but formal finery, he in black velvet, she in blue, and smiled politely. On the way they noted that the previous days' storms had done surprising damage, uprooting small trees and scattering roof tiles.

"Not a good omen," Emma murmured. "I have caught such looks and mutterings... The people know who I am."

"'Tis the commoners' love of a good fight," sighed Sir William. "They'd be delighted if you and Mrs. Nelson brawled in the street. Indeed, they'd lay wagers."

"Then brawl is the last thing I must do," whispered Emma.

"Exactly," Sir William replied. "Be every inch a lady, every moment."

The noisy parade pulled the coach up the gravel driveway to the front door of the new Nelson house, and the head of the crowd rapped peremptorily on the front door. "Open!" he shouted. "Open for the Lord Nelson, just returned from the sea!"

Nothing happened. The door remained shut.

Bewildered, the self-styled herald rapped the knocker and shouted his pronouncement again. The crowd rumbled in puzzlement. Nelson, Emma noted, began to wear a subtle look of relief.

At length the door opened, but what appeared was a simple porter, who gawked at the crowd in amazement. To the barrage of shouted questions he admitted that he was one of the workmen who had brought the furniture to make the house ready, and that Lady Nelson wasn't there at all, but was with her father-in-law in the city.

"Where?" demanded Nelson, in his best command voice.

LOVE OF GLORY

"Er, at Nerot's Hotel, in King Steet, St. James," the bewildered porter answered. "That's the last I heard."

"Well," said Nelson, in the ensuing stunned silence, "It seems that Fanny has made a muddle of things, again." He stood up to announce to the crowd: "My apologies, my friends. We'd best turn the carriage around and re-hitch the horses, for I must go on to London after all."

The crowd dutifully followed his instructions, grumbling and muttering as they did.

"Respite," murmured Nelson, as he resumed his seat.

"I believe," Sir William whispered to Emma, "that Lady Nelson has done herself no favors with her confusion."

Emma only nodded, but said nothing.

"I say, good Horatio," he went on, "I have to make a courtesy call upon my nephew, Charles Greville, if only to see how he is managing my properties. He should be at Paddington Green just now, and could certainly put us all up for a day, if you'd like to accompany us."

"Certainly," Nelson replied, with a note of relief in his voice. "I could do with a bit of rest before dealing with...London society. Ah, and isn't this the nephew who built the port and dockyard at Milford Haven? I'd certainly like to speak to him about that."

"Excellent," smiled Sir William. "Ah, and Emma, you might wish to visit...Miss Carew whilst we are in the neighborhood."

"Oh. Yes," Emma responded, feeling a flash of guilt for having neglected her daughter so long. "I should like to see her again." *She'll be nearly twenty now*, Emma realized. *Greville swore he'd do well by her...*

"Then we go first to Paddington Green, and then on to London proper. I shall inform the driver at our next comfort stop." Sir William leaned back in his seat, looking perfectly innocent.

Chapter 8
Charles Greville and Little Emma

Sir Charles Greville's house at Paddington Green was stuffed with antiquities and scientific curiosities, some of which Emma recognized as gifts Sir William had shipped from Italy. Sir Charles himself had aged noticeably in the fourteen years since Emma had seen him last. Graying, balding, decidedly paunchy, he seemed close to his uncle's age. Looking at him now, Emma wondered at her own youthful passion for him. Greville, in his turn, couldn't seem to take his eyes off her. They made polite small talk until late, when Nelson and Sir William went off to their respective guest rooms. Mrs. Cadogan duly followed Sir William. Emma lingered, as did Greville, until at last they were alone.

"Well," Greville broke the silence, "you look very well, Emma."

"And you, Sir Charles," Emma lied smoothly. She couldn't help adding, "I wonder that you never did marry, after all."

Even in the dim light, Greville blushed visibly. "Ah, well," he temporized, "you know, I truly did woo Henrietta Middleton, but in the end, she refused me."

LOVE OF GLORY

"Indeed." Emma tried to sound sympathetic, remembering that it was in hopes of winning the rich young heiress that Greville had foisted her off on Sir William. *I daresay I got the best of the bargain*, she smiled inwardly. "But did you never try again?"

Sir Charles looked away. "Er, no," he replied awkwardly. "The rejection rather discouraged me, and now I believe I am too old."

Emma bit her lip to keep from laughing aloud. Sir William had been older still when he'd married her, no doubt to Greville's dismay.

But now Sir Charles was staring at her bulging belly as if he couldn't quite believe his senses. "And is it true that you are with child to...my uncle?" he ventured.

Emma spread her hands wide with a smile. "You see my condition," she said, letting him draw what conclusions he would.

Greville chewed his lip in turn, and glanced significantly at the ceiling—above which Lord Nelson could be heard moving about in preparation for bed. Emma only continued to smile, and after a moment Sir Charles shrugged his thought away. "Well," he said dryly, "at the rate of one child every sixteen years, you cannot be accused of overbreeding. Little Emma is at Blackburn house at the nonce, if you wish to visit her."

"Indeed, I do!" Emma brightened. "I've not seen her in all these years, nothing but occasional letters: I so wish to see how she has grown. Is she quite well, Charles?"

"Quite," Greville sniffed. "She soon will be done with her schooling, and I expect to obtain a position for her as governess to a respectable family."

"Excellent," Emma murmured, wondering if he had placed the tiniest bit of emphasis on the word 'respectable'. "I will call on her tomorrow. Does your coachman know the way to Blackburn house?"

Greville blinked, as if he hadn't expected Emma to commandeer the use of his coach, but he yielded with good grace. "Certainly," he managed. "I have been there to pay the girl's fees, often enough. Do go in the late afternoon, for she then will have arrived home from school."

That direction, Emma guessed, was to give him time to warn the Blackburns of her coming. She began calculating just what dress and shawl she would wear for the visit.

"Ah, well," said Greville, rising from his chair, "the hour grows late, and I have much to discuss with Sir William in the morning. Good evening, Emma."

A quick bow, and he was gone. Emma stared after him for a long moment as the fire sank down to coals in the grate, wondering how Greville remembered their time together. He'd been happy enough to possess her then, pleased enough with her youthful beauty, flattered that other men—including the great painter, Romney—were so smitten by her and so envious of him.

Yet she knew perfectly well that he'd been eager to pawn her off on his uncle, in exchange for becoming Sir William's heir. He'd been coldly calculating then; what did he think of his clever plotting now? Did he regret anything? Could she even consider him still a friend?

With a sigh, Emma got up and made her way to the stairs.

*****

The carriage that stopped at the Blackburns' modest house had been brushed to gleaming, as had the matched bay horses. The lady who stepped out of the carriage was a study of subdued elegance in her blue woolen long-sleeved Empire dress and fur-trimmed cloak. The housemaid who let her in gaped for a moment, then bowed repeatedly. The Blackburns, forewarned, had gathered in the parlor along with their ward,

LOVE OF GLORY

Emma Carew, but whatever self-possession they'd assembled was blown away like feathers on the wind as Lady Hamilton entered. Emma greeted the husband, then the wife, graciously, but her attention was riveted on her daughter.

Little Emma had grown into a lanky young woman, chestnut-haired and passably pretty, but with none of the striking beauty her mother had possessed at the same age. Her shell-pink gown, no doubt her best dress, revealed that she hadn't inherited Emma's sense of style, either: its indifferent fit and fussy furbelows did nothing to accentuate her figure, and the color made her skin appear sallow and her pale eyes look washed out. Emma ached with pity for her, but showed none of it.

"My dearest child," she said, taking the girl's hands in her own, "how well you look. I'm so pleased to see you at last."

"And y-you too," Little Emma mumbled, blushing.

"Oh, I've so much to tell you of our adventures in Italy and in the empire, but first tell me of yourself. How goes your schooling?"

While the girl blushed and stammered, the Blackburns took advantage of the moment to order tea and biscuits. The maid dithered so pitifully that Mrs. Blackburn hurried to help her. Mr. Blackburn excused himself to go outside and smoke his pipe, and mother and daughter were left momentarily alone.

Little Emma seized the moment to ask boldly: "Is it true what they whisper about you, at school?"

"Why, what do they say?" Emma asked innocently, guessing that she already knew.

"Th-that you...were Lord Greville's mistress, and that's where I come from."

Emma bit her lip, knowing that there was more whispered than this. Also, she was sure it were best that her daughter never know that Emma had had a lover other than Greville. "It is true, child," she said carefully, "that Sir Charles refused to marry me, for I had no fortune. He'd hoped to wed the Middleton heiress, so he sent me away. He did, however, promise faithfully to do well by you—as I hope he has."

"Yes," Little Emma admitted.

At that point Mrs. Blackburn and the maid returned with the tea service, and the talk shifted to politer topics. "Little Em does so well in school," Mrs. Blackburn gushed. "Her teachers simply adore her, and she won the medal for Elocution last spring."

One would scarcely believe it now, thought Emma, observing the fumbling girl before her. "I'm so pleased to hear it," she said, as expected.

Mrs. Blackburn prattled on, between sips of tea and bites of biscuit, and Emma filled the gaps with murmurs of appreciation. Eventually Mrs. Blackburn caught herself repeating the same comments, and escaped through the obvious route of saying: "Ah, but I'm sure you two wish to be alone for a while, to catch up, and all that..."

Alone again with her daughter, Emma for a moment could think of nothing to say.

Little Emma brought up the topic for her. "All your letters," she almost whispered, "about Italy, and being the ambassador's wife, and the war with the French and all, I read them over and over. They were like fables, or fairy-tales."

Moved by an impulse of generosity, though she knew it was unwise, Emma asked "Now that I'm back in England, would you wish to come live with me and Sir William? We have an establishment here in London..."

"Oh, no!" Little Emma gasped, clearly frightened. "I couldn't! All among the high lords and ladies—all politics and intrigue and... Please, no. Besides, I—I'd miss my school friends, and I'm doing so well there, and—and Lord Greville said he'd have a position for me as soon as I've finished, and... I really couldn't come away. No."

LOVE OF GLORY

Emma heaved a great sigh, partly in relief, partly in pity. Greville had done no more nor less than he'd promised; he'd given Little Emma a 'respectable' upbringing and set her to a 'respectable' future. He'd never promised to teach her fine manners, nor art, nor to make her a lady, as he'd done for Emma. The child would indeed be 'respectable'—perhaps happy and safe—and nothing more. She would live and die in obscurity, and be content with it.

As I was not, and never could be; but she is not me. With a tearful smile Emma embraced her daughter, and then let her go.

She took her leave graciously of the Blackburns, promised to write again to Little Emma, and returned to the carriage.

All through the ride back to Greville house she wept quietly, but by the time she alighted at the front door her eyes were dry.

Chapter 9
Fanny Nelson

The respite at Greville house apparently heartened Nelson sufficiently to face the lions, and the Hamilton party returned to London on November 9th, where they found the Grosvenor Square house not yet ready for habitation. They sent Mrs. Cadogan, Miss Knight, Tom Allen and their baggage to a hotel on Albemarle Street, but for themselves—as requested—they went straight to Nerot's Hotel to meet Nelson's family. Sir William was dressed in a suit of black worsted, and Emma wore a subdued dark blue woolen long-sleeved Empire, artfully draped in a lighter blue-and-gold jacquard shawl. She'd been careful to dress her hair in a simple chignon and wear but the lightest of face-paint; for this role, she knew, she must be discreet and retiring. Nelson, of course, wore his full formal uniform.

And of course they were recognized in the street, for who in all of Britain could fail to recognize Nelson by now? Crowds hurried after them and congregated around Nerot's to watch them disembark, giving ample warning of the arrival to all within.

LOVE OF GLORY

Indeed, they had scarcely set foot inside the elegant lobby when a familiar figure in a naval uniform came hurrying toward them.

"Ah, Hardy!" Nelson recognized him. "Fancy meeting you here. How have you been?"

"Please, sir," Captain Hardy fumed, "where the mischief have *you* been? We heard you'd landed at Yarmouth, and then nothing more. I was about to set off for there myself, guessing the reason—"

At that point he caught sight of Emma, blushed red as a turkey's wattles, and said nothing more.

"Why, the last I'd heard from Fanny was to come to Roundwood house in Ipswich," Nelson said smoothly, "so I repaired thence. Imagine my chagrin at finding no one home."

Hardy paled as quickly as he'd blushed before.

"I then turned toward London," Nelson went on, "but given the state of the weather, and the roads, I only arrived this morning. I trust the family is at home?"

"Yessir," Hardy managed to croak, "in the main suite."

"Then let us proceed there directly," Nelson said with a stiff smile. "As per her invitation, I've brought my friends, Lord and Lady Hamilton. Come along, my dears."

As Emma swept past Hardy, she considered that if he kept turning red and white and red like that someone might mistake him for a barber-pole.

To the main suite they went, where Nelson paused for only an instant before rapping on the door. The door swung open to reveal a middle-aged woman in a somewhat rumpled Empire dress, who promptly asked: "What news, Hardy?" before she recognized the man standing in front of her. Her mouth dropped open, and she had nothing to say.

"Greetings, wife," boomed Nelson, smiling rigidly. "I'm home from the sea, at last."

Fanny Nelson took a faltering step backward, and Emma got a good look at her for the first time.

At first impression, Emma was struck by the woman's resemblance to the Emperor Francis; the woman was likewise flabby, sallow, long-nosed, and beginning to run to fat, with a face shaped by a common expression of petulance.

At her best, she was no competition. And she knew it.

"Ah, Fanny," Nelson went on smoothly, "allow me to introduce to you the Crown Ambassador to Naples, Lord William Hamilton, and his wife, Lady Emma Hamilton."

"...No..." Fanny whispered, staring.

"Lord and Lady Hamilton," Nelson continued, deliberately not hearing, "my wife, Lady Frances Nisbet Nelson."

"How delightful to meet you," said Sir William, stepping forward and giving his best ambassadorial bow.

"Most charming," said Emma sweetly, giving the necessary degree of a curtsey.

"A gift, to the lady of the house," said Sir William, holding out the neatly wrapped package of laces. Fanny cringed away from it as if it were a snake.

"Ah, what might that be?" asked an older gentleman, lumbering up from behind Fanny and shamelessly taking the package.

"Some fine lace, to trim a court gown," said Emma, very politely.

"Ah, and now my father, the Reverend Edmund Nelson. Father, Lord and Lady Hamilton," Nelson went on through the introductions. "Captain Thomas Hardy you already know. I'm surprised that my brother William and stepson Josiah aren't here."

"*Adopted* son," Fanny hissed, blushing furiously. "and you know quite well why they aren't here."

"Ah ha ha ha ha ha! William is afraid that you intend to ask him for money," old Father Edmund laughed, "though I should think you'd not be lacking, after all the prize money you've got from your victories, eh?"

Nelson cracked a genuine smile. "Why, I have not the full rights to that until after I've visited the Admiralty," he said, "which I really must do this afternoon."

"As must I repair to the Foreign Office," Sir William added. "We truly cannot stay long."

At that, Fanny Nelson looked infinitely grateful.

"Then by all means, let's to our luncheon," urged the old minister, rubbing his hands.

"Er, yes, let's," added Captain Hardy, blushing again.

*****

Luncheon was a frosty affair, with Fanny glowering at Emma every moment, Emma smiling politely back, Sir William smoothly conversing with Father Edmund about their travels, Nelson tossing in occasional comments, and Hardy looking utterly miserable. Everyone ate perfunctorily, with only Father Edmund seeming to actually taste—let alone enjoy—the food.

It was Hardy, sweating under his collar, who put an end to the ordeal by reminding Nelson that he really *must* get to the Admiralty soon.

"Ah yes, I suppose I must," said Nelson, artfully pulling back from the table. "Heaven knows how late I shall be kept there."

"And I also," added Sir William, rising smoothly. "Come, Emma: we must be off about our duties."

"Ah, pity," smiled the oblivious old Father Edmund. "Do come again soon, won't you?"

"When we can, surely," said Emma demurely, rising and taking Sir William's arm. The two of them began moving toward the door, Nelson in tow.

LESLIE FISH

"One moment, Horatio!" Fanny snapped. "A word with you, before you go."

Nelson halted and turned, frowning. Hardy looked as if he were about to faint.

"*Arrivederci*, then," said Sir William, steering Emma and himself out the door. As it closed behind them he halted and leaned close. "I daresay," he whispered to Emma, "that the sounds of battle will be audible from here."

Sure enough, even the thick wood of the door didn't muffle Fanny's howl of: "Husband, how dare you bring your—your pregnant *whore* into my house?!"

Father Edmund's shocked voice cut in: "Fanny! Such language!"

Then followed Nelson's unmistakable growl: "Because you, madam, invited the Hamiltons. And what did you mean by that little comedy of inviting us to Roundwood, where all of Ipswich saw us arrive at an empty house?"

"Please, sir! Madam!" Hardy wailed.

"Nelson seems to be holding his own," chuckled Sir William. "Now let us make haste to our carriage to wait out the storm."

A light drizzle of rain was indeed falling as the Hamiltons got into their carriage, but they both knew that wasn't the storm he meant.

It was a good ten minutes before Nelson emerged, looking darkly furious, with Hardy trotting nervously behind him. They climbed into the carriage, whereupon Sir William spoke up first. "My dear sir, let us stop by the Albemarle Street hotel and let Lady Emma out before continuing on. We shall both doubtless be long at our reports, and there is no point obliging her to wait for us."

"Yes, indeed," snapped Nelson. "And I should pick up Tom while we are there."

A quick word to the driver had the coach rattling off at a good trot. There was silence for several long minutes before

LOVE OF GLORY

Hardy, pale again, dared to mumble: "I'm truly sorry for all that, sir. Truly."

Nelson gave him a cold look. "Can I assume, Captain," he said, "that you had no part in... ah, fanning the fire?"

"No, milord!" Hardy paled further. "I—I came to the hotel expecting to find you, to remind you of the impatience of the Admiralty. 'Twas Lady Nelson who importuned me to find you, I swear."

"I see," said Nelson, looking little mollified.

"In fact, sir, in fact..." Hardy stammered, beginning to blush again, "you are not expected at the Admiralty so late in the day. Tomorrow will do quite well."

Nelson stared at him for a long moment, and then broke into a thunderous laugh.

*****

As the carriage drew up to the Albemarle hotel, Emma noticed a familiar figure walking hastily away from the door. She caught Sir William's arm and pointed. "Will'um, isn't that Captain Troubridge, whom we last saw in Palermo?"

"It is, indeed," murmured Sir William, peering through the drizzling rain. "I wonder what he is doing here. If he meant to renew our acquaintance, I wonder that he did not stay."

The mystery was partly solved when the party reached their suite to find a mess of letters waiting, Tom fluttering about repacking Nelson's gear, and Miss Knight and Mrs. Cadogan faced off like a pair of tigers—which ended the moment Sir William came through the door.

"Ah," he said mildly, "I take it there has been some news while we were out?"

"Oh yes," Miss Knight gushed, pointing to the uppermost letter. "The house at Grosvenor Square is finished, and we shall be able to move the household into it tomorrow."

"Excellent," said Sir William. "And what did Captain Troubridge have to say?"

Mrs. Cadogan quickly filled the ensuing silence. "He came to see Miss Knight, sir, rather than you."

"Ah, to press a suit perhaps?" Emma volunteered.

Miss Knight said nothing, but only blushed.

"Milord Nelson," Tom Allen cut in, "where shall I be moving your gear? We had a note saying that the house your wife rented at Dover Street isn't ready yet."

Nelson blew out a breath slowly. "Then we are here for the night, I daresay, and off to Nerot's again tomorrow, after I've finished with the Admiralty. Sir William, I do hope your apartment here has room enough."

"I'm quite sure of it," said Sir William, "and for Captain Hardy as well, if he should be so inclined."

Hardy was quick to decline, claiming he had lodgings of his own elsewhere, and beat a hasty and grateful retreat.

*****

When everyone else was settled, Emma went quietly to Nelson's chamber. They lay cuddled together, though her advanced pregnancy forbade them anything but to hold each other.

"This shall be our last night for a long time," he told her quietly. "I am obliged to stay with Fanny and my father, at least for a while. It will be...difficult, not seeing you."

"I am sure to be obliged to attend at least a few social functions with Sir William," Emma murmured. "We can at least see each other, at least speak..."

"You must tell me when the child is born."

"Indeed, you will have an invitation to the christening."

"And afterward..." He frowned into the dark. "I don't know. I simply don't know."

LOVE OF GLORY

Emma hugged him fiercely, and they said nothing more.

Chapter 10
Cross Currents

In the morning Sir William and Lord Nelson dressed formally, Nelson in his best dress uniform and all his medals, and set out for their respective ministries. They left Tom to carry Nelson's baggage off to Nerot's, at which he seemed none too pleased. Emma, Mrs. Cadogan and Miss Knight arranged the packing of the Hamiltons' baggage, and conducted it to the house now lent to them by Sir William Beckford.

The house was a relatively new Georgian brick structure, well trimmed and elegant, furnished with quite good paintings and small sculpture such as an art-dilettante friend of Sir William's might be expected to own. The cabinets and clothes-presses were ample, and Miss Knight hastened to fill them with the Hamiltons' gear. The rooms had been aired, the linens freshly cleaned and the pantry well filled, and Mrs. Cadogan soon had fires burning cheerily in the kitchen and parlor.

With the men gone and Miss Knight mysteriously avoiding her, Emma was left alone to pace irritably through the new house. Eventually her mother took her in hand, sat her down firmly by the fire and served her an herbal infusion that settled her stomach and calmed her nerves.

LOVE OF GLORY

"What, then?" she asked gently. "Are ye dismayed by the welcome ye got from Nelson's family?"

"Oh, not for myself," Emma snapped. "I never had a moment's doubt that he'd change his heart... And certainly not for the welcome his wife gave him."

"Hmmm, then do ye worry for fear of what society shall say of you?"

"No." Emma smiled grimly. "Between Nelson's glory and my own skills, I've no doubt I can hold my own among them."

Mrs. Cadogan paused a moment in thought, and then guessed: "Eh, and how did ye fare with Little Em, then?"

"Oh, Mother," Emma burst into tears, "there is nothing of glory about her. She plans to be a governess, and probably marry a shopkeeper, and do nothing more with her life—and that is all that she wants. She's nothing like me!"

"Ah, well, ye're nothing like me, either," Mrs. Cadogan chuckled. "Ye got some lucky drop o' some long-ago king's blood, I daresay. Besides, Little Em is also Sir Harry Featherstonhaugh's daughter, nay?"

Emma only nodded, thinking of her early love-life.

"Well, I've ne'er heard it said that Sir Harry had much of either looks or brains. The cleverest thing he e'er did was take you for a mistress, and then yield ye to Sir Charles when ye got with child. And the cleverest thing Sir Charles did was trade ye to Sir William, in exchange for a mess o' pottage. I'd say joining your fortune to Sir William be the best thing that e'er happened to ye."

Second best, thought Emma.

"I daresay, until ye met Sir William ye didn't find a man fit to breed at your own level." Mrs. Cadogan grinned pointedly at Emma's swelling belly. "If I'm any judge, this child shall be the prettier—and the more ambitious. Leave Little Em to her humble contentment, and think on the future."

"I will, that," said Emma, considerably cheered, and sipped her herbal tea.

A few minutes later, the clatter of wheels outside announced the return of Sir William's carriage. Emma straightened up and took care to smooth her hair.

"Ah, what a day it has been," said Sir William, plodding into the parlor with a pronounced limp. "Lord, but I've been kept standing about waiting, and trotting from chamber to chamber, until my old bones are sore. Good Mrs. Cadogan, would you fetch my basin, and my slippers? I've no wish to walk or stand again until I must." He dropped gratefully into one of the tapestried chairs, tossed his hat aside and unbuttoned his waistcoat.

"How did the ministers receive your report, Will'um?" Emma asked, as her mother went off to fetch the requested items.

"With much interest," he said, rubbing his hands. "My commentaries upon the state of the Holy Roman Empire appeared to coincide with observations from other, ah, travelers, and I got the distinct impression that the crown is engaged in most secret and intense discussions with the Czar. It is our general consensus that the empire cannot hold Bonaparte for more than five years, at most. After that, it shall be up to England—and hopefully Russia—to defeat him, and I pray we can build up our armies to a sufficient force by then. This shall be a long conflict, my dear. I pray I live to see the end of it."

"Surely you will," said Emma, clasping his hand. "And what of Nelson?"

"I've no doubt the Admiralty will keep him until late," Sir William shrugged. "I saw part of the welcome he got. Again, crowds recognized him, cheered, and plagued him for speeches, which he dutifully gave, until his agent, Mr. Alexander Davison, rescued him. I hear that he has been invited to the Lord Mayor's procession and the banquet afterward." Sir William

LOVE OF GLORY

frowned briefly. "I've not heard of any such invitation for ourselves."

"I see," said Emma, as if it were nothing to her. "And are our duties now ended, that we may repair to private life?"

"Not entirely," said Sir William, giving her a wry look. "I expect that there will be invitations soon enough. And of course, Nelson will be coming here for dinner early this evening before attending. I expect he wants a respite from...all the attention."

"Of course," smiled Emma.

"Oh, and Sir Charles will be visiting too. Doubtless he and Nelson shall have more to talk about, concerning Charles' harbor."

And Charles Greville's presence, Emma privately reflected, would be excuse enough for Nelson to dine with the Hamiltons, if any gossips were listening.

*****

Nelson returned to the Hamiltons' apartment in far better humour than he'd left it, arriving just before Sir Charles. They both settled down at the dining table to discuss such technicalities as dock widths and dredging. The rest sat and listened in polite attention, while Tom Allen was left to serve the dishes.

Emma noticed that Miss Knight flicked her gaze continuously back and forth between Greville and Nelson, and wondered what that portended.

Over the dessert Nelson joked about his reception in London. "I've never seen the Admiralty behave with such deference," he said. "They fairly seemed to tiptoe around me. I'd expected to be sent back to sea almost at once, but they practically insisted that I stay in the city for some months, making the social rounds."

"Not surprising," Sir William commented. "As the only man ever to beat Napoleon, you are a great symbol of hope to the populace. Of course the Navy wishes to show you off. I daresay your presence will be requested at every *soirée* in London for the next half-year."

Emma saw that Miss Knight was fidgeting with her spoon, and wondered if she should ask about the woman's nervousness.

"Ah, enjoy fame whilst you can," Greville laughed. "Society's favor is as fickle as the wind. In another turn of the moon, some new sensation may drive you from the public mind or alter your reputation altogether."

"Indeed," piped up Miss Knight, setting down her spoon. "Your pardon, Lady Hamilton, but I must be gone to Albemarle Street."

"Truly?" Emma blinked. "And when shall you return?"

"Not at all, I think," said Miss Knight, rising, ignoring the dark look that Mrs. Cadogan threw at her. "As Captain Troubridge warned me, you are sailing into dangerous waters, milady. I've no wish to be there when the storm strikes. Good day to you."

With that, she turned and walked quickly, quietly, to the front door, and out and away.

In the ensuing shocked silence, Mrs. Cadogan muttered, "I'd wondered why she left her luggage there."

Nelson, annoyed, reached for his wineglass. "What a damned bitch Miss Knight is," he growled to all and sundry.

"There are, alas, all too many like her," Greville considered.

"I am constantly amused at the hypocrisy of the age," murmured Sir William past his cup. "We all know, very well, that there is not a man in all the ministries who doesn't either keep a mistress or go a-whoring in the discreet clubs. One should think they would grant their finest warrior the same privilege."

LOVE OF GLORY

"Perhaps," said Greville, giving his uncle a shrewd look, "one would do well to investigate the privy doings of Lord Nelson's chief opponents, possibly to gain the names of their paramours or sporting-houses. Such knowledge might make a useful counterweight to hypocrisy's calumnies."

Sir William leaned forward, smiling. "Could I trust your discretion in such information gathering?" he asked.

"I will certainly see what I can do," Greville shrugged, spreading his hands.

"I hate to leave, actually," grumbled Nelson, "but I must go and prepare for the Lord Mayor's festivities. Tom, time for us to pack up and go. Milords, milady, I hope to have the pleasure of your company again soon."

With many assurances to meet again, Nelson and Tom Allen, soon followed by Sir Charles, made their departures.

"I must go hire some proper maids," Mrs. Cadogan said, heading for the kitchen. "And I wish Miss Knight scant joy of her Captain Troubridge."

When they were alone Emma turned a thoughtful eye to Sir William. "How severe do you think the scandal is?" she asked quietly.

"We shall know only when we note which hosts invite us, and which snub us," he answered, taking a last sip from his cup. "I notice, for example, that I, as a returning ambassador, was not invited to the Lord Mayor's banquet, nor have I heard aught about being presented at court, much though the Foreign Office was pleased with me. Well, we shall learn soon enough who our friends are."

"I had thought that Captain Troubridge was our friend," Emma said mournfully. "and Miss Knight, for that we took her in when her mother died and brought her safe to England."

"My dear," sighed Sir William, "the only sin which approaches pride in its extent is ingratitude."

LESLIE FISH

*****

The next day brought better weather in the morning, two new maids at noon, including a Nubian named Fatima who could speak Italian, and Mrs. Cadogan bustling in with news.

"I've never seen the like," she reported. "As Lord Nelson followed the Lord Mayor's procession, the folk cheered him like the very thunder. Then they unhitched the horses and pulled his carriage themselves up Ludgate Hill to the Guildhall, where the mayor presented him with an engraved sword. Himself made a pretty speech of gratitude, but could scarce be heard for the cheering. Aye, and he has been invited to a morning meeting at St. James' Palace, where he is to be presented to the King."

"How interesting," Sir William murmured, "that as a returning ambassador, I received no such invitation."

"Just who might our enemies be, precisely?" Emma pondered.

"I daresay Sir Charles may have some news of that tomorrow," Sir William considered. "But, after dealing with the court of Naples, I believe we can manage the simpler intrigues of London."

Emma said nothing, but pressed a hand to her belly, where she felt the child kicking.

The next day's enforced idleness ended when Greville, as promised, appeared.

"Lord Nelson's presentation was not a success," he noted wryly over a glass of port. "He wore all his decorations, which actually annoyed His Majesty—who was not pleased with the Neapolitan medals, nor the spray of Turkish diamonds pinned to Nelson's hat, nor to Nelson's holding the title of a Sicilian duke. The King merely asked concerning Nelson's health, and then turned to chat merrily for half an hour with an unsuccessful general. It was not very flattering, and all the court noted it. It was also noted that Lord Nelson was...disappointed that yourselves were not invited."

"It is not well that the King is at odds with his greatest military hero," Sir William commented. "Recall the unfortunate case of Belisarius in Byzantium."

"The balance of power is somewhat different here," Greville hastened to say. "It is well known that His Majesty is...not well, and suffers from...fits."

"How did he appear?" Emma asked.

Greville tapped his fingers thoughtfully on his glass. "I have heard his physiognomy compared unfavorably to that of the Emperor Francis," he said carefully. "As you know, the King's... indisposition caused the creation of the Regency, which is ruled by the highest of the peers—and that sort are, to say the least, conservative in their views. There is a growing party in support of the Prince of Wales, intending to give him *de facto* control of the Regency, which may in time become official."

"Indeed?" Sir William's eyebrows climbed. "This seems to have been done with much discretion. I confess, I've heard nothing of it until now."

"One thing the English do know how to be is discreet." Greville shot a wry glance at Emma. "It is also well known that, whatever the King may think, His Royal Highness, the Prince of Wales, is delighted with Nelson, and intends to meet him formally."

"In what fashion, do you think?" Emma asked, clenching her hands on her napkin.

"Patience," Sir Charles smiled, enjoying his moment. "The First Lord of the Admiralty is entertaining the Nelsons at his home this evening, upon which I shall doubtless have news for you tomorrow. Meanwhile, Sir Alexander Davison plans a grand dinner at his house in St. James's Square tomorrow, to which yourselves are certainly invited—as well as the Prince of

Wales, and Lord Nelson, and five cabinet members—including no less than the Prime Minister."

"What?!" Sir William marveled. "What does this portend?"

"Why, simply that Lord Nelson is to take his seat in the House of Lords at the end of the month." Greville paused to take a sip of port and let the import of that sink in. "After which, from what I hear, the East India Company has invited him—and you—to a dinner at the London Tavern on Ludgate Hill, where Nelson is to be honored with a dramatic presentation of some sort. As I said, the Prince's faction waxes as the King's wanes, and Nelson is to be a gem in the Prince's crown."

"I see," murmured Sir William, sitting back in his chair.

So did Emma. "You must tell me," she said to Sir Charles, "how Lady Nelson dresses and behaves at Lord Spencer's dinner tonight, so that I may trim my sails accordingly."

"You may play Cleopatra to her Octavia," Greville said cautiously, "but take care not to be too flamboyant. English fashion is more subdued than Italy's, or the Empire's."

"Only be beautiful," murmured Sir William. "Beautiful, and noble."

"I believe I can manage that," said Emma.

*****

Emma spent most of the next morning ensconced with her mother, examining her wardrobe, jewelry and cosmetics, and plotting the uses of what Mrs. Cadogan called "a woman's armory." Sir William briefly commented on the similarity between Italian court politics and English women's politics. At length Emma put on a simple gown for dinner, and awaited word of her enemy's armaments and dispositions.

The news, when it came, was brought not by Sir Charles Greville but by an old friend of Nelson's, Vice-Admiral Cuthbert

LOVE OF GLORY

Collingwood. The balding but still impressive old gentleman greeted Sir William first, then gave Emma a frankly appraising look which ended in an appreciative smile. As the three settled in for luncheon, he happily recited what he'd learned.

"At Lord Spencer's dinner last night," he said, helping himself generously to the roast gamecock, "Lady Spencer noted that Nelson treated his wife with, as she put it, 'every mark of dislike, and even of contempt'. He was morose and spoke little, whilst Lady Nelson fussed over him as if he were an invalid, which did not in the least improve his temper. Indeed, his rebuffs of her solicitousness drove her to tears. Afterward, whilst the men remained over wine to talk of the Navy, Fanny followed Lady Spencer into the withdrawing room and unburdened herself at great length."

"I can imagine," Sir William commented drily.

"Indeed, her language became rather intemperate, at which Lady Spencer was much taken aback."

"Not terribly discreet of her."

"Pray tell me, sir," Emma cut in, "how was Lady Nelson dressed?"

Sir Cuthbert wrinkled his forehead in surprise. "Rather severely," he recalled. "She wore a gown of virginal white, which did not flatter her complexion, and restrained herself to but few jewels. She seems determined to take a martyr's pose in society, which rather exacerbates the embarrassment of Lord Nelson's position."

"I see," murmured Emma, calculating what she would wear that evening. "Am I to understand that she will not be present at Sir Alexander's dinner party tonight?"

"Indeed not," the old Vice-Admiral laughed. "She is a trifle outgunned, and so far prefers not to engage the enemy directly. So sail on boldly, my good dame. These waters may be deep, but you should find only allies upon them tonight."

Emma smiled, catching the allusions. "You shall find me well-rigged, sir, I assure you," she said.

Sir Cuthbert laughed so uproariously that he overturned his wineglass.

*****

Sir William's timing was impeccable. Lord Nelson had entered through the carved double doors of Davison's grand house a full three minutes earlier, allowing time for the assembly to greet him properly. Sir William waited quietly until the cheering stopped, and then stepped toward the doors with Emma on his arm. The steward announced them no more loudly than he had anyone else, but the crowd in the reception room beyond hushed at once.

Emma paced beside Sir William, chin held high, knowing what an impression the two of them made. The ambassador looked quietly elegant in black velvet, adorned only with his badges of office and honors. Emma wore a shimmering white Grecian gown, with the largest of her embroidered shawls draped—like a classical Greek *peplos*—around her right hip and bunched at the waist, coyly concealing the bulge of her belly, up over her left shoulder, where it was held by a diamond pin, and then trailing down her back. With it, she wore plain white kid slippers, her long kidskin gloves and her diamonds. Her face-paint had been applied with meticulous subtlety, and her hair was caught up by a white satin ribbon in an elegantly simple Psyche knot. She was, she knew, an image of classical elegance. Those in the crowd who had seen those paintings of her from 15 years previous would recognize her now and not find her wanting.

The reaction of the assembled guests was all that she could have hoped. Stunned and admiring faces followed her as she and Sir William made their way toward the chair where Sir

LOVE OF GLORY

Alexander waited to greet his guests. On the slow and stately march toward their host, Emma caught fragments of whispers:

"...Romney's muse..."

"...no sylph now, but Venus..."

"...no wonder..."

She dared not glance to left or right, but knew that somewhere in that crowd Nelson stood watching her.

And then they reached the chair, where Sir William performed his bow and Emma her curtsey with long-practiced ease. With the proper words said, the Hamiltons bowed again and took their formal steps back, then turned to their right and proceeded to their expected place in the waiting line. For one instant Emma caught a glimpse of Nelson, staring openly at her and smiling. Only a glance, and Emma politely turned her gaze back to the open length of hallway and the next guest to be announced. She managed to keep her smile slight, no more than mannerly, but inwardly she was gloating. No, there had never been a chance that Nelson might change his heart and return his true passion to his wife.

And her own beauty had bolstered Nelson's reputation, no matter what tales Lord Keith had told. She might have left England as no more than Romney's model and Sir Charles' mistress, but she had returned as the ambassador's wife, a reigning beauty, and the mistress of the greatest hero in all Britain. Let the self-righteous gossips contend with that.

Eventually the formal greetings ended, the doors to the dining room opened, the musicians in the gallery struck up a stately tune, and the assembled party followed their host to the long table. As so many times before, Emma found herself seated between Nelson and Sir William. They smiled knowingly at each other, recalling other banquets in other lands, aware of exactly how to play this game.

The meal was long, elaborate and full of toasts to Nelson. He met the salutes with brief speeches, well-rehearsed after his tour through Europe, and the company smiled appreciation. Emma, covertly watching the guests from behind her wineglass and utensils, noted no less a personage than the Prince of Wales casting an unmistakably lustful eye upon her. She saw that Nelson also noted this, and frowned, so she took care to glance at the Prince no more than at anyone else. In fact, it was easier to keep her eye upon the Prime Minister, since the formidable Sir William Pitt was given to long toasts and longer speeches.

Eventually the dinner ended, and the guests withdrew to assorted waiting-rooms for half an hour. Emma took the time to visit the necessary room, where she took care to repair her face-paint and hair. She returned just in time for the announcement of the dancing, hurriedly took Sir William's arm and paced beside him into the ballroom. The musicians struck up a stately waltz, in which everyone joined.

Emma dutifully trod the measure with Sir William, who looked as if his feet were already paining him, and was grateful enough to seek a chair and sit beside her husband for the rest of the dances. She noted with approval the position of the nearest chandelier, mounted with its galaxy of candles, their light enveloping her in a soft glow.

She also noted, with amusement, that as soon as she was seated the footmen came hurrying to her bearing trays of exquisite small cakes and flute-glasses of champagne. Emma graciously accepted a plate and glass, and pretended not to notice the servants' looks of wide-eyed admiration.

Nor were the gentry far behind. A bold youth approached her, blushing, introduced himself as "a student of the great Romney" and begged leave to sketch her portrait. Emma graciously declined, on the grounds that her modeling days were far past, but thanked him for the compliment. Another would-be artist, she noted, kept his distance but sketched furiously on a small hand pad with a lead pencil. A pair of stammering girls, just old enough to be out in society, came

LOVE OF GLORY

leaning on each other for moral support to ask about her the source of her marvelous gown. Her gentle reply, concerning dressmakers of Trieste and Vienna, sent them off speculating furiously as to who in all of London could create anything similar.

As a stately elderly couple approached, Sir William whispered in Italian, "For God's sake, charm that old dragon; she is the infamous Lady Hale." Emma racked her memory for any word of who Lady Hale was, and why she was infamous, as the old gentleman went to Sir William and chatted with him about the political reliability of the Saxon states. Lady Hale said nothing, but raked Emma with a cool and calculating eye. Emma only smiled and spread her hands wide, as if to say that she was concealing nothing. Lady Hale responded with a twitch of a smile, and a nod that could have been a salute from one equal to another.

When the old couple had departed, Sir William explained—again in Italian—"She had children by so many different lovers that none but herself could keep track of them."

"Ah, so that is why she approved of me," Emma considered, in the same language.

"Indeed," Sir William said with a trace of mirth, "she had most liberal ideas about breeding for health, beauty and vigor. ...Oh, but here now is another admirer."

This one was a saucy youth who asked Emma if she would perform any of her famous Attitudes at the ball. Emma smilingly replied that such had not been requested nor anticipated, but once settled in London she might indeed give performances at concerts of her own. Close on his heels jostled a blushing young fellow who wished to invite her to a formal dinner at Lady Amherst's house—his mother, he took care to say—a fortnight hence. Emma smiled fondly and said she would be happy to accept, but must first ask her husband's secretary if they had previous engagements. Next came two middle-aged ladies with questions about Italy, but who couldn't take their eyes off her diamonds.

And on, and on, as the musicians played and the dancers paced, guest after guest came to pay informal respects to Emma and her husband. She fielded them all with the skills she had gained in Italy and the empire, taking care to show herself in the best light at every moment, cheered on by Sir William's occasional comments in Italian. At length she saw Nelson approaching, alone, and though her heart thundered her demeanor remained unchanged.

Nelson paused before the two of them, gave Sir William a bow and smile, then turned his eyes back to Emma. "You are looking well, milady," was all he said, but his tone implied much.

"In your honor," Emma replied, voice pitched so that none but Nelson—and Sir William—could hear it. They smiled at each other in perfect understanding.

"I shall send word," said Sir William, just as softly, "as to when it will be politic to make a visit."

"'Politic' it may never be," Nelson grimaced, casting a glance sidelong. "The gossip has spread like plague. I've been nagged by more wives than my own... Ah, damme, there comes another. I bid you good evening."

He turned, not too abruptly, and walked off, not too quickly, but enough to escape a fat and righteous-faced dowager in taffeta, who rustled after him like a pursuing ship under full sail.

"That is the Lord Chaplain's widow, I believe," noted Sir William, in Italian.

"Oh, that they should vex him so!" Emma replied fiercely. "He that has won more battles against England's foes than any man living!"

LOVE OF GLORY

"Vanity, envy and spite," Sir William began, intending to lead into a fitting quote in Latin. He broke off as the Prince of Wales himself approached.

Prince George Augustus Frederick was a robust man in his late 30s, blessed with thick dark hair and a sturdy figure beginning to run to fat. His clothes were elaborately cut, and decorated with thick ruffles of lace and gold embroidery. He walked with a touch of a swagger, and the gaze he turned upon Emma was more than appreciative. He smiled widely as he asked smoothly: "Lady Emma, may I have the honor of the next dance?"

Emma didn't need Nelson's worried glance from afar or Sir William's warning squeeze on her arm; her instincts, honed by decades of practice among the wealthy and powerful, set off her private alarms sufficiently. "I am indeed honored, your Royal Highness," she replied sincerely, "but my delicate condition precludes any more such activity than I have already done tonight."

The Prince blinked, then stared at the bulge of her belly under the artfully-draped shawl, and gave an amazed laugh. "Oh, indeed," he chortled, still staring. "I hadn't realized—Ah, some other time, perhaps?" He turned and strode away, still chuckling, much to Nelson's visible relief.

"Could it truly be that he didn't know?" Emma asked Sir William, in Italian.

"His Royal Highness is not noted for being terribly perceptive," the ambassador replied. "Still, you may be sure, after tonight no one in London shall remain ignorant. The child's parentage, however, should remain in doubt until we are better situated."

He followed that with a quote in Latin, of which Emma caught only a reference to vigor and age.

"I fear that must be only a dozen weeks more, at best," Emma murmured, feeling the child kick again.

Chapter 11
Dramatic Rivalry

On November 20th Nelson was formally seated in the House of Lords, introduced—to considerable applause—by the Foreign Secretary and Lord Romney. That was followed by another social triumph for Emma, the lavish dinner at the London Tavern, where a magic-lantern show of transparent paintings of Nelson's battle at Aboukir Bay was displayed. Fanny Nelson did not appear at that either gathering, and Emma dared to wear more colorful dress. Still more admirers gathered to speak to her, and Nelson could scarcely take his eyes off her—save when he was drawn into a corner to confer quietly with Sir William and Lord Greville. Though the Hamiltons drove home alone, Emma felt as if Nelson's presence were still with her.

"I pray I've done my part well," she said to Sir William as they alighted at the Grosvenor Square house.

"That you have, my dear," Sir William assured her, "Well played. Very well played, indeed."

Right then a sudden motion to their right caught Emma's eye. She turned in time to see a young street lout hurl something at her. "Whore!" he shouted, just as the missile—a fresh horse-turd—spattered her dress.

LOVE OF GLORY

"Be damned to you!" roared Sir William, raising his walking-stick as if it were a sword.

Quick as a cat, Emma bent down and sideways, grabbed a fragment of paving-stone from the street, and hurled it at the lout. Her aim was true; it caught him on the forehead and knocked him backward, howling as he clasped the suddenly bleeding cut.

By that time Sir William had gotten within reach of the youth and given him a sharp rap on the pate with his walking-stick. The lout, seeing the odds so disastrously against him, turned and reeled away, moaning.

Sir William hurried back to Emma, who was feeling about for another stone, and took her by the arm. "Into the house, my dear," he said, reaching for the knocker, "and quickly."

The maid who let them in gaped at the obvious despoilment of Emma's dress, and Sir William—once the door was safely closed—ordered her to fetch a robe for her mistress. With that, he helped Emma get out of the dress, right there in the hallway. "I had thought," she grumbled, letting the wide skirts pool around her feet, "that Englishmen were better behaved than the street urchins and Lazzarone of Naples."

"There is more going about here than meets the eye," murmured Sir William, taking the robe from the maid and wrapping it about Emma's shoulders. "It is not simply hypocritical self-righteousness, but an underlying war of factions. Those of the King side with Fanny Nelson; the Prince's side with Horatio and you."

"And doubtless every man in England joins one team or another!" Emma steamed, handing the smirched dress to the maid. "Can we not be shed of such foolishness?"

"Not quickly." Sir William narrowed his eyes in thought. "I believe we should change residences, without announcing that fact to all and sundry."

"Eh, Sir Will'um," said Mrs. Cadogan, as she entered the hallway holding an envelope, "this was delivered an hour ago. I'm told 'tis an invitation for yourself and Emmy to come to the theatre with Lord Nelson."

"Indeed?" Sir William took the note, opened and read it, and frowned tightly. "The game moves on," he muttered. "Nelson's wife shall also attend."

*****

A distant bell chimed the hour after noon, and Emma still sat before her dressing-table, staring at the mirror, wondering what role to play at the theater that night and how best to dress for it. Her hand, almost of its own accord, skittered to a dish of sugared almonds as if the sweets could settle her mood.

"Child," Mrs. Cadogan admonished from behind her, "ye must stop comforting yerself with food, lest ye grow big as a house."

Emma pulled her hand back guiltily.

"That, and gambling," her mother continued, "they'll be the death of ye, do ye not exercise some caution."

"Should I indulge in drink, then, as so many do?" Emma retorted irritably.

"Indulge in nothing." Mrs. Cadogan shook her head. "Keep yer wits about ye at all times, my girl, for ye've set yerself on a perilous road and shall find enemies at every turn."

"I know," said Emma, meeting her mother's eyes in the mirror. "Well, I wished for an adventurous life, did I not?"

"The choice of Achilles," proclaimed Sir William's voice from the doorway. "The post has come, and the paper with it. You may find it interesting, I daresay." He held out the offending paper, opened to a particular page.

Emma took it and looked. Prominently displayed at the top of the page was an etching that showed a recognizable

LOVE OF GLORY

caricature of Sir William peering at a collection of sculpture and antiquities, while on the wall above and behind him hung two portraits of herself and Lord Nelson, attired as Cleopatra and Mark Anthony.

"Rather well done, I do admit." Sir William deftly caught the paper as Emma thrust it away in disgust. "Note that not much scorn is heaped upon Horatio or yourself. The artist's pen describes you both as great beauties, and myself as but a nearsighted old *cognoscente*, unaware of the intrigues about him. There could be worse roles, I daresay."

"So that is how it is to be played," murmured Emma, pondering the power of art and public imagination.

"Just so," said Sir William, settling on the nearest chair. "The King's faction represents age, settled wealth, stolid virtue —and the concealment of its multiple breechings."

"Like Lady Hale," Emma remembered.

"Aye. Hypocrisy is the tax which vice pays to virtue. Meanwhile, the Prince's faction represents youth, vigor, adventurousness, and a certain forthright honesty about private matters. That is where we find ourselves, my dear—and I expect the whole game shall be on display at the theater tonight, for news of our presence with the Nelsons has spread, and all the able penmen of the daily papers are expected to attend."

"To report on the battle, no doubt." Emma glowered into the mirror. "Well, I played this game cleverly enough in Naples. Mother, pray do lay out my blue satin gown and the headband with the several feathers."

She reached decisively for her rouge-pot, certain now of what role she would play.

*****

It took careful planning to maneuver the Hamiltons' carriage in right behind the Nelsons', especially through the enormous crowd milling about the front of the theater, but the clever coachman managed. Sir William waited until the Nelsons stepped out onto the pavement, and watched while the company cheered their hero.

Fanny Nelson, Emma noted, wore a severe gown of virginal white and a simple turban of violet satin. The effect suggested was clear enough, but the combination of cut and colors was not flattering.

Emma smiled as she awaited the right moment, then stepped out of her carriage with quiet dignity. All heads turned, and many jaws dropped. Emma kept her smile restrained, knowing how her voluminous blue dress, gold-embroidered shawl and headdress of feathers contrasted with her rival's display. No one in the crowd could look at the two of them and not understand why Nelson preferred her. Fanny Nelson's frozen expression revealed everything. So did Nelson's smile as he reached out a hand to invite the Hamiltons to join him. The crowd pulled back respectfully as the two couples swept into the theater.

"Round one: success," Sir William whispered in Italian as they paced up the stairs to the Nelsons' private box.

The play itself was a trifle, a frothy comedy of mistaken identities and half-heard conversations, and Emma scarcely noticed it. Her attention was held by the quiet but constant murmuring of the audience, who strained to look up at the Nelsons' box far more often than to watch the play. Emma, settled between Sir William and Lord Nelson, discreetly gripped Horatio's hand under the concealment of her shawl. Fanny sat at Nelson's right side, near his empty sleeve.

At the intermission, as soon as the curtain came down and before anyone could rise from their seats, the band struck up a lively tune and a tenor strolled out on the stage to sing a rousing ballad about Nelson's victory on the Nile. Nelson, with

LOVE OF GLORY

a fleeting expression of amused annoyance, stood up to accept the tribute and saluted when it was over. The crowd cheered.

As Nelson sat back down again, Emma felt an urgent need for the necessary room. She passed a quick word, in Italian, to Sir William and pulled herself to her feet. Nelson, startled, asked where she was going. "I feel a trifle faint, and need a bit of fresh air," Emma temporized, moving out of the box.

"Oh, you can't step outside alone," Fanny Nelson said quickly, rising also.

Something about her eagerness warned Emma not to let her rival get too close. She hurried out of the box, then left down the corridor that led to the stairway. Fanny hastened after her, momentarily hampered by her close-cut skirt, and aimed herself toward the stairs, clearly assuming that Emma would go that way.

Instinct warned Emma not to let that woman get above her on the stairway. She hurried on down the corridor, making a good guess from her own days in the theater that there would be a private jakes for those who could afford private boxes. And yes, ahead she could see the familiar small unmarked door. As she pattered past the stairway without turning, she heard a hiss of frustration from the woman behind her. Suspicions confirmed, Emma all but ran to the small door and pushed it open.

Yes: behind it lay, not just a board over a cupboard, but a proper seat and a washbasin. Thanking whatever theater-manager had been so sensitive to comfort, she shut the door behind her and locked it. Her relief, when she pulled up her skirts and sat on the seat, was far more than physical.

Did she truly believe she could do it and escape unscathed? Emma wondered, feeling a trifle lightheaded. No doubt the King's faction of the nobility would readily accept the idea that a pregnant woman falling down stairs to her death could be purely an accident, but the commons would guess otherwise.

Surely Nelson too would guess. *The woman has no sense,* Emma concluded as she washed her hands. *But, that makes her no less dangerous.*

Someone jiggled the doorknob, then knocked politely. An unknown male voice asked if the closet would be occupied long. "Just leaving," Emma promised, hastily drying her hands. She opened the door upon the surprised smiles of two young gentlemen, one of whom hastened past her with only a brief word of apology. The other gallantly offered to escort her back to her seat. Since a quick glance down the corridor showed Fanny Nelson still lurking by the stairs, Emma accepted the offer. She returned to the theater box with Fanny trailing sourly behind, and politely introduced the delighted gentleman to Nelson. The encounter was brief, since the play was about to resume and the young gallant had need of the privy himself. Emma settled between Nelson and Sir William as primly as if nothing had happened.

But as the second act began, Emma whispered to Sir William, in Italian: "Can we avoid any further encounters with that woman?"

Sir William barely raised an eyebrow. "I shall see what I can do," he promised.

*****

Despite Sir William's best efforts, the Hamiltons were invited a few days later to attend another play with the Nelsons. "I suspect 'tis for public show, my dear," the old ambassador apologized as Emma distractedly brushed her hair. "We must remain amiable before the crowd."

"Would not doing so reflect badly upon the Prince's faction?" Emma grumbled, fussing with a recalcitrant lock.

"Most certainly," sighed Sir William. "Time is Prinny's invincible ally. Because all know that he will ultimately win, he

LOVE OF GLORY

must soothe the fears of the King's faction lest they commit desperate stupidities as their power ebbs."

"I will do my best," Emma promised, "But I shall need some assistance if I am to be put within that woman's reach again."

"I believe," Sir William smiled, "that we may safely include the estimable Mrs. Cadogan in our party."

*****

The play was *Pizarro*, a popular melodrama. Again, the crowds cheered Nelson and the theater orchestra struck up a salute for him, and again he acknowledged their adoration with good grace. This time Fanny Nelson was in severe black and white with a plain gold cross prominently displayed. Emma wore her wine-colored wool gown with a contrasting blue jacquard shawl and her diamonds, and smiled pleasantly at everyone. Mrs. Cadogan was seated at Sir William's other side, wearing a subdued but elegant dove-gray gown with jet earrings and a single cameo brooch. She also sat leaning slightly forward in her seat so that she could look across the box to see everyone in it, and she glanced often at Fanny Nelson. Fanny, for her part, darted poisonous glances at Emma—until she caught Mrs. Cadogan intercepting them, then she subsided. To all of this, the men seemed oblivious.

Emma and Mrs. Cadogan, having used the necessary room just before entering the theater-box, felt no need to leave during the intermission. Fanny did, and insisted that Nelson accompany her. Apparently he met with more admirers on the way, for he returned in good humor, while Fanny appeared, if anything, more sour than before.

"Frustration does not suit her," Sir William commented, in Italian.

"She might do better," Mrs. Cadogan replied in the same tongue, "to accept with good grace what she cannot change."

"One might say the same of the King's whole party," Sir William murmured.

The play resumed, trotting through an assortment of intrigues and betrayals in flamboyant style. At one point the Wronged Woman of the piece declaimed on how a woman's love can turn to hatred, and Fanny gave a theatrical sigh and sagged in an equally theatrical faint. Nelson only gave her an irritated look, grumbled, "Oh, what is the trouble now?" and signaled for an usher to fetch a glass of water. Emma pretended to be absorbed with the play and to notice nothing.

After the play they parted company amiably, Nelson being caught by a crowd of admirers while the Hamilton party made good their escape. Once safely ensconced in their carriage riding homeward, Emma ventured to ask what Fanny had hoped to accomplish.

"To wring some pity from the audience, and from Horatio, no doubt," Sir William judged. "If so, I daresay she was disappointed in the latter."

"She may not yet be done," warned Mrs. Cadogan. "Even so, the fool woman is going about this all wrong. Everyone knows ye catch more flies with honey than with vinegar."

Emma thought of what it would be like to have Horatio and then lose him, and felt a spasm of pity for Fanny. "Poor thing," she murmured. "Poor thing."

"Emma, my dear," said Sir William, patting her hand, "your kindness does you credit. But then, you have always had a good heart."

"Aye," sighed Mrs. Cadogan. "if only the head would match."

*****

A week later, after much ado in the House of Lords about military spending, another invitation arrived.

LOVE OF GLORY

"This one is for dinner at the Nelsons'," Sir William frowned. "It might be an attempt at peacemaking."

"I'd best come along anyway," said Mrs. Cadogan. "This little war is far from ended."

So it was that the Hamiltons, wearing formal but subdued clothing, arrived at the Nelsons' apartments that evening braced for a session of subtle diplomacy. Tom Allen, looking more careworn than when they'd last seen him, ushered them in with the air of one approaching a battle at sea. Horatio's father happily welcomed them to the sitting room with glasses of excellent port. In a spirit of almost desperate amiability he regaled them with bits of gossip from the local church, and Sir William diplomatically encouraged him. Nelson looked bored to the point of tears, and Emma sympathized entirely. Mrs. Cadogan nodded and smiled and sipped her port, but her eyes tracked alertly around the room.

At last Tom Allen, with a desperate glance at Nelson, came to announce that dinner was served. The company rose gladly—old Father Edmund with some help from Tom—and they paraded into the dining room.

Fanny Nelson stood behind the chair just to the right of the head of the table, and she had obviously set the scene with care. Two silver candelabra and what appeared to be all of the household's silver cluttered the table. Flowers had been stuffed into every available vase, and tall white tapers burned in the candleholders. Fanny herself was decked out in a voluminous silver-and-green jacquard satin gown, which flattered neither her figure nor her complexion, and what appeared to be every piece of jewelry she owned. Her hair had been done up in an elaborate pompadour with—oh, heavens!—a small model of a full-rigged ship pinned on top. She had plainly been trying for an impression of opulence and splendor, perhaps to intimidate her rival, but the total effect was pathetic. Emma found herself honestly pitying the woman.

LESLIE FISH

Fanny imperiously guided Father Edmund to the head of the table and Horatio to the seat beside her. Mrs. Cadogan, with apparent innocence, took the chair directly opposite her, obliging Sir William to sit across from Nelson, with Emma at the table's foot. Fanny shot her a frown, but dared say nothing. Tom Allen hurried off to the kitchen to fetch the first dishes. Father Edmund happily took his seat and the rest followed. He also intoned a long and elaborate blessing for the meal. There was then an awkward silence which Sir William, ever the diplomat, hastened to fill with a question to the old minister about his church's charity work. Father Edmund expounded happily until Tom Allen came back with the soup course.

The soup was a sorry attempt at oyster bisque, which the Hamiltons managed to swallow without grimacing. Emma considered that Fanny would have done better to cook a good hearty chicken broth with barley, such as any English housewife could make, and wondered if the woman had hired a local cook specially for the occasion or had risked doing the cooking herself.

Sir William expanded the conversation to include Horatio by asking him about his experiences to date in the House of Lords, at which point the talk became a little livelier. Emma caught Fanny throwing bitter glances at her, saw that her mother was quietly taking note of them, and continued to smile pleasantly. Tom cleared away the soup bowls and tureen, and returned shortly with the fish course, which was steamed river-mussels. The little shellfish had at least been cooked tender, but had almost no flavor. Nelson made wry comments about getting clear and honest answers out of assorted peers on the subject of expanding the British army, and Sir William was offering helpful hints, when the salad course arrived: an uninspired collection of shredded cabbage, lettuce and roots.

Emma was looking about for any sign of salad dressing when she felt the child in her belly give a ferocious kick. She

LOVE OF GLORY

dropped her fork and paled, horrified at the thought that the baby might be coming early. Nelson noticed, and broke off in mid-complaint to stare at her. The child kicked again and Emma felt it ram at her stomach, setting off a wave of nausea. She pushed hastily away from the table and wrenched herself to her feet.

"My dear?" Sir William queried gently.

"W-which way is the necessary?" Emma gasped, feeling her stomach heave insistently.

"Down the hall, last door to the right," Father Nelson pointed. "Oh dear, I hope the mussels weren't upsetting."

Mrs. Cadogan, likewise shoved back her chair, shot a thunderous look at Fanny Nelson, and demanded: "Emmy, what did you eat that I did not?"

Too busy fighting her stomach to speak, Emma only hurried down the indicated hallway. She heard her mother come clattering after her, and Nelson's voice snarling, to someone: "What have you done?!"

Emma made it to the last door on the right, into the necessary closet and all the way to the cabinet before her stomach erupted. "Stay there!" said Mrs. Cadogan, closing the door behind them. "Bring up everything! Water... Lord, where's a cup?"

Emma only hung over the cabinet's seat-hole, gasping, until she felt her belly quieting. "I am quite well now," she panted. "The babe kicked me, most royally hard, that was all."

"Are ye sure?" he mother peered at her. "'Twasn't a bad mussel, was it? I'd not put it past that woman..."

"Just a monstrous kicking, Mama," Emma reassured her, pulling upright. "'Tis all done now. Ah, I need to wash my face."

They could both hear furious shouting from the distant dining room.

"Wash well," said Mrs. Cadogan, pouring water in the basin. "Take your time, dear. Let's wait for that storm to pass."

But the shouting didn't cease, though they waited several minutes. At length Emma decided it would be more politic to come out than to stay hidden. She and Mrs. Cadogan strolled out of the chamber and down the hallway, and reentered the dining room just in time to hear Nelson say: "—what *you* never gave me!"

Everyone fell silent as Mrs. Cadogan, followed by Emma, came back into the room. They saw Horatio and Fanny on their feet, facing each other across a good six feet of distance, both red-faced and looking a little disheveled. Father Edmund was cowering in his chair, looking terrified. Sir William was likewise seated, his hands raised helplessly. He smiled in relief as he saw the two women come in.

"Ah, Emma dear," he said consolingly. "I trust you feel better?"

"Oh yes," Emma hastened to say. "Just the result of my condition."

Fanny said nothing, but turned beet red.

"Ah, well," said Sir William, getting to his feet, "I confess to feeling a bit under the weather myself. Might I ask to make an early evening of it, my good host?"

Father Edmund seemed too frightened to answer, but Horatio replied: "Of course, my good sir. We can always dine again at another time."

"Let us be away, then. Tom, do be so good as to fetch our wraps. Father Nelson, I thank you for your most enlightening news of the church..." With more smooth phrases Sir William steered Emma and Mrs. Cadogan out the door and swiftly away. He didn't drop his unctuous chatter until they were safely into their carriage and trotting off toward Grosvenor Square, whereupon he sagged like an understuffed pillow and mopped his brow with his kerchief, though the night was chill.

"Ah, was it very bad, then?" Mrs. Cadogan enquired.

LOVE OF GLORY

"Terrible," murmured Sir William, stuffing his kerchief back in a pocket. "We shall have to change lodgings as quickly as might be arranged."

"But we must inform Lord Nelson of where we are going!" Emma fretted.

"I suspect there will be no need of that," Sir William made answer.

Nothing more was said as the Hamilton party arrived at their rented house and went inside. Only as Emma and her mother prepared to go upstairs did Sir William call to Mrs. Cadogan: "Madame, please see to it that the fire in the sitting-room is kept up, and have some brandy present. I expect we may have a late guest tonight."

Mrs. Cadogan hurried off to comply. Sir William headed into the sitting-room himself, and Emma hurried upstairs to change out of her formal clothes and into a lounging robe. That done, she sat before her dressing-table and distractedly brushed out her hair. She dearly wished to know what had passed between the other diners while she and her mother were in the necessary, but feared to ask Sir William directly. Heaven knew what insults Fanny might have thrown at him, too.

Time passed and the hours grew late, but none of the three could sleep. Silent, nameless tension hung over the house like a waiting thunderstorm.

Close upon midnight a knock sounded on the front door.

The sound was soft, but it made Sir William flinch and Emma jump out of her chair. She all but ran to the door and recklessly threw it open.

On the doorstep stood Horatio Nelson, in the same clothes he'd worn earlier, looking inexpressibly tired—though he smiled when he saw who had come to greet him.

"I've left her," was all he said.

Chapter 12
Tria Juncta in Uno

No one was awake early the next morning except Sir William, who penned several letters and sent them out in quick succession. The first went to Nerot's hotel, asking Tom Allen to bring Nelson's kit to the Hamiltons' house. Others went to various friends and allies, asking politely for invitations that would take Nelson and the Hamiltons out of London as quickly as possible. Still others went out to other acquaintances, seeking fitting but discreet lodgings away from Grosvenor Square—quickly.

Of course, the news was all over London by the next day.

Rescue arrived in the form of a letter from one William Beckford, inviting Nelson and the Hamiltons to come spend Christmas—and many days before—at his mansion in Wiltshire. Most gratefully, the Hamilton party set out for the Beckford mansion on the 19th of December.

As they passed through Salisbury, they were met by a welcoming committee: an escort of local volunteer cavalry, a band playing patriotic tunes, and cheering crowds.

LOVE OF GLORY

"'Tis all for you," Emma smiled at Nelson, who looked a little dismayed.

"'Tis the price of glory," Mrs. Cadogan remarked.

"Simply smile through the formalities," advised Sir William, "as you must surely have learnt to do by now, and give the speech we wrote out yesterday. Accept the pageantry as your due, sir, and all shall be well."

Nelson sighed and once again accepted the burden of his fame.

When he finally returned to the carriage, bemusedly holding a huge gilded key, Sir William offered him a drink from his flask and briskly ordered the driver to hurry on. Nelson gladly accepted the drink, and sank back in the cushions. "What am I to do with all these symbolic keys—to towns which have neither walls nor gates?" he asked plaintively.

"Keep them handy," Sir William answered. "If ever you need to vote several times in one election, you can ride from town to town, showing your keys..."

Nelson laughed, and reached for the brandy flask again.

"The people make this show for love of you," Mrs. Cadogan noted.

"Much more such love, and I am undone." Nelson wiped his mouth and handed back the flask. "Yet heaven knows when the Admiralty shall send me to sea again."

Emma shivered with an inexplicable chill. "How long...?" she ventured.

"Our admiralty has been known," said Sir William, "to keep able officers ashore, cooling their heels on minimal pensions, for years at a time."

"And then it wonders," Nelson added darkly, "why officers fight over the prize money for captured enemy ships."

"Yet I think the high admirals will not keep you ashore too long, my dear fellow." Sir William eyed Nelson keenly. "So long as Napoleon and his allies have any ships at sea, the admiralty shall need you abroad to hunt them."

"Ah, but I pray not too soon!" Emma breathed.

Nelson smiled at her. "No, not too soon," he agreed.

*****

William Beckford held no title but had an enormous fortune, built upon the West Indian trade, and he spent it on his eccentric tastes. His house at Wiltshire, called Fonthill Splendens, was an enormous mansion in the Palladian style with a perfectly huge Gothic "folly" attached. He also had a crowd of other Christmas guests waiting to meet Nelson and the Hamiltons: his architect, the President of the Royal Academy, opera singers, poets, actors and artists. He had planned lavish entertainments for all of them, but most especially for the Hamilton party. At the grand Christmas Eve fête Emma was even persuaded to perform some of her 'Attitudes', which she managed quite well, despite her advanced pregnancy, thanks to considerable draperies. Nelson was impressed, and a little dismayed, by the extent of the celebrations. Sir William noted the fascinated respect paid to Nelson, to Emma, and even to himself. Mrs. Cadogan, however, observed that the local gentry kept away from Fonthill Splendens, which drew primarily an intellectual/artist crowd.

The pleasantries ended the day after Christmas, when all of them were obliged to return to London. Sir William had arranged discreetly for the rental of a house on Clarges Street, in Piccadilly, and Nelson learned that his wife had rented a house in Dover Street.

Wearing a resigned look, Nelson hired a carriage to take himself and Tom to the Dover Street house "To deal with legal formalities," he explained, rubbing his head.

LOVE OF GLORY

"Not divorce, not yet," Tom whispered to Mrs. Cadogan, who duly reported the exchange to Emma.

Emma busied herself with settling into the new house, arranging for a midwife, and listening to what gossip Mrs. Cadogan and Sir William could pick up concerning Nelson's progress. There was a tale, related by Nelson's solicitor, that Fanny had given him a flat ultimatum—Emma or herself—and Nelson had chosen Emma and walked out of the house for the last time. There was another, which Sir William confirmed, that the admiralty had moved with extraordinary speed to appoint Nelson vice-admiral and second in command of the Channel Fleet—his duties to begin on New Year's Day, 1801.

"I suspect," Mrs. Cadogan commented, "that they mean to get him away from Emmy as fast as possible."

"In any case, he has the commission he wanted." For a moment Sir William wore an almost smug look. "I daresay he is sure to find plenty of French ships to hunt."

"Ah, but he will not be here for the birth of the child," mourned Emma, looking down at her protruding belly.

"He will be in steady communication, though." Sir William waved a freshly opened letter. "This details a code by which the two of you can say anything without danger of being compromised, should the letters be intercepted. Ah, he also warns you to beware of the Prince of Wales, who has a lecherous reputation."

"He need not worry," Emma laughed, and then felt the child kick again.

*****

After New Year's, with Nelson gone to his ship and the social whirl ended for a time, peace settled over the Hamiltons' house. Emma abandoned her fashionable finery for simple Empire shifts and voluminous robes, and stayed indoors by the fire. She dutifully ate the dishes her mother prepared for her, picked out infant's clothes and a christening robe, and otherwise spent her days reading books Sir William had picked for her—or Nelson's letters, when they arrived, and which she answered with all the outpouring of her fervent heart. His letters, she was delighted to see, were as full of passionate yearnings and remonstrances as any opera or melodrama. No, there was no doubting his love.

The house's anonymity kept pests and gossips away from their door, and Sir William and Mrs. Cadogan kept the papers away from Emma, so that she saw none of the scurrilous caricatures or commentaries about Nelson and herself. The last weeks of her pregnancy were spent in drowsy comfort and warm expectations.

On the last day of January Emma felt the unmistakable signs of approaching labor, hurried to her bed and sent for the midwife. By that evening the child was born, a healthy girl, and Emma wrote a triumphant letter to Nelson. The next morning Emma engaged a Mrs. Gibson as nurse, and the day after that received Nelson's ecstatic reply.

As she'd promised, Emma named the girl Horatia.

Fleet duties kept Nelson busy until the end of February, when he finally got three days shore leave. He wasted no time hurrying to London to see Emma and their little daughter, not stopping to so much as speak to anyone else. He burst in through the door of the Clarges Street house like a whirlwind, and embraced Emma so fiercely that Sir William warned them to take care lest they both fall down. He stared, awed, at his baby daughter and kissed her sleeping forehead as carefully as if she were made of the finest porcelain, then tiptoed away. For the next two days he never let Emma out of his sight.

Sir William and Mrs. Cadogan conferred quietly in the library, and the household ran smoothly around the smitten lovers.

LOVE OF GLORY

On the third day of his leave Nelson lingered as long as he dared. "I can scarcely bear to part with you," he whispered in Emma's ear, "but I have orders to sail for the Baltic. I believe that if I can achieve a great victory there, I can obtain a divorce on my return."

"Oh, but be careful!" Emma murmured back. "I fear so much for you when you are at sea, and I shall pray ceaselessly for your return."

"Nothing could keep me away," Nelson promised. He kissed her one last time, and then hurried to his carriage. Emma watched until it had vanished completely down the street, then shivered in the cold and returned to the house.

Sir William was in the sitting room, frowning at a clutch of papers. Emma helped herself to a glass of port and sat down beside him. "Much though we hate to see him leave, my dear," he said, "'tis just as well that Nelson has departed for sea just now. The czar's Armed Neutrality aids France entirely too much, and the Swedes, Danes and Prussians move to join it. Czar Paul is fickle in his alliances, I fear. A show of strength is needed now to make it clear that the Armed Neutrality is unwise, and Nelson is surely the man to do it."

"I fear for his safety," Emma admitted, "yet I also fear to distract him from his duties."

"In that case, my dear," Sir William frowned, "you had best put down these latest rumors flying about that the Prince of Wales is paying court to you. It will do our friend no good to be distracted by jealousy, you know."

Secretly, Emma was worried by the Prince's attentions. His approval of Nelson sanctioned their unorthodox alliance; if his admiration turned to rancor for any reason, the Prince was in a position to cause much harm, not only to her and Sir William, but to Nelson.

"I have not the least intention of disporting with the Prince of Wales," Emma sniffed. "but now that the fashionable season is starting again, I *must* go out and hold my own in society."

"Be careful, then, what invitations you accept."

Emma resolved to do just that.

*****

Invitations did indeed trickle in for the next month, all from members of the artistic set, none from the political aristocracy. Sir William noted that this was to be expected of the King's faction. He was also perturbed by the news that Czar Paul had been assassinated and promptly succeeded by his heir Alexander, who might take a more solid position on France, one way or another.

In early April they got the news that Nelson had thoroughly trounced the Danes at Copenhagen and was now moving toward Sweden. London celebrated Nelson's victory in subdued fashion, not having seen the Danes as much of an enemy, but Emma was ecstatic. Soon afterward came word from the Admiralty thatNelson had been given complete command of the fleet, that he had intimidated the Swedes into compliance and was sailing for Russia. Nelson also wrote to Emma that he had been slowed in his progress only by catching a nasty cold. Emma replied with a letter full of endearments, congratulations on his victories, and concerns for his health.

Soon after Emma received a flurry of new invitations, and Mrs. Cadogan began to chide her about eating too well and spoiling her figure.

In May came news that made Sir William cackle with glee; Nelson had relied upon diplomacy, of all things, to win Czar Alexander's agreement to disband the Armed Neutrality. Soon after that Parliament made Nelson a viscount and granted him leave to return home.

LOVE OF GLORY

Emma heard of this while at a dinner party, and happily danced the tarantella for an hour—first with Sir William, then with the actor Kemble, then with all the other guests, and then with the servants, including Fatima. Everyone was impressed with her stamina, if not her propriety.

And on July 1st Nelson returned to London.

*****

"The public opinion of the three of us appears to have stabilized," commented Sir William, as he flicked his baited hook a little further out into the river. "Upon opening the paper, one is as likely to encounter gentle mockery as applause. In sum, the general attitude is approval—gained, no doubt, by your notable victories, sir."

Emma, sitting with her back against a tree, said nothing. Nelson, lying with his head in her lap so that she could soothe away his headache, smiled lazily. "Nonetheless," he said, "I am delighted to be out of London, avoiding not just the annoying gossip but also the heat."

"The weather is lovely here at Staines," Emma agreed, running her fingers through Nelson's hair.

"Years ago, when I was aground with no commission in sight," Nelson went on, "I thought country life an utter bore. Now, I daresay, I've developed a taste for it. Indeed, I have it in mind to buy a country house..." he looked up at Emma, "where the three of us could live quietly, just as quietly as this, and be perfectly content."

"It sounds wonderful," Emma murmured.

"Seriously, Em, could you endure being away from the social whirl of London, where you've cut such a swathe?"

"Of course I could. There are times, I swear, when I find social obligations a burden. And I would be with you. What other society would I want?"

"Besides," Sir William mused, "I daresay, if you wished it, you could attract society to yourself, wherever you might be. See how well William Beckford managed... Aha! He's taken the bait!"

Emma laughed in delight, watching the elderly ambassador wrestle enthusiastically with the river trout on his line.

Nelson sat up and looked at the sloping riverbank behind them, where his brother William and family sat eating luncheon on a spread blanket. Nelson's new aide, young Captain Edward Parker, sat chatting with them and tossing occasional admiring glances at the fishing party.

"A reminder of my duties," Nelson sighed, turning back to Emma. "Young Parker brought me a summons from the Admiralty this morning."

"Oh! Why didn't you tell me?" Emma pouted.

"I didn't want to spoil the day's outing. Nonetheless, we leave tomorrow for London. Bonaparte has been massing troops and barges on the Channel coast, and there is widespread fear of an invasion. I am wanted to lead the fleet out to deal with it."

"Invasion?" Emma sat up, alarmed. "When do you think it will occur?"

"Never, I expect," Nelson smiled. "This show is only to test our defenses and see how swift we are at implementing them. That, I daresay, Old Boney will soon learn."

"You will be sailing vigilantly up and down the Channel, then? So close, and yet so far away... Oh, I shall write to you every day!"

"Pray, don't expect long answers." Nelson ruefully stretched out his arm. "My hand can write only so much."

"A bare word will be enough." Emma leaned close and kissed him.

"Also, I expect to see some action. I confess, I miss you less when I'm engaged in battle."

"Please, please, don't risk yourself for my sake!"

"I swear myself to be prudent. Meanwhile, my dear, see if you can find a suitable country house for me. I did mean what I said about the three of us living together, quietly out of sight of London gossips."

"I shall do all that I can," Emma promised, knowing that nothing would stop gossip, but that one could at least keep distant from it.

"Aha!" Sir William shouted in triumph, holding up a wriggling fish. "Four pounds, I swear! We shall indeed have an excellent last dinner together."

Nelson cocked an eyebrow at him. "Sir William," he couldn't help asking, "how did you know this would be my last dinner ashore for a while?"

"Why, by the letter that arrived for you today, and by Captain Parker's subsequent impatience." Sir William smiled. "I have not been an ambassador these many years for nothing."

Nelson and Emma burst out laughing.

*****

The Hamiltons returned to the house in Clarges Street and sent out a housing agent to seek country properties for sale. Their whereabouts could not be kept entirely secret, and letters arrived from old friends as well as from Nelson. Dinner invitations were fewer but various artists and collectors called regularly, and Emma's reputation as a hostess for the intelligentsia spread quietly. Mrs. Cadogan fussed over dinner menus, warning Emma to watch her weight, and Fatima was kept busy trimming and altering her gowns. Emma duly practiced her dances and poses, but a long look in the mirror informed her that she would never again be the sylph who had fascinated the great painters of her youth.

An unexpected but welcome guest was Sarah Nelson, William's wife, who had enjoyed touring the countryside with them. She appeared at the door in plain country dress, not at all intimidated by Emma's finery, but eager to share news and gossip of Nelson's family. Emma gladly invited her to tea, where Sarah eventually revealed her true intentions.

"'Tis the children," she confided over her teacup. "Of course I want the best schools for them, but my Will is only a country parson with a pitiful income. How can we maintain young Horatio—yes, we named him for his famous uncle—maintain him at Eton, and have a good school for little Charlotte? 'Twas Fanny who first put her into Whitelands House at Chelsea, persuading Will that 'twas the best in the land for guarding the health and morals of young ladies, all without a thought as to the cost. I intended to beg your Horatio for help, but he is reserving his money for some project of his own."

Emma set down her teacup with a twinge of guilt, knowing why—and for whom—Nelson had been saving the money. "Surely the Admiralty has rewarded Horatio's family for his exemplary service...?" she queried.

"If so, none of it has gone to my Will," Sarah gloomed. "All bequests have gone to Fanny and her son, who is none of Horatio's."

"That wretched Tom-Tit," Emma fumed. "So much for her love of Horatio's family! Ah, but what can I do?"

"You have friends," Sarah implored, "and Sir William has more. Can you not persuade them to give my Will a better position?"

Ah, so that's it, Emma smiled, remembering how relatives of friends had shaped her own history. "Indeed," she said, "for what Lord Nelson has done for crown and country, the Ministers should have made his brother an archbishop! Of course I shall speak immediately to my husband, and we shall write to our various friends."

LOVE OF GLORY

"Oh, thank you!" Sarah said sincerely.

"Can you stay with us for a while?" Emma asked, patting her hand. "Indeed, could you join our household for a time? We should be able to accomplish much by joining together."

As Sarah happily agreed, Emma caught sight of her mother in the doorway, nodding her head in approval. *Another conquest*; she might as well have said it aloud.

Meanwhile, Nelson's letters to Hamilton house told of his intentions to destroy the French fleet, alternating with endearments to Emma and discussions of the house they would have together. Sir William kept track of events in Austria and Russia, muttered sourly to himself, and said nothing about them to Emma.

Mid-July brought bad news; Nelson had attacked the French fleet at Boulogne, but had been driven off again with some 150 casualties—Parker among the injured. The young captain would recover, but his left thigh was shattered. Emma wept when she read the reports of how Nelson, at the funeral of his troops killed in the abortive attack, followed their coffins with tears running down his cheeks. She was furious when she read accounts in the papers which hinted that Nelson might have mismanaged the assault, and cheered at Nelson's own pert replies.

Then came good news; her agent had found an excellent house for sale. It was a small and slightly run-down mansion at Merton, an hour's drive southwest of the Admiralty, right on the river Wandle. It had extensive gardens and five bedrooms. Emma visited the house, loved it at first sight, and wrote eagerly to Nelson. Trusting her judgment, he had his lawyer draw up the papers and make the first payment. He also wrote to Emma, begging her to meet him in Deal when he got his next leave at the end of the summer.

*****

LESLIE FISH

The seaport of Deal was windy and chill, even in the last days of August, but when Nelson came ashore there he found the Hamiltons and his sister eagerly waiting for him. They had reserved three rooms at the Three Kings, the best inn in the city, and greeted him with such enthusiasm as made him blush. Emma was delighted that Nelson looked to be in good health, not so thin as when he'd left, and with good color in his cheeks. Nelson, in turn, was quite pleased that Emma had befriended his sister-in-law.

Dining that evening in one of the private rooms, Emma reported progress with the Merton house and her attempts to improve his brother's situation. Nelson explained his concern for his two wounded officers, Edward Parker and Frederick Langford, currently hospitalized in the city. Emma faithfully promised to visit them and see to their welfare, and Sarah agreed to join her.

After dinner they retired to their assorted rooms. Nelson hadn't long to wait before Emma joined him.

She locked the door, set her lamp down on the bed-table and whispered "My love," before pulling off her robe and sliding into bed beside him.

Nelson said no word, but seized and kissed her fiercely. After so long without him, Emma's passion matched his in ferocity. They made love furiously while the hard wind off the sea rattled the windows.

Afterward, holding him in her arms, Emma felt his silent tears warming her breast. "Love, what is it?" she whispered. "But tell me, and let me do whatever may give you ease."

"It is young Parker," he sighed. "His wound has become infected. The doctors fear that the leg must come off right up to the hip, and I know what that means. Lord, the pain..." He clutched the stump of his right arm.

LOVE OF GLORY

"We shall find a way to comfort him," Emma promised, stroking his back, "Both before and after. Let us plan to take Sarah and go see him, starting tomorrow."

Nelson drew a deep breath and let it out slowly. "I've seen so many," he murmured. "Fine young officers... They become like sons to me, who have none of my own. And then they die. So many, and now Parker."

"He may yet live, if I have any power over it. And... you may yet have a son of your own. Now kiss me, hard."

Nelson rolled up onto her and kissed her as fiercely as before.

*****

Next morning Nelson, Emma and Sarah went to visit the little house where the two naval officers were recuperating. Langford clearly was on the mend, but Parker didn't look well. His splinted thigh seemed swollen under the bandages, his eyes were sunken and his color was poor. Nonetheless, he brightened considerably when Nelson strode into the room— and both of the young officers stared, open-mouthed, when Emma and Sarah followed him. Emma was dressed in a gown of buttercup-yellow satin, with a red-and-white brocade shawl, and seemed to fill the air with sunlight. Even as Nelson was making the proper introductions, she lifted the large basket of fruit that she'd brought with her and set it on the bed-table between the two invalids.

"Eat well, my brave lads," she beamed, "for I've seen myself that fresh fruit can speed a body to recovery."

Sarah, not to be outdone, brought forth her vase of fresh-cut flowers and set it behind Emma's basket. Nelson pulled out a bottle of good port and set that beside the women's offerings, then went for wineglasses and chairs. Emma led the conversation with all the skills she'd learned as a diplomat's wife. The visiting party stayed for an hour, and left the two wounded officers thoroughly charmed and dazzled.

"We must return soon," said Nelson, as the party walked back toward the inn. "The boys seemed much cheered by our visit."

"We shall return this very afternoon," Emma decided. "and visit at least once a day hereafter, as long as we remain in town."

"Emma, you are a treasure," Nelson sighed, gripping her arm.

That night, in contrast to the previous evening, he was remarkably tender with her.

Emma and Nelson, often accompanied by Sarah, spent the next week visiting Parker at least once a day, despite his doctor's fussing about the excitement of having guests. Parker's spirits certainly rallied, but his leg didn't improve. The doctors finally informed him, and Nelson, that to save his life the leg must come off.

Emma sat with Nelson in the garden of the recovery house while the doctors performed the amputation. Despite drinking rum until he was nearly insensible, Parker groaned loudly at the pain, and both Nelson and Emma could hear him. Nelson clutched his own stump and wept silently in Emma's arms.

By evening the sounds had ceased, and they waited in growing impatience to hear from the doctors. At last Nelson could bear the tension no longer, told Emma to stay in the garden, and went into the house himself. Emma waited, studying the last of the late-summer roses, and eventually Nelson returned. He sat down heavily beside her on the bench, and let out a mournful sigh.

"Parker sleeps peacefully now," he reported. "They took off his leg near the hip, and it will be buried with the midshipmen who died in the fighting. Whether he lives or dies now is in God's hands."

LOVE OF GLORY

"We must all pray, then," said Emma, clutching his arm. "Poor dear Parker... We must keep visiting, and continue to scour the town for fresh fruit."

"Ah, my dear..." Nelson patted her thigh absently. "I must return to my ship on the 20th of September. One way or another, I expect to know by then."

"Ah, and Sir William has arranged for us to leave on the 20th, also. I can scarcely bear the thought of leaving you..." Emma drew a resolute breath, "but Sir William has work to do in London, and I must see to the house in Merton, and both of us are suborning friends everywhere to procure a better position for your brother."

"I know. Duty lays her chains upon all of us. Consider the poet's words: 'I could not love thee half so much, loved I not honour more'."

He turned to give her a long, thorough kiss.

*****

Parker clung to life but didn't improve, despite the amputation and Emma's earnest care. By the 20th of September, when the Hamiltons departed, he was no better. Emma threw herself into the work she had promised Nelson, and received some hints in her correspondence that William Nelson would indeed receive a better paying position—at which Sarah was boundlessly grateful.

The news from the broker and Nelson's lawyer was less promising. A surveyor reported that the Merton house to be in a wretched state; the purchase price plus the repairs would cost all of ten thousand pounds. Sir William discreetly offered to help, but the cost was still appalling.

A week later came word that Parker had died. Nelson, on his flagship but refusing to sail until he had news of Parker, attended the funeral—which he himself paid for, since the

Admiralty wouldn't. Sir William found that last bit of miserliness particularly disgusting, and wrote several pointed letters to his connections—and the papers.

Emma was stricken by the description of Nelson following Parker's casket to its grave, with silent tears running down his cheeks. "Oh, my poor dear," she whispered. "And does he grieve like this for all the men who fall in battle, or as a result of it, under his command?"

"Any commander who doesn't grieve for his fallen men is no leader at all," Sir William stated.

"Oh, how does he bear it?" Tears spilled from Emma's eyes too. "He has need of so much comforting, and yet the Admiralty sends him back to sea again."

"I daresay, he drowns his sorrows in battle—as I used to drown mine in work." Sir William gave her a soft smile. "But indeed, there are better comforts."

*****

As the autumn progressed, the Hamiltons received variable news. The house at Merton was in poorer condition than they'd originally thought, and would need extensive—therefore expensive—work done. Sir William Pitt resigned as Prime Minister, replaced by Lord Henry Addington, who was negotiating a treaty with France—a treaty whose terms left Nelson aghast over all the territories to be returned to their former rulers. The only good part of it, as Sir William noted, was that French troops would also withdraw from Naples.

Another bit of good news was that the Admiralty would allow Nelson to go ashore in late October. Fired by his enthusiasm, Emma and Sir William moved into the Merton house to await him, bringing Nelson's brother and niece with them. Sir William happily reported to Nelson that the house was well repaired and well furnished. "I verily believe that a

LOVE OF GLORY

place more suitable to your views could not have been found," he wrote. "It would make you laugh to see Emma and her mother fitting up the pig-sties and hen-coops, and already the canal is enlivened with ducks..." He added: "Your Lordship's plan as to stocking the canal with fish is exactly mine. I will answer for it, that in a few months you may command a good dish of fish at a moment's warning."

Nelson, for his part, could scarcely wait to reach his pastoral paradise. He came ashore promptly on October 22nd and rode all night, reaching the house at 8 o'clock the next morning. The Hamiltons, Nelson's brother, and his niece Charlotte were surprised but delighted by his early arrival. All of them were ecstatic at how well he looked, and happily took him on a tour of the house and grounds.

Nelson duly wended his way through the spacious rooms, noting how cleverly Emma had lightened them with placement of windows and mirrors. The walls were hung thickly with ornaments, and with a slight shock Nelson recognized the flagstaff of the *l'Orient*. There were polished plates and medallions which, on closer inspection, showed scenes and quotations relating Nelson's victories. There were coats-of-arms for the titles he'd been granted, from Bronte to Burnham. There were paintings representing his naval battles, and others showing scenes from antiquity—except that the faces of the chief characters were those of himself and Emma. A portrait of a younger Emma dressed as Cleopatra hung beside an armored Mark Anthony with Nelson's face. Everywhere were tributes to his glory and Emma's love.

Slightly overcome, Nelson wandered out into the newly planted garden and along the path by the ornamental canal, wearing the look of one who had wandered into heaven. Emma heard him murmur, wonderingly, "Is this, too, mine?" and beamed with joy.

"There will be local celebrations, you know," Sir William warned him. "And of course the gentry will fall all over themselves inviting you to dinner."

"I shall be happy to attend," Nelson smiled.

Emma gave him a keen look, and saw that Nelson was indeed happy. This was the life he had secretly wished for himself: to be a well-to-do country squire, surrounded by a loving family and cordial neighbors and tributes to his achievements. Given this, he could leave the sea without regrets and lie content on his laurels. She had given her lover his heart's desire.

Chapter 13
Days of Glory

In the ensuing days Nelson settled quickly and happily into his new role. He left Merton only briefly, to formally take his place in the House of Lords on the 29th and again to give a speech concerning the war on November 3rd. He quickly grew accustomed to living his public life by day in London, and his private life by evenings and weekends at Merton.

There were indeed invitations to local dinners and dances, one of them featuring fireworks, which delighted little Charlotte. On Sundays the whole household attended the local church, and afterward went fishing in the garden's canal. Neighbors dropped by with small gifts and bits of local gossip and to proffer invitations, some few of which Nelson accepted. After William Nelson departed, the days passed in lazy contentment.

The only cloud on the horizon was the leftover problem of Fanny and Father Edmund. The old man wrote letters gently but solemnly chiding Nelson for having abandoned his wife, which would leave Nelson troubled for hours afterward. Emma wrote to Sarah, enlisting her help in prying Father Edmund away from Fanny's control, but received no encouraging news.

LOVE OF GLORY

Finally Nelson invited his father—alone—to come visit the Merton house.

The old man arrived on November 18th, and Emma took great care to receive him warmly. Nelson, though equally cordial, was disturbed at his father's frailty. Emma noted that Father Edmund was feeble and inclined to sleep much; nevertheless he had the energy to visit the local church. In every word and action the old minister was kindly and amiable, and said nothing about the family scandal.

Only by the absence of any commentary about his dismantled marriage did Nelson realize that his father had finally given up any hope of reconciling him with Fanny.

When Father Edmund departed for Bath, the whole household breathed easier. A letter from Fanny was returned unread, and Nelson settled totally into his new life.

Emma, waking early to study her sleeping lover in the morning's light, noted with approval that he had put on flesh and smiled contentedly even in sleep.

Christmas at Merton was a cozy affair. Certain well-to-do neighbors attended: Abraham Goldsmid, the banker, James Perry, the editor of the *Morning Chronicle*, and John Pennington, the cotton merchant—this last, having lived through the Terror in Paris, had fascinating stories to tell. William and Sarah Nelson came too, bringing their son Horatio, who promptly squabbled with his sister Charlotte. Father Edmund sent a cordial letter, but admitted he was too old to venture out in winter weather. As a surprise, Lord Minto appeared for a Twelfth Night dinner and reminisced happily with Sir William.

In the subsequent weeks Sir William returned often to London to visit the museum, the Royal Society and the house he maintained in Piccadilly, leaving Emma and Nelson largely alone in the Merton house. The lovers spent the snowy weekends cuddled in bed, rising only to eat and bathe and read the papers, not bothering to put on anything but their dressing-gowns. Mrs. Cadogan artfully arranged for their meals, and kept the other servants away from them; and so the winter passed slowly in a drowsy contentment.

Sorrow intruded in late April, when Nelson received letters from his brother-in-law George Matcham saying that old Father Edmund was ill and not expected to live. Nelson was upset that his father hadn't written to him directly, nor asked him to come for a last visit. He was not invited to the funeral either. He could express his feelings only by writing to Matcham to take great care with the coffin and the grave—which was to be right before the altar in the old man's church at Norfolk.

Emma, understanding perfectly, organized a memorial service at Merton. The neighbors attended respectfully, though only the aged vicar of the local church had actually met Father Edmund, and the service calmed Nelson considerably.

After that, Nelson ordered subscriptions from the town news agent for the *Monthly Review*, guaranteed to interest Sir William, the *European Magazine* to keep all of them apprised of current affairs, and his own favorite, the *Naval Chronicle*. That last, Nelson was amused to see, carried constant mentions of himself—usually tributes, but often snickering cartoons about his relationship with the Hamiltons. The cartoons upset Emma more than Nelson, who merely laughed at their references to his potency.

The three of them were also delighted by visits from artists, particularly Sir William Beechly, who wanted to paint Nelson's portrait. Emma and Sir William chatted warmly with the painters, and Nelson was pleased at their wide knowledge and unrestrained conversation. No less of a personage than Benjamin West, President of the Royal Academy, came by for a visit, and Nelson personally praised his famous painting.

LOVE OF GLORY

"I never pass a print-shop where your Death of Wolfe is in the window without being stopped by it," he commented. "Why have you not painted other such scenes?"

"Because, my lord," West smiled, "there are no more such subjects."

"Dammit, I didn't think of that."

"My lord," West continued gravely, "I fear that your intrepidity may yet furnish me with another such scene, and if it should, then I shall certainly avail myself of it."

Emma paled, and frowned at the painter as if he'd aroused the attention of the Fates.

"Ah, will you, Mr. West?" Nelson enthused, offering him a glass of champagne. "Then I hope I shall die in the next battle!"

"Oh, say not so!" Emma wailed, horrified. "Please, love, keep far from battle and live as long as God allows to mortals!"

"There, there," Nelson soothed, patting her hand, "we must all die eventually, and how better than of a swift wound, in some glorious battle?"

"Ah, how like an earlier Horatius," Sir William noted. "he who held the bridge against the armies of the Etruscans... Yet I recall that he survived to die comfortably in old age."

"However glorious, let it not be soon!" Emma insisted, clutching his arm. "Only rest on your laurels, my dear, for surely you've earned them."

"I have, at that," Nelson murmured.

Emma threw a glance at Sir William, who replied with the briefest nod of acknowledgement. With whatever influence and powers of persuasion they possessed, they would see to it that Nelson received in full all the glory he deserved.

*****

As spring rolled on, more honors descended on Nelson. The Lord Mayor of London invited him to ride in the mayoral carriage through the city for the inaugural procession, and Sir William urged him to accept. Enormous crowds turned out, cheering, to watch the spectacle—and again the people unhitched the horses and dragged the carriage themselves, all the way up Ludgate Hill. The Hamiltons and little Charlotte watched from the sidelines, ecstatic, as the crowds cheered thunderously, waved handkerchiefs and shouted "Nelson forever!" Nelson, well taught by Sir William, accepted the adulation graciously.

Scarcely had they all returned to Merton when word arrived that Oxford University wished to confer honorary law degrees upon Sir William and Nelson. Emma and Sir William made the arrangements between them, taking care to invite Nelson's brother and sister and their families to attend the ceremonies. They set off for the college town in mid-July, with only Sir William being unsurprised by the crowds that gathered along their route to cheer them as they passed.

Emma, entertaining a happy suspicion, privately asked her husband why, not how, he had quietly arranged this.

"First, my dear," Sir William smiled, "our beloved hero deserves his rewards for his exemplary efforts on behalf of the crown. His efforts in earlier years went unrecognized for the most part, and I wish to rectify that injustice.

"Second, you may note that whenever Horatio speaks he stresses the importance of utterly defeating Napoleon, something of which our lords and allies need to be reminded constantly.

"Third..." he gave Emma an apologetic look, "to armor our reputations. None shall dare cry 'cuckold' or 'whore' or 'adulterer' in the light of such glory. If Nelson is seen as greater than ordinary men, his uncommon privy arrangements will not be judged in ordinary terms."

"I see." And Emma thought she did. "It requires a hero to defy convention."

LOVE OF GLORY

"At least to do so successfully," Sir William agreed.

On the 22nd of July Sir William and Nelson received their honorary degrees with full ceremony, which prompted a spate of witticisms in the newspapers. The *Morning Post* quipped that Nelson should also have received a Doctorate of Divinity "because of his knowledge of cannon law." Nelson's brother William did indeed receive a Doctorate of Divinity, and with it the tacit promise of a better living, at which Sarah was ecstatic.

Their enjoyment was dampened by their reception, or rather lack of it, from the local peer, the Duke of Marlborough. Sir William was surprised and hurt at the rebuff, Emma was furious, and Nelson cynically remarked that this sort of snobbery was only to be expected from the nobility. They continued on to the Welsh border, receiving joyful welcome from the common folk at every town as they passed, and Sir William noted the irony.

"How remarkable," he said dryly, "that the nobles sympathize with Napoleon, who climbed to power on the French Revolution, which made haste to execute every noble it could catch, while the commons cheer for Nelson, who so well opposes Old Boney. We must wonder if the Quality are so impressed with Bonaparte's title of 'Emperor' that they cannot see the threat that he truly poses."

"'Tis no more than their usual snobbery," Nelson glowered. "All know that I rose through the ranks from a common family."

"They are stupid ingrates," Emma fumed. "But for Horatio, Napoleon might well have invaded long since, and then where would their noble heads be?"

"Intelligence is not a requirement for a Peerage," Sir William concurred. "Indeed, I often wonder if, in its obsession with long-ennobled bloodlines and its abhorrence of outcrosses, the peerage is not inbreeding itself for stupidity."

That made Nelson laugh uproariously, and his good humor continued through the tour.

Finally they arrived in Milford, where Sir William met with Charles Greville and went off to inspect the family estate. In contrast to Marlborough's treatment, the local Earl of Cawdor welcomed the Hamiltons and Nelson warmly, and invited them to local festivities. They attended a banquet commemorating Nelson's victory at the Battle of the Nile, where he rose to the occasion by pronouncing that Milford Haven was every bit as fine a harbor as Portsmouth, and would surely flourish in coming years. Sir William was invited to lay the foundation-stone of a new church, and the party attended a regatta and a cattle show.

In the refreshments tent at the cattle show, Greville managed to encounter Emma alone.

"I see you are doing well, my dear," he smiled at her over his wineglass. "Your fame precedes you everywhere."

"And notoriety, no doubt," Emma matched his smile, "which is another reason why Sir William takes care to fan the flames of Nelson's glory."

Greville raised an eyebrow and saluted her with his glass. "In truth, you have managed with as much good taste as Lady Hale ever did. But all such machinations aside, Emma, have you considered what you will do when my uncle dies?"

"No!" Emma's expression of shock couldn't have been counterfeit. "I never think of it! And no more does Nelson. We both love him dearly."

"Well..." Greville blinked, and regrouped. "I beg you to think of it now, my dear. You know you will not inherit the bulk of his fortune."

"Of course not. I know that Sir William gave you...your portion when he chose to marry me, so that you might build up the port here at Milford." Emma favored him with an appreciative smile. "And indeed you seem to have done well with his money."

Greville nodded his acceptance. "His collection of antiquities and *objets d'art* shall go to various museums. Have you not thought of what he shall leave you to live on?"

"No, never. I know him to be goodhearted, and not one to leave me penniless, and that is enough for me."

"Let us hope that to be so." Greville drummed his fingers on his glass. "When my uncle is no more, do you intend to marry Nelson?"

"We both have intentions in that direction," Emma admitted, "though there is still the little impediment of his wife."

Greville leaned closer. "There is speculation that Nelson hopes to win another great victory, and thereby have sufficient...ah, political backing—not to mention money—that none shall dispute him when he asks Parliament for a full divorce from Fanny."

Emma caught her breath, considering that—and remembered Nelson's chilling words to Dr. West. "I know he thinks of that," she said, "but his previous victories have not so availed him. That being so, I would rather that he remain safe on land, and be no more than his mistress, than that he risk himself in battle again so that I may be his wife."

Greville gave her a long look. "I have never doubted your good heart, Emma," he said, "but only your practicality. Still, I promise you, for the good service you have done to me and to my uncle, I shall see to it that you never starve."

"I thank you, Charles—" Whatever else she would have said was cut off by the arrival of the Earl and his party, who descended happily upon the refreshment table. Emma was swept up in their company, and had no further chance to speak with Greville. In the merry entertainment Emma soon forgot Greville's troubling words, and thought no more about them.

*****

LESLIE FISH

Nelson and his entourage made their slow progress through Wales, stopping to give a speech at the war memorial in Monmouth, which Emma followed by leading the crowd in singing "Rule Britannia." From there they went on to Hereford, where the Duke of Norfolk ritually bestowed the freedom of the city upon Nelson. This caused Sir William to remark privately that the more intelligent of the Peerage seemed to be coming around to Nelson's point of view—and to the Prince's faction. On they went, through Ludlow and Worcester and all towns in between, where the crowds turned out to cheer their hero. At Birmingham, Nelson and the Hamiltons attended the theatre, where their arrival halted the performance for several minutes of applause. They continued on to Warwick, and finally home, reaching the peace and quiet of Merton by the 5th of September.

Emma was delighted to learn that little Horatia was now eating solid food, and could come to join her parents at Merton. Sir William was likewise pleased to hear that much had changed in the political scene; Napoleon had made himself "First Consul for life"—in effect, permanent dictator of France—and the Foreign Office was worried. Nelson duly went up to London to meet with the Prime Minister and discuss the threat to Britain. He returned happy that his appeal for permanent pensions for common sailors had been seriously heeded, but less than pleased that his own pension was smaller than that of other admirals who had won lesser battles.

Emma arranged a birthday celebration for Nelson including a dinner party and musicale, at which she sang a ballad of praise for him. Everyone present, including the editor of the *Morning Chronicle*, considered the party a great success.

Only afterward did Sir William make a quiet complaint to Emma.

LOVE OF GLORY

"My dear," he commented over the breakfast table, "I own that your party was a great triumph, but we cannot continue in this fashion."

"What?" asked Emma, surprised. "Have we not politicked sufficiently well?"

"We have indeed done that," Sir William sighed, cracking open an egg, "but it must end. My funds and Horatio's cannot sustain this pace any longer."

"Oh dear," Emma cried, suddenly remembering Greville's words.

"I no longer have the income of an ambassador, nor Nelson that of a working admiral. Also, after all these years, I rather tire of never having fewer than a dozen guests at dinner. Frankly, I seek a calmer and quieter life now—and from what he has told me, I daresay Nelson does too."

"I see," said Emma, wondering just what sort of economies she would have to make, and deciding to ask her mother about the subject. "We shall have no more parties then, not until Christmas at least."

"I pray you do not overwhelm the household purse for Christmas," Sir William responded with some heat.

"In that I shall be conservative," Emma promised, and got up to look for Mrs. Cadogan.

On her way to the kitchen Emma was halted by the sight of Tom Allen at the front door, ushering in a young man whom Emma recognized as George Parsons. She ducked into an alcove behind a potted palm and paused to listen.

"I really must see him," Parsons was insisting. "I was midshipman on the *Foudroyant*, and served in the landings at Egypt. I have surely qualified as lieutenant, and Lord Keith promised me my commission, but now the war has ended and my commission has not been signed after all. I've no hope if Lord Nelson won't help me."

"Aye, isn't that the usual way o' the Navy," Tom gloomed. "When there's war, they'll be press-ganging men off the streets, but when there's none they'll cast you off to fend for yourself. That happened to Himself, more than once."

"Then surely he must sympathize?"

"Mayhap not. He's been vexed more than a little by requests of old friends and old sailors begging for his help. Yet... I shall see what can be done. Pray step this way..."

Tom led young Parsons to the door of Nelson's study and left him there to go in and announce the guest. Emma, stealing shamelessly closer, heard Nelson's exasperated voice grumbling loudly about being "pestered to death" by his former shipmates —and saw Allen's expression drooping.

It occurred to her that Nelson didn't realize what power he had, and how it could be wielded. She moved out of hiding and paced silently toward the waiting guest and the study door, considering how she should best handle this.

A moment later Tom came out, looking sorrowful, and ushered Parsons into the study—at which point he caught sight of Emma and his expression shifted to something nearer hope. She paced up to the door, holding a finger to her lips, and entered right after the young midshipman.

Nelson, who hadn't yet had time to form a polite refusal, brightened as he saw Emma come in. "His Lordship must attend me," she smiled, brushing past Parsons. And then, to Nelson himself, "Think, my dear, that it will cost you nothing from your purse to assist an able ally here."

While Parsons gaped at her, Nelson only looked puzzled. "And how should I accomplish that?" he asked.

"My dear," said Emma pressing close to him, "though you may sit in the House of Lords, you have greater power yet among the commons: power enough that you need not scruple to ask a favor of the First Lord of the Admiralty. Indeed, I think

LOVE OF GLORY

that he will be more than pleased that you allow him to grant you such a reasonable request."

"...request?" Nelson murmured, a trifle distracted by her stroking his shoulder as she spoke.

"Simply write a letter to Lord St. Vincent—I can help you compose it, if you wish—giving a strong certificate for young Parsons and requesting favorable attention to his commission. I've no doubt that he will grant it."

"Hmmm," said Nelson, reaching for a pen, "As simple as that? Good Lord, I'd forgotten that I'm both an Admiral and a Peer."

"And...a national hero," Emma said softly.

Despite Nelson's clumsiness at writing left-handed, the letter was finished in short order. Emma handed it to the blushing Parsons and said: "Now, my young friend, obey my instructions minutely; send this to Lord St. Vincent at Brentwood, timed so as to reach him on Sunday morning."

Parsons took the letter, stuttering his gratitude, and Tom Allen—giving Emma a look of admiration—hurried him out of the study. The door closed with finality behind them. Emma turned back to Nelson and stroked his hair.

"My love," she crooned, "your humility shall do you credit in heaven, but here in England you would do well to remember what power you now have—and make good use of it."

"And doubtless you will be glad of the opportunity to guide me on how to use it, eh?" he grinned toothily. "Oh, come here, you fascinating witch!" With that, he pulled her into his lap.

"Oh Horatio, mind the chair!" Emma giggled, hearing the furniture creaking under their joined weight.

"I will indeed," he said huskily, setting her back on her feet. He brushed aside the pen and inkwell, and pressed Emma back onto the desk. She laughed recklessly as she felt his hand slide under her skirts and lift them.

LESLIE FISH

*****

The next day, Mrs. Cadogan and Fatima went up to London with a heavy purse for Mrs. Gibson, and returned with little Horatia in tow. The toddler was a pretty child, but despite the joyful welcome she received at the house, her expression remained sullen.

"Come greet your mother, dear," said Mrs. Cadogan, nudging the girl toward Emma.

Horatia dug in her heels and responded with a distinct "No!"

"Ah, patience," said Mrs. Cadogan, sweeping up the child in her arms. "She knows no one but the good nurse, as yet. But give her time, and she may yet come to know and love ye well."

Fatima hurried after them, up the stairs and off to the prepared nursery, leaving Emma alone with her thoughts. This was the second daughter who had been raised apart from her, and who had little love for her.

"But how could it have been avoided?" Emma wailed softly to the unhearing walls. "I had to concern myself with Horatio, and Will'um..." She sighed as she thought of all the roles she'd had to play: model, mistress, wife, secretary, hostess, and even politician. How could she have done all that, and been an attentive mother as well?

Nelson, though, was delighted with the child. He greeted her effusively, swept her up on his arm and swung her until she squealed, and promised to take her out rowing. Horatia appeared to be awe-stricken by him, and in subsequent days toddled about after him, fascinated. Sir William was charmed by the little girl as well, and promised to teach her how to fish. Horatia warmed to all their attention, but still remained sullen with Emma.

"I try to be kind and loving with her," Emma sighed, "but she seems determined to have none of it."

LOVE OF GLORY

"I believe the little minx is jealous," Mrs. Cadogan said slowly. "She has been used to being the beauty of the household, and you've displaced her in that regard."

"Oh heavens! The last thing I need is a rival under my own roof!" Emma laughed, but at heart she was troubled. She knew well how to deal with an adult rival, but what to do with a child? She would keep on being kindly and loving, she determined, no matter how ill Horatia might take her overtures; she would teach the child music and languages, literacy and fine manners, and raise her to be a lady. Eventually Horatia would be grateful, and learn to love her. "Love and patience shall wear her down," she promised herself.

Chapter 14
Sir William's End

In November, as Nelson was preparing for the opening of the House of Lords, came terrible news. It was not just that Napoleon was moving again and had recently annexed Piedmont in Italy, but also that an assassination plot had been exposed. A group of men from all over Britain had been caught conspiring to kill King George on the day that he formally opened Parliament. The ringleader was Nelson's old friend from the western colonies, Colonel Edward Despard.

"Good Lord," Nelson confided to Sir William over the morning newspapers. "I've not seen the man in twenty years, but I can't imagine how he could have descended from an honest colonial administrator to... this!"

"You must decide how you will testify," Sir William replied, "for it is assured that you will be called upon to bear witness when he is brought to trial in the Sessions House."

"I will speak as to his good character," Nelson decided. "He was a decent man when I knew him last."

"Then for heaven's sake do not let your position be known until after you've spoken in favor of Lord St. Vincent's enquiry into the chicanery of prize agents!"

LOVE OF GLORY

"The irony is that I have also placed a lawsuit against St. Vincent over prize-money due to me."

"Then leave that until after the founding of the commission of enquiry. You are an honest man, Horatio—and for just that reason you need a guide through the wilderness of politics."

"Well do I know it," Nelson sighed. "At least all this business will be postponed until after Christmas. I believe Emma has planned a party for the event..."

"More of Emma's parties," Sir William gloomed. "I must have a look at the account books."

The Christmas party proved to be a hectic affair, although happily, not excessively expensive. Emma provided much of the entertainment with her singing and her Attitude poses, which everyone appreciated. Nelson enjoyed himself hugely, as did the invited neighbors. Even little Horatia was delighted by the celebration, and complained noisily when Fatima and Mrs. Cadogan took her away to bed.

After the merry Christmas, somber duties descended again. The commission of enquiry was founded, but Nelson lost his lawsuit against St. Vincent; and on February 7th Despard's trial opened, with Nelson called as the first witness for the defense. The judge, noting that Nelson hadn't seen the man for more than twenty years, restricted all testimony to comments upon Despard's general character.

"No man could have shown more zealous attachment to his Sovereign and his country than Colonel Despard did," Nelson claimed. "I formed the highest opinion of him at that time as a man and an officer."

Cross-examination only confirmed that Nelson had known nothing of Despard in the twenty years since their service together, and he was soon dismissed.

Two days later, Despard was found guilty of treason and sentenced to be hanged. The only effects of Nelson's testimony and plea for mercy was that Despard was to only be hanged, not drawn and quartered, and his widow was granted a pension. The execution cast a pall of gloom over the Merton house, and Sir William suggested that the family move to London, to the house in Piccadilly, for the rest of the winter. While the men attended the House of Lords, Emma gave a grand end-of-winter party, wherein she sang and played piano for a hundred guests. Her performance impressed the editors of the London papers, delighted the children as well as the adults, and cheered Nelson considerably.

Sir William attended the Queen's birthday reception, but came home with a cold.

*****

Through the long weeks of March, Sir William's health didn't improve, but grew slowly worse. He weakened steadily, growing ever less able to take food. The eminent Dr. Moseley, summoned from Chelsea, admitted that there was nothing that he could do to benefit the ambassador. Emma, frantic, sent for Charles Greville. Uncle and nephew remained closeted for an hour, and when Greville emerged he told Emma that his uncle wanted no priests fussing at his death-bed, but only the company of his closest friends.

Emma hurried in to sit by her husband, weeping bitterly. "Oh Will'um," she sobbed, clutching his hand, "you cannot die! Our *tria juncta in uno* cannot lose you!"

"Hush, my dear," Sir William said quietly. "for I must ask for your forgiveness."

"Forgiveness?" Emma puzzled. "Surely you have it, but why ever would you need my forgiveness?"

"For using you," the old man whispered. "I made use of your beauty, your charm, your bravery, your...sort of innocence, even to this day. I used you for my own political purposes...charming this king and that queen..."

LOVE OF GLORY

"Oh my dear, you married me; you made me a great lady and a diplomat's wife. How could I do otherwise than be a helpmate to you?"

"It was not by accident that I introduced you to Nelson."

"Ah Will'um, you brought me such happiness, and glory..."

"'It was all in the service of crown and country. I did use you, dear Emma."

"If so, I was honored to be so used! My dear, my husband, you've done nothing to ask forgiveness for."

"In truth, I have loved you, Emma." He squeezed her hand.

"And I you, dearest Will'um. I shall not leave your side." With that, she pulled off her dressing-gown and slid into bed beside him.

Nelson found them like that, asleep, with Emma's arms wrapped around Sir William, when he came back from Parliament that evening. With only a few words to Mrs. Cadogan and the rest of the household, he settled himself on Sir William's other side and lay down to await the finish.

A few days later, Nelson wrote to his agent Davison: "Wednesday, 11 o'clock, 6th April, 1803. Our dear Sir William died at ten minutes past ten this morning, in Lady Hamilton's and my arms without a sigh or a struggle. Poor Lady Hamilton is, as you may expect, desolate."

*****

It was Mrs. Cadogan who sent for Sir Charles Greville. Greville, as Sir William's heir, took charge of the funeral arrangements, which Emma was too distraught to manage. Nelson assisted quietly, staying out of the limelight. Among other things, little Horatia was given a proper christening—under the fictitious name of Thompson and the polite fiction that she was Nelson's god-daughter. Sir William's body was placed in an elegant coffin and taken by hearse to the churchyard in Pembrokeshire where his first wife was buried. Emma, veiled and grieving in voluminous black, accompanied the coffin and attended the small funeral. If any of Sir William's other relatives had any complaints about Emma, the grim presence of Nelson and Greville kept them silent.

James Perry's obituary in the *Morning Chronicle* paid tribute to both Sir William's long years of public service and Emma's devotion.

After that came the settling of the will. Sir William's remaining estate paid Emma's outstanding debts, gave her the furnishings from the rented house in Piccadilly and an annuity of 800 pounds per year. It also left a little enamel portrait of Emma to Nelson. The antiquities and art treasures, as Greville had predicted, went primarily to the British Museum and secondarily to the Royal Society. Emma wept afresh to see the art pieces leave for their new homes. She insisted that another house be rented in Piccadilly and the furnishings moved there, since she could no longer bear to stay in the house where Sir William had died.

She wept again when Nelson quietly moved, not into the new Picadilly house, but into a nearby flat above a saddler's shop, though she could not fault his logic; without Sir William's presence, Nelson could not live in the same house with Emma and maintain any semblance of propriety.

"'Tis all hypocrisy," Mrs. Cadogan tried to comfort her, "yet it must be done. What was it Sir William always said? 'Hypocrisy is the tax vice pays to virtue'."

"Virtue," Emma sniffed, wiping her eyes, "is a shabby overlord, and some vice is less cruel—and more honest—than ever the church would admit. Oh mother, what shall I do now?"

"Soon enough, my gel, ye'll return to Merton. There Milord Nelson may come to ye as he list, so long as you both be discreet about it."

LOVE OF GLORY

"Discretion will be difficult enough," wailed Emma, rubbing away fresh tears. "I'm pregnant again."

Then on the 14th of May the Admiralty sent Nelson orders to take command of the Mediterranean fleet. Two days later, Britain declared war on France.

Chapter 15
All At Sea

On May 18th Nelson arrived in Portsmouth and hoisted his flag on his new ship, the *Victory*. He was, as he wrote to Emma, delighted with the ship, which was the fastest and most powerful that the Royal Navy could provide. In another letter, two days later, he promised: "I assure you, my dear Emma, that I feel a thorough conviction that we shall meet again with honour, riches and health and remain together till a good old age." With that Emma had to be content, and soon afterward she closed up the Piccadilly house and moved back to Merton.

With neither Sir William nor Nelson present, Emma lost her taste for entertaining and grew desperately lonely. Mrs. Cadogan and Fatima doted on little Horatia, but the child still hadn't warmed to her mother. Emma took to fussing with the furnishings of Merton, trying to make it into a grand home worthy of Nelson, and writing him passionate letters several times a week. His equally warm replies, as they arrived, were the height of her days. Her pregnancy proved more troubling than the previous two, and often left her sick for hours. Mrs. Cadogan insisted that this was the result of brooding and worrying, but even that could not keep Emma from fretting at

LOVE OF GLORY

Nelson's absence. Merton had been her paradise the year before, but now it was a hermitage where she could only pace out her days in near-solitude, yearning for Nelson's return.

Adding to her worries were the notations, in Nelson's letters, that he was not only miserable with seasickness but troubled by growing problems with the vision in his remaining eye. As he hunted for French ships up and down the Mediterranean, his letters spoke more and more often of retiring permanently before his sight gave out.

Spring slid into long hot summer with no change; Nelson was still at sea, with no decisive victory. Emma's loneliness grew excruciating.

In desperation she wrote to Nelson's sister and sister-in-law, and even to Sir Charles Greville, begging them to come and stay at Merton. All of them politely but firmly refused. Writing long passionate letters to Nelson every day could not fill all of her time, and neither could playing with Horatia. Emma took to visiting the various neighbors and attending their parties, where she was often drawn to the card tables.

On one evening she found herself losing nearly a hundred pounds to James Perry, who chided her gently for betting beyond her means. Emma was about to make an angry reply, but then remembered that Perry's *Morning Chronicle* had always been sympathetic to Nelson, and herself.

"Oh, I do know," she admitted, staring miserably at the damning cards. "I'm no longer an ambassador's wife, but a widow on a small income. Yet I'm so lonely with everyone gone... 'Tis only at gay parties like these that my spirits are lifted, for they recall our wonderful days in Italy. Perhaps I dream too much of that time, and lose recall of where, and when, and how I live now."

"I understand," synpathized Perry. "Perhaps you should give more entertainments of your own, inviting artists and musicians such as used to flock around you in London. Surely such society would gladly come to you."

"Sir William warned me against too many extravagant parties," Emma worried.

"Can you not practice a little clever economy, and see to it that such entertainments are not unduly extravagant?"

"I'm not sure I know how. 'Tis my mother who always handles the payments for such things... Oh, I can't bear waiting for Nelson to return!"

"Ah, there now," Perry offered. "I shall come to visit you myself, and I'm sure our friends the Goldsmids would be happy to visit also—and make certain suggestions for economy. You have friends, Emma; only let them help you."

Emma could only nod agreement, though in truth she could not see how to invite guests without providing the sort of receptions she had been used to during her years with Sir William.

Perry, as good as his word, arranged for the wealthier neighbors to drop in on Emma unexpectedly, giving her no time to plan any elaborate entertainments for them. Also, various artists and musicians resumed their visits, usually asking no more than a tour of the house and grounds—and perhaps introductions to other of Emma's acquaintances. She got in the habit of keeping the wine-cellar and the meat-locker well stocked, which still made inroads into Sir William's legacy.

The Christmas party at Merton that year was a subdued affair by Emma's standards, since Nelson was still at sea. Even so, Mrs. Cadogan clucked at the expense.

Shortly after New Year, Emma felt the first warning symptoms and sent for the midwife. The child, another girl, was born during a thick blizzard, and the midwife worried that the baby was small and underweight. Worse, in her first week of life the tiny girl developed a severe cough, and nothing the doctor could do improved it. While Emma wept and wrung her hands, and the whole household grieved, the child died before she was a month old. Emma could scarcely bring herself to write the news to Nelson.

Nelson, having chased the French ships as far as the Caribbean and back again, still could not come home.

*****

The year of 1804 crawled slowly past Merton. The papers were filled with reports of Napoleon's victories on land and Nelson's at sea, while—as Sir William had predicted—the Holy Roman Empire slowly crumbled. Emma wrote anxious letters to her old acquaintances in Europe, most of which garnered no reply. Only Queen Carolina and her daughter, Empress Maria Theresa, responded regularly; their letters, though, were filled with lugubrious accounts of more land and troops lost to Napoleon. Nelson's numerous letters were little better, for they spoke of his frustration at not being able to catch the French fleet for a decisive victory, and complained of his failing health and eyesight.

A sense of gloom settled over Emma, much as she tried to distract herself with entertaining visitors of the artistic set. She busied herself with tutors for little Horatia, but the child remained sullen and uninterested in her. Emma gamely taught Horatia piano and the rudiments of French and Italian, but the little girl preferred to speak them with Fatima. William Nelson now had an excellent "living" as Prebendary of Canterbury, where—he claimed—his duties kept him too busy for visiting. Sarah Nelson wrote warmly to Emma, but could not get leave from her husband to come to Merton. The Matchams and the Boltons likewise begged off, and Emma came to realize that their only interest in her was her connection to their illustrious brother-in-law. She saw herself as being alone in the world, save only for her mother and Nelson.

Taking Perry's warning, she stayed away from card-tables. Still, she spent money on improvements to the house, determined to make the place perfect for Nelson on his return. Mrs. Cadogan wailed further about expenses.

To his credit, James Perry stopped by at least twice a week, and his newspaper carried gossipy accounts of the artists and musicians who frequented the Merton house. He was also keenly aware of Emma's loneliness and desperation.

"You must know, dear Emma," he tried to cheer her one afternoon, "that your little gatherings here have had a most remarkable effect upon fashions in London. The younger set look to you to set the styles in dress, home décor and even dinner menus."

"Ah, Prinny's faction, you mean?" Emma smiled, recalling Sir William's analysis. "Unfortunately, 'tis the old King's faction which still holds power."

"Remarkable," Perry murmured, setting down his wineglass. "I could almost believe that both the Old Guard and Napoleon conspire to keep you and Nelson apart. Together, you make formidable allies to His Royal Highness—and there is some quiet gossip that the Prince hopes to challenge His Majesty's competence and take control of the Regency. Nelson's views on reform, particularly of the Navy, are well known. Do you see how this connects?"

"Indeed!" Emma saw it. "With Nelson's backing in the House of Lords, the Prince's hopes might well be accomplished." She didn't add her hopes that the Prince, in gratitude, might then speed Nelson's divorce from Fanny.

"Then you can appreciate the Admiralty's position. Whilst they keep Nelson at sea, he cannot meddle in politics. However, should he win the victory he seeks over the French, his influence would be immense—and the longer he stays at sea, the greater his chances of defeating the French utterly."

LOVE OF GLORY

"They should let him come home on leave, then—sometime when Parliament is not in session."

"That is precisely what my paper shall suggest," Perry smiled. "I wish you good fortune, Emma."

*****

The *Morning Chronicle* did in fact urge Nelson's return, but Napoleon didn't cooperate. He forced Spain to declare war on Britain and put the Spanish navy at his disposal, making an invasion of England possible. Various French ships managed to escape the British navy's blockade and sail off to unknown destinations, either in the West Indies or the captive ports of Italy. Nelson remained at sea for another Christmas.

All through early 1805 French squadrons ducked and dodged through the Mediterranean, the eastern Atlantic and the Caribbean, keeping Nelson busy chasing them. Not until August, when the British navy had the French and Spanish ships bottled up in their own ports again, was Nelson able to take leave and come home.

Emma had ample warning of his arrival by announcements trumpeted in the papers. If Nelson had departed as the nation's hero, he now returned as its near-godlike champion. Everyone extolled his incredible feat of pursuing the French from Egypt to the West Indies for a full two years while keeping his ships and crews sound and fit. Choirs sang and masses were said in his honor. Wherever he went, crowds turned out to cheer him.

Emma, making a good guess as to his preferences, for once held no grand *soirée* to celebrate his return, but awaited him in the quiet house with only his own small chosen family to welcome him home.

When Nelson strode through the front door, early in the morning on August 22nd, Emma was there waiting for him. She was stricken by how thin and worn he looked.

"Oh, love!" she cried, running to him, "you've lost flesh."

"Ah, and you've gained it," Nelson smiled, holding her back to look her up and down. "So in total, we've lost nothing." With that he embraced her so fiercely that she wondered if they could reach the bedroom before yielding to Nature.

A child's exuberant screech interrupted them, and Horatia, hotly pursued by Fatima, came running through the hallway to throw herself at Nelson, howling "Papa! Papa!" at the top of her healthy four-and-a-half-year-old lungs. Nelson bent down to hug her, declaring that she'd grown too big to pick up. Horatia squealed with joy, covered his face with childish kisses, and prattled brightly about how she'd been learning "tongues and music."

In a moment of sharp insight, Emma laughed: "Good heavens! She rivals me for your affections."

Nelson laughed too, but the child shot Emma a fierce look.

"Oh now come, *Bebe*," crooned Fatima, deftly prying loose Horatia's hands. "let your parents be together *tout seuls* for a while. You will see more of your Papa at *dîner, bien sûr*."

Horatia set up a howl of frustration as she was carried away.

Nelson cast a fond look after her, and then turned back to Emma. "A lovely child," he said, "but no rival for what I wish of you—right now."

Emma smiled and led him—quickly—up the stairs.

Their private reunion was fierce enough to leave bruises on her hips, but it was not prolonged. Nelson's siblings, having heard of his return, began arriving before noon, bringing their assorted wives, husbands, in-laws and children with them. Neighbors soon followed, and even a visiting Danish historian who had come to present Nelson with a copy of his account of the Battle of Copenhagen. Emma was obliged to get up, get dressed and play hostess. Nelson, as the innocent historian noticed, was not terribly pleased by the visiting crowd.

Next morning, Nelson and Emma hurried off to London.

LOVE OF GLORY

*****

They went first to the rented house in Piccadilly, much to the dismay of the resident housekeeper who had been given little warning of their arrival. While Mrs. Cadogan, Fatima and the housekeeper stripped away dust-covers, aired out rooms, applied linens and chased after Horatia, Nelson went to call on Lord Barham at the Admiralty. Even then, some of Nelson's relatives—two Bolton nieces from Norfolk—learned of his whereabouts and came to call on him. Emma hid her annoyance and played the charming hostess. Nelson spent a busy day with official appointments, then collecting his nieces and went shopping with them for presents for Horatia. It was late evening before Nelson and Emma were at last left alone together, whereupon they went straight to the master bedchamber.

"Ah, no rest for the weary," Nelson sighed, pulling off his shoes. "Now that Pitt is Prime Minister again, he is moving quickly against Napoleon. The Foreign Office has persuaded the old alliance of Russia, Prussia and Austria to support Britain, but there is some question as to how effective they will be. I shall be asked to many more meetings, I fear."

"Make certain such appointments are restricted to daytime," Emma soothed, slipping out of her gown. "Return to me each sunset, and I shall assure your rest."

"Rest, is it?" he smiled wolfishly as he pulled off his waistcoat. "I'd call it healthy exercise, befitting a Navy man. Come help me haul on the sheets, my love."

"Aye, and show me your cannon," Emma laughed merrily, matching him garment for garment.

"If I do, I shall give you a full broadside," he promised.

"I expect nothing less. Give me the full charge of your balls!" she laughed, pulling down the bedcovers.

"And I'll shiver your timbers, and cover your decks with brine!"

"Oh, and sink me beneath the waves!"

"Gladly! Ah, kiss me hard!"

Not bothering to blow out the candle, Nelson toppled her into the sheets. In short order, the bed was creaking and groaning like a ship under full sail.

Chapter 16
An End to It

Next day, at the discreet order of the Ministry, Nelson officially moved into the Gordon's Hotel in Albemarle Street—which was within short distance of Emma's house on Clarges street, where he was seen visiting almost every evening. The crowds that recognized him, and gathered whenever he appeared on the street, made discretion impossible. Understanding that, Emma took care to always appear in public looking her best. The crowds came to recognize her too, and smiled openly, even if they dared not cheer.

By day Nelson labored through the labyrinth of English politics, in the evenings he attended various parties with Emma, and at night he retired to her bedchamber. After a month in London, he and Emma returned to Merton to find it thankfully empty and quiet. The daily hour's ride up to London and back suited him better than remaining in the city, even though relatives and old friends still made the effort to seek him out. His brother William visited occasionally to thank Nelson for his promotion. The Matchams and the Boltons came calling more often, usually with their children in tow. Nelson

LOVE OF GLORY

delighted in these family gatherings, and Emma took care to be the charming hostess.

One thing never mentioned at these gatherings was the state of Nelson's marriage. Divorce was almost exclusively the province of the Church of England, and, despite William Nelson's elevation to Prebendary, the Church was not pleased with Horatio. Discreet inquiries from his lawyers revealed that annulment would not be granted, since there was no question of too-close blood relationship, insanity, or—often mentioned with a chuckle—impotence. Legal separation *a mensa et a thoro* (literally 'of table and bed'—living separately, but still legally married) was certainly possible, since Nelson had undoubtedly committed adultery, but such would not permit him to remarry. Nelson's only real hope was to take the separation for now and later persuade Parliament to grant a complete divorce that would allow remarriage. So far, precisely because of his careful neutrality from either Whig or Tory party, he didn't have enough political support to guarantee that— especially since the adultery was entirely on his part, and not his wife's. Neither could he, for fear of the scandal, use the old common-law custom of selling his wife. "After all," he commented gloomily to his lawyers, "who would buy her?"

That problem aside, life at Merton was everything Nelson had hoped for. His house was lovely, his household doted on him, his family warmly surrounded him, and his little daughter was growing like a weed. On returning from work in London, he would change out of his formal military uniform and put on the sober and simple clothing of a country gentleman and stroll about his property, often with Horatia skipping along ahead of him. And of course there was always Emma—the loving hostess by day and the passionate lover by night.

His only distraction was the problem of France. He discussed tactics with the Prime Minister and with various

LESLIE FISH

Navy officers, both in London and when they came to visit at Merton.

This disturbed Emma, for Nelson had mentioned in passing that if the French ships did manage to break out of their blockade, the Prime Minister wanted him to lead the fleet that would meet them. She knew there was no dissuading Nelson from taking that role, so she put it out of her mind and concentrated on enjoying the summer at home with her glorious lover in all his contentment.

*****

The end to their interlude came early on the morning of the 2nd of September. With a clatter of hoofbeats and a grinding of wheels, a muddy post-chaise rolled up to the door at Merton, and a young Captain Blackwood came running from it to see Nelson. He was carrying dispatches to the Admiralty, and had stopped to warn Nelson of what they contained. Nelson, already awakened by the sound of the carriage arriving, took one look at the travel-rumpled young officer and guessed at his mission. "I am sure," he said, "that you bring me news of the French and Spanish fleets, and that I shall have to beat them yet."

"True, sir," Captain Blackwood panted. "Villeneuve has left port and joined with another fourteen sail from Corunna. He sailed for Cadiz, and presently lies in anchorage with another thirty French and Spanish ships. We fear he is waiting to join forces with the other squadrons, whereupon... Well, anything may be possible."

"Pray, wait until I dress," said Nelson.

Within the hour, he was following Blackwood to London. Emma watched him go, clutching a kerchief as if she would strangle it and softly reciting prayers for Nelson's safety.

Nelson returned on the 12th, for a farewell dinner with James Perry and Lord Minto. Emma could not be her usual

LOVE OF GLORY

vivacious self but constantly brushed tears from her eyes, which the guests could not help but notice: Minto with suppressed sneers and Perry with sympathy.

Next morning, while Tom Allen and Mrs. Cadogan packed his gear, Nelson took Emma to the town church. The early morning attendance was small, but Nelson insisted that Emma take communion with him. As they knelt at the rail, waiting for the vicar, Nelson pulled two plain gold rings out of his pocket and held them up to be blessed. Emma gasped as she looked at them, realizing that—law or no law—Nelson meant to formally seal their union.

When they had taken the communion Nelson caught the priest's eye and held it, then took Emma's hand and said aloud: "Emma, I have taken the sacrament with you this day to prove to the world that our friendship is most pure and innocent, and of this I call God to witness." Then he placed one ring on her finger and held out the other, his intention plain.

Eyes bright with tears of joy, Emma placed the other ring on his hand.

Afterward there was one last family dinner, at which Emma tried to put up a brave front, followed by a quiet prayer at the bedside of the sleeping Horatia. At half-past ten o'clock, he descended the stairs to his waiting chaise and drove away. Emma watched, weeping silently, until his carriage-lights disappeared among the trees.

*****

Merton House grew quiet again with Nelson gone, and Emma's only solace was reading the papers and writing letters that begged for any news of him. She heard of his arrival at Portsmouth, and the crowds that gathered to cheer him aboard the *Victory*. She read of how he set sail on September 15th and proceeded next day to Weymouth—from which he dispatched another passionate letter to her. From there he proceeded on to Plymouth, then out into the Atlantic, and finally reached Cadiz on the 27th. There he found the French and Spanish ships still bottled up in the harbor, and settled down with his own fleet to wait for them to come out.

The waiting preyed upon Emma's nerves to the point where she could no longer stay at Merton. She sent little Horatia to her old nurse, Mrs. Gibson, and went herself to visit William and Sarah Nelson in Canterbury. William and Sarah welcomed her warmly, and Emma reconsidered that they might indeed be fond of her as more than just Horatio's mistress. Besides, they were united to her by a desperate concern for him. Letters and reports came sporadically, and Emma and Sarah hung upon every word.

On October 23 they received a letter saying that Nelson had sighted the last of the French and Spanish ships leaving Cadiz, and he was setting his fleet to pursue them, certain that this would be the decisive battle. Emma calculated that the letter had taken at least a day to reach them, possibly two. The decisive battle had already been fought; perhaps it had already been won.

William and Sarah hastened to the house chapel to pray for Nelson's victory, but Emma could not join them. She knew that Nelson's fate had already been decided, and no prayers would alter it. She could only wait to hear what that fate might be.

The long day dragged past, the sun sank and the Nelsons went to dinner, but for once Emma could not eat. She felt frozen in time, suspended, waiting for the word that would give her a future, good or ill. She slept only fitfully that night and was up at dawn to sit by the window, waiting. That day, too, stretched endlessly. Sarah and Mrs. Cadogan tried to entice Emma to eat or to leave her post by the window, but she refused to stir, accepting only glasses of tea or wine.

LOVE OF GLORY

Toward sundown came the clatter of hooves and wheels, and a muddied chaise pulled up by the door. Emma recognized the man in the carriage as Mr. Whitby, from the Admiralty. Instantly she scrambled to her feet and hurried to the front door, not waiting for the maid to answer it. Even before the first knock sounded she flung the door wide. There stood Whitby, rumpled and pale, holding a pair of letters.

"Horatio?" she whispered.

The man's face began to crumple. "We have gained a great victory," he began.

"Never mind your victory!" Emma cried. "My letters—give me my letters. Tell me if Nelson lives."

Whitby held out the letters with a trembling hand, tears spilling down his cheeks. "Dead," was all he whispered.

Emma gave a wailing scream, and fainted.

Chapter 17
Widow of Glory

Word spread through the house like fire through tinder. Whitby and Fatima carried Emma into the parlor, Mrs. Cadogan fetched brandy and smelling salts, Sarah came running to see what the disturbance was, then ran even faster to her husband to tell him the news. Tom Allen arrived while they were reacting, and Whitby thankfully handed over to him the task of dealing with the bereaved. Emma wakened slowly to the sounds of dismay and lamentation, and remembered everything. She couldn't speak, and her eyes felt dry as sand, but she gave her mother an imploring look. Understanding, Mrs. Cadogan caught Tom's sleeve in a fierce grip and insisted: "Tell us how it happened. Leave nothing out."

"I had this from wounded sailors who saw it," Tom fumbled. "They were transferred with the dispatches to the schooner that put in last night. I heard..."

"Say it!"

"Yes, milady. It was in the thick o' the battle, goin' up against the *Redoubtable*, when a sniper's bullet took him in the left shoulder clean through to the back. Two sailors and a marine sergeant carried him down to ship's surgeon on the

LOVE OF GLORY

orlop deck. On t'way the Lord Nelson made them stop at the middle deck whilst he gave orders to a midshipman for adjusting the tiller-ropes. When they got him below, he looked at the surgeon and said: 'Mr. Beatty, you can do nothing for me. I have but a short time to live...' And whilst the surgeon cut away his coat and examined his wound, he said: 'Remember me to Lady Hamilton. Remember me to Horatia. Remember me to all my friends. Doctor, remember me to Mr. Rose...' That will be his solicitor, I'm sure—"

"Yes, yes. Go on."

"Aye, ma'am. He said: 'Remember me to Mr. Rose; tell him I have left a will and left Lady Hamilton and Horatia to my country.'"

Sarah Nelson burst into tears. Mrs. Cadogan gave her a thoughtful look, and then urged: "Go on, go on!"

"Aye. The doctor asked summat of what he was feeling, and he was hot. They brought him lemon-water and wine, and fanned him as best they could. Then they all heard cheers from above, and after a bit Captain Hardy came down to shake his hand and tell him that they'd got fourteen o' the French and Spanish ships, and would have the rest shortly. Milord Nelson said: 'I am a dead man, Hardy. I am going fast. It will all be over with me soon. Pray let my dear Lady Hamilton have my hair and all the other things belonging to me.' He meant a lock of his hair he'd put by, and I'm sure I don't know what else."

Mrs. Cadogan noted the glances shot between William and Sarah.

"Captain Hardy went back up topside, and the surgeon talked briefly with Milord again, and Himself said: 'God be praised, I have done my duty.' Then he said: 'What would become of poor Lady Hamilton if she knew my situation?' And then there was the boom of a cannon recoiling just above, and little else could be heard for a while. Captain Hardy returned soon and took milord's hand, and congratulated him on his brilliant victory, and they spoke of who would command the fleet and how they should anchor for the coming storm."

"A rising storm?" William Nelson cut in. "They'd have had to jettison—Oh, tell me they didn't just cast his body overboard!"

"No, sir! No. Captain Hardy promised they'd not. Then milord Nelson said: 'Take care of my dear Lady Hamilton.' The sounds of wind grew stronger, and I heard milord murmur something that sounded like 'Kismet, Hardy'—but he took it to mean 'Kiss me, Hardy', for he did so."

Kiss me hard, Emma thought, making her own guess as to what Nelson had truly said, and where his dying thoughts had been.

"And after a bit of mumbling he asked the steward to turn him on his right side to ease his pain. He said summat more to the doctor, and then told him: 'Remember that I leave Lady Hamilton and my daughter Horatia as a legacy to my country.' The chaplain and the purser lifted him up a little, and he said again: 'Thank God I have done my duty.' Then he muttered for more drink, which was given, and he said no more. The surgeon pronounced him dead just as the cannon-fire ended."

"He died at the height of his triumph," William Nelson pronounced, patting his wife's hand. Mrs. Cadogan didn't spare a glance for him. "And what then?" she asked.

"Captain Hardy wrote the victory and the loss in his log-book. Then the storm struck in force, and most of the captured ships sank in it. When 'twas over, the ship's crew mourned most bitterly and swore that as they'd brought him out, they'd bring him home. They put his body into a great cask o' brandy—or perhaps 'twas rum—and lashed the barrel to the main-mast, with marines guarding it and his cabin day and night. And so they sailed to Gibraltar, where they met the schooner and sent her forthwith to England with the wounded and the dispatches. The fleet is coming after, bringing our Lord Nelson home."

LOVE OF GLORY

There was a long silence as the tale ended. At length William Nelson drew a deep breath and asked: "Has the news reached London, then?"

"No formal word," said Tom, "but Whitby's coming means they know. With the fleet limping home, it might not bring the official dispatches for another week or more, though surely the schooner's sailors will talk…"

"Then we must prepare for the formal mourning, and the celebrations of victory," said William, drawing himself up as if about to give a sermon; his look was calculating.

"And we must go to London," pronounced Mrs. Cadogan, startling him. "Come, Emma; we must pack. We will fetch little Horatia and be waiting in the house on Clarges street, for surely the Admiralty will send its formal condolences there."

Yes, thought Emma, pulling herself to her feet. *I and his daughter. We must be seen, and remembered—as he wished.*

As the two women paced toward the stairs, William Nelson and his wife exchanged another glance: his bewildered, and hers scowling at him.

"You know," she said quietly, "I never liked Fanny."

"My dear!" gasped William, astounded, "What an odd thing to say, and at such a time, too!"

"While planning your sermon," Sarah added, walking toward the door, "you might dwell a bit on avoiding the sin of ingratitude."

William only blinked after her, wondering what on Earth she'd meant by that.

*****

Early in the morning of November 6th, the news came formally to the Admiralty at Whitehall, in dispatches carried by two travel-worn naval officers. The word went quickly from the First Lord of the Admiralty to the Prime Minister and the King, by way of his keepers. His next letter went to Nelson's still-legal wife, but he'd delegated the Controller of the Navy Board to send the announcement to Emma, at the house in Clarges Street. After that, the news went to the *Gazette*, from which the rest of the press heard it.

Emma, already dressed in black, had been awaiting the letter. Its arrival was the signal for Mrs. Cadogan to drape the house in black crepe and funereal wreaths. Fatima was left to explain to little Horatia that this meant her papa would never come home again, at which the child was first puzzled and then angry.

Meanwhile, the city around them both celebrated and mourned throughout the day and into the next night. Gunfire salutes were fired from the Tower and in Hyde Park. Church bells began to ring ceaselessly. Lamps were lit everywhere and hung out in the streets. Abe Goldsmid lit only two rows of lamps on the façade of his town house in St. James' Square, and set out to commiserate with Emma.

He found her sitting in her parlor, dressed in full formal mourning, with nothing on the small table beside her but a single candle, a decanter, and a single glass half full of wine. There was a second chair, and Goldsmid took it.

"My condolences upon your loss, Lady Emma," he began.

Emma gave him only the briefest of nods.

Goldsmid sighed and hitched closer, knowing this would be difficult. "Emma, despite your pain, you must take action. Already, political factions shuffle about to make use of Nelson's victory, and his death."

Emma grimaced, reached for the glass and took a sip of wine.

"You must plot and move also, lest you and your child be shunted aside. Soon his funeral shall be held, and already the King's faction has refused you an invitation."

That made Emma raise her head, eyes flashing.

LOVE OF GLORY

Heartened, Goldsmid continued. "But write a letter to His Highness the Prince of Wales, who always liked you, and ask him to accompany the widow 'Amy Hart' at the funeral. Do you but wear a thick enough veil, and none shall recognize you. Even if any do, you shall be on the Prince's arm and no one dare refuse his partner. Do you understand?"

"I do," Emma murmured. "I shall write him directly—but how can I be certain that the message shall reach him in time?"

"Give it to me, and I will see to it," Goldsmid promised. "You must also be present at the reading of Nelson's will, for he confided to me that he had left you provision in it. Take a good ally with you—I would suggest James Perry—as witness to your legacy, so none may deny it. Also, there are many witnesses that Nelson asked the crown to provide for you, but no such official pronouncement was made, and the King's faction may choose not to honor his wishes. You must gain help within the Prince's faction, and for that you must make use of your popularity with the commons. Can you do that?"

"I...know not where to begin," Emma sighed.

"First, the theatres are already creating tributes and hymns to Nelson; you must attend at least a few of them. I shall accompany you when I can, and I daresay I can persuade John Pennington to help where I cannot, but even if you have no other chaperone than your mother, you must go. Attend every tribute to him that you can find—and take Horatia with you when you can. You must show yourself to the crowds as the epitome of the grieving faithful lover, and mother of his child—his only true child." He carefully added: "There is more at stake than just yourself and your future, Emma."

"What do you mean?" she asked, attentive now.

"In the House of Lords, Nelson was careful to remain neutral—partly because he knew not how to navigate the treacherous waters of politics, and partly because, as I know, Sir William cautioned him thus. He aligned with neither the

LESLIE FISH

Whigs nor the Tories, but only made passionate pleas for reform of the navy and opposition to Napoleon. Even so, these positions and his own history placed him solidly in the Prince's faction—and thus among the Whigs. The King's faction, knowing that the Prince's must ultimately triumph, do all that they can to retard that inevitability by setting policies that will restrain the future plans of their opposition. They cannot deny Nelson's victory, nor the price he paid for it, nor the great influence this gives to his wishes in life—but they will try to deflect his policies wherever possible, and they will begin with you."

"With me?!" Emma snapped, indignant.

"Certainly. As his mistress, you represent something of lawlessness—of rebellion against the established order. As a single woman of limited means, you may be disregarded as a political influence—and such will be done under the guise of propriety and righteousness. Can you not see that, my dear?"

"I think so," said Emma, blinking back tears. "Pray come with me to the study, where I will write whatever letters you ask. Indeed, might you dictate my handling of the more delicate political matters?"

"Gladly," said Goldsmid, assisting her to rise. "And afterward, you must be prepared to admit callers who come to pay their respects."

*****

Emma, accompanied by a sullen Horatia and Mrs. Cadogan, all dressed in deep mourning, did indeed appear at a public tribute to Nelson at Hyde Park, where the crowds saluted her and gave her a wreath amid flourishes of trumpets. She went to the theatre, accompanied by her neighbor John Pennington, where the crowds cheered her.

LOVE OF GLORY

A peculiar tribute arrived in the form of newspaper cartoons, one of which—by James Gillray, who had often lampooned Nelson in life—showed him dying upon the deck in the arms of a weeping Britannia, who bore a striking resemblance to Emma.

"His pen made you look rather fat, my gel," complained Mrs. Cadogan, "But then, he does not flatter the King, nor the Prince, either."

Emma, sitting as far from Fanny as possible in the crowd, also attended the reading of Nelson's will. She had not expected any great sum, and was gratified to learn that he had left her the ownership of Merton, an annuity of 500 pounds per year, and control of the interest from the 4000 pounds he left for Horatia. Fanny Nelson, having received a good bit more, had the sense not to say anything.

George Rose, Nelson's advocate in the Admiralty, did discreetly ask if the Ministry would heed Nelson's wish that Emma receive a pension for her services to the crown while in Naples, and was told only that the question would be "taken under advisement."

"That," James Perry warned Emma that evening, "does not bode well for your chances. You may very well have to make do on the legacies left you by Nelson and Sir William. Meantime, continue attending every tribute to Nelson where you can gain entry. Mayhap something may yet be made of the public adulation."

"I shall need assistance," Emma sighed. "I cannot keep track of all these things, nor of whom shall be my companion, nor whether I should sing or not, nor... Oh, I'm lost without him!"

"You need a social secretary," Perry considered, "you who always were one yourself..."

"I can't think," Emma groaned, resting her face in her hands. The tears that came so often now spilled down her cheeks.

LESLIE FISH

"There, there," Mrs. Cadogan soothed, "I can take on some of that work."

"And, invited or no," Emma pronounced resolutely, "I shall go to Nelson's funeral."

*****

It was on November 4th that Nelson's body came back to England. His body had been placed in a coffin made from the mainmast of the *L'Orient*, and when the patched and dismasted *Victory*, towed by other ships of the line, came limping into port at Spithead, this was set inside another coffin of lead. When the ship had made its slow way up the Thames and arrived at the Royal Hospital in Greenwich on the 6th, yet a third coffin of finely carved wood enclosed the other two.

William Nelson, now an Earl and very conscious of his new rank and standing, fussed endlessly over the details of the procession and funeral. He sent no invitation to Emma.

After lying in state for three days in the Painted Hall at Greenwich, the triple coffin was escorted to a funeral barge by 500 naval pensioners, many of whom had known Nelson personally. The barge was his own, from the *Victory*, pulled by his own crew, followed along the riverbank by ever-growing crowds of mourners. A southwesterly gale sprang up as the barge approached Saint Paul's, and as the cannons boomed in salute their roar was matched by the wind.

Thousands packed the streets to watch as the coffin was landed at the Whitehall stairs and taken to the Admiralty. There the coffin stood all night, to be taken out in the morning for the funeral and burial. The long sad progress had taken a full two months, and among the many veiled and black-draped women who had followed its course, nobody noticed one more.

Late in the morning of January 9th, 1806, the funeral procession set out to St. Paul's. The coffin, draped in black

LOVE OF GLORY

velvet, was borne through the streets of London on a funeral car designed and painted to suggest a ship of the line. Sailors from the *Victory* marched ahead, bearing the flag the ship had flown at Trafalgar; the wind held it open, showing the holes shot through it. After them came the military band playing the Dead March on fifes and muffled drums. Close behind the coffin marched Nelson's civilian friends and 31 admirals and 100 captains, followed by over ten thousand soldiers. As they passed through the streets the massed crowds were dead silent, save for the faint rustling as men removed their hats when the coffin passed. The head of the procession reached the cathedral before the end of it left Whitehall.

Inside the cathedral hung a chandelier of 130 lamps, and the floor of the aisle was dug open to reveal the crypt and a black marble sarcophagus originally meant for Cardinal Wolsey three centuries earlier. The bishop and his attendants waited at the altar, the Prince and assorted peers filled the waiting seats, and if the seat next to Sir Charles Greville was discreetly filled by a heavily veiled woman—who in fact had been waiting in the cathedral all night for this opportunity—no one noticed or complained.

The funeral took four hours, all done with the most lavish pomp and ceremony that Earl William Nelson could arrange. Only at the end was there any departure from formal ritual. When the 48 sailors from the *Victory* were told to fold the battle-flag and place it on the coffin, they instead tore it into 48 pieces; each man then took his section and thrust it into his shirt. The peers looked a trifle dismayed by the action, but did nothing.

Finally, as the choristers sang, the coffin was lowered into the crypt. The organ played the Recessional and the crowd slowly emptied out of the cathedral. If a veiled woman was seen pausing to drop a single rose into the crypt, nobody noted it.

After all, other mourners also paused to drop flowers or ribbons into the crypt as well.

Emma didn't begin sobbing aloud until they were out in the open air. Greville steered her hastily to his carriage and handed her in, then mounted with some alacrity and signaled the coachman to drive away.

"That was nicely done, Emma," he dared to say, once they were headed back onto Clarges Street. "I confess, I feared you meant to make a scene."

Emma only shook her head, and wiped her eyes with an already damp black kerchief.

"By all means, show yourself—and Horatia—openly hereafter at the various tributes. Even if you cannot win the pension Nelson wished for you, you might well win friendship and sympathy from others. Still, I would advise you to leave London as soon as the public mourning has ended, for you know you have enemies here."

"I pray I also have friends," Emma whispered. "Surely no one can doubt how I loved Horatio."

"No indeed," Greville sighed. "No one can doubt that at all—and that, indeed, is the problem."

Chapter 18
Loss

Another major tribute that Perry managed to arrange for Emma to attend was a viewing of the life-sized wax effigy of Nelson, newly constructed and displayed at Westminster Abbey. He took care to conduct her there himself, with Mrs. Cadogan bringing little Horatia. He noted with approval that Emma was exquisitely dressed and, whether by nature or artifice, looked as beautiful as she had the year before. The crowds stepped back respectfully as he led her toward the glass case where the effigy sat, wearing one of Nelson's own uniforms.

As she saw it, Emma gasped and clutched Perry's arm with desperate strength. He gripped her hand firmly, hoping that she wouldn't faint.

Little Horatia caught sight of the effigy and ran toward the glass case that surrounded it, crying: "Papa! Papa!" She pressed against the case until Mrs. Cadogan drew her away, and then began to wail softly.

This scene, Perry considered, would play wonderfully in the streets, but not in Westminster Abbey.

LOVE OF GLORY

Fortunately, at that moment the artist stepped forward, and Perry recognized her as Catherine Andras, the medallion-maker for whom Nelson had posed just before leaving London for his ill-fated voyage. "Please, milady," Catherine asked, "is the likeness accurate?"

Perhaps Emma's years of familiarity with art and artists guided her, but she straightened and took a calming breath. "The direction and form of the nose," she managed to say, "the mouth and chin and general carriage of the body, they are exactly his." Unnoticed tears flowed down her cheeks. "Only, please, might I rearrange that lock of hair about his forehead more to the way he usually wore it?"

The vicar obligingly opened the case, letting Emma step within. She stared at the image for a long moment and gently re-arranged the artificial hair. Then she bent closer, and her intention became plain.

"Pray do not kiss it!" the vicar cried, alarmed. "The color is not yet dry!"

Emma caught herself, drew a deep breath and stepped back. The vicar hastily closed the case again. "The likeness is perfect," Emma managed to say to Catherine, and then broke into hopeless sobs.

Perry carefully guided her out of the Abbey, covertly noting the reaction of the crowd of viewers. Yes, they showed immense respect to the weeping mistress and orphaned child. Perhaps the press could make something of that, to stir the Ministry in favor of giving Emma that pension. The crown had, after all, awarded Nelson's brother William an earldom and a grant of 99,000 pounds, not to mention what it had awarded to William's heirs, to Fanny and to Nelson's sisters. If only Prime Minister Pitt were not ill, he might have been moved to do something.

Still, the King's faction held enough power to make that doubtful.

LESLIE FISH

*****

"It is as we feared," said Abraham Goldsmid, pacing back and forth across the parlor. "Sir William Pitt has died, and with him the last hope. No, the Ministry will not give Emma the pension that Nelson asked."

Emma took another sip from her glass, which Goldsmid guessed held something stronger than wine, and said nothing. She looked distracted, undone.

"What of his daughter, Horatia?" Mrs. Cadogan asked sharply. "Have they forgotten that she is Nelson's only blood child?"

"No, but she is only a daughter, and a bastard at that," Goldsmid sighed. "The Tories have no sympathy for by-blows, nor for the whole feminine sex. They look to Nelson's brother to maintain the family bloodline."

"The greater fools, they," snorted Mrs. Cadogan.

"That is not to be doubted," Goldsmid said drily, then turned to Emma—who was sipping the brandy again. "Emma, you must understand. Between Sir William's legacy and Nelson's, you have at best 1500 pounds—that, and the furnishings of this house, and Merton. You must learn to live upon that, within your means. Sir William warned you against extravagance—"

"Sell the furnishings and close this house," Emma roused herself to say. "I shall go back to Merton and end my days there. Merton, where we were so happy..." Her tears renewed, and she reached for her glass again.

Goldsmid exchanged a glance with Mrs. Cadogan. "If you wish, I will handle the sale of the furnishings," he offered. "I haven't appraised any of it, but with luck we might realize another 2000 from the sale."

"May we rely upon you to invest it wisely?" Mrs. Cadogan implored, her expression saying more than her words.

"Yes," Goldsmid agreed. "I shall always be your friend, my good ladies. Never doubt it."

"Oh, enough!" Emma wailed. "Be done, both of you, and leave me to mourn in peace! Lord, Lord, he is gone and I have no one..."

"Let me see you out," Mrs. Cadogan said hastily, rising. As Goldsmid duly followed her into the hallway she whispered to him: "She grieves so sorely, I fear for her."

"Keep myself and Mr. Perry apprised," said Goldsmid. "And... you might do worse than to send for Sir Charles Greville again. He was ever her friend, I believe."

"Friend, aye," Mrs. Cadogan muttered darkly, "but not much of a lover."

"How say you?" Goldsmid paused at the door.

"What, didn't ye know? He kept her less than four years, much though she loved him, and then traded her to Sir William in exchange for that good old man's paying his debts and making him his heir."

Goldsmid raised his eyebrows. "I daresay Emma got the best of the bargain, then," he said.

"Aye, if only Sir William had succeeded in teaching her prudence."

*****

Back at Merton, Emma seemed to recover somewhat. Throughout the rest of the winter she remained secluded in mourning, obsessively re-reading Nelson's old letters, and Mrs. Cadogan managed to keep the household budget within safe limits. Fatima and the various tutors took care of Horatia, who often didn't see Emma for days on end. Mrs. Cadogan plotted shamelessly with Perry and Goldsmid to invite Emma to their early spring parties, not only to draw her out of the house but to preclude any thoughts Emma might have had about entertaining the neighbors herself.

Still, Merton attracted visitors: artists who had admired her portraits and followed her career, old friends of Nelson's, and historians who came to see the various tributes to him that decorated the house. Emma gradually grew accustomed to meeting these guests, giving them tours of the house and grounds and a light supper afterward—often of fish pulled from the ornamental canal. As spring wore on to summer the guests became more frequent, and the household budget began to strain.

"Ye've made the house a very museum to Nelson," Mrs. Cadogan said one afternoon, as she and Emma sat in the garden watching Fatima play with Horatia. "P'rhaps you should list it with the universities, and charge admission. 'Twould fatten our thin purse a little."

"Would that not seem to cheapen his memory?" Emma asked, fanning herself futilely in the muggy heat. "I've noted that the peers, and their imitators, fancy it beneath their dignity to handle money directly."

"So it may be, but proper society has cast you out long since, my gel. It can do ye no further harm to handle coin like a shopkeeper."

"I must ask Perry or Goldsmid about it, but don't trouble me now."

"Why Emmy, what else have ye to do? I've seen: ye do naught but write letters all day, when no guests are present. Neither work brings in money."

"It keeps me conversant with old friends," Emma sighed. "Oh mother, what am I to do? I have no husband and no lover, and I don't know what to do with myself."

LOVE OF GLORY

"Ye might comfort yourself with your children," Mrs. Cadogan said, a little sharply. "Hadn't ye heard? Little Emma has become a governess to a good family."

"I did hear of it." Emma shrugged. "I suspect that she lacks the pluck to court and marry one of the men there. She seems determined on a life of genteel obscurity."

"Well, you still have little Horatia." Mrs. Cadogan pointed. "See how merrily she plays with Fatima, and ye've seen well to her education and connecting her to her relatives."

"Kitty Matcham adores her," Emma admitted, "and Sarah would have her to visit more often, but William has become such an ass since he has been made an earl, and he refuses to allow it."

"Nonetheless, in all your letter-writing, keep steady words with Kitty and Sarah. Keep their love, for ye may need to rely on them sometime. Pray give me that fan; this heat's unbearable."

"Look at Horatia gamboling about with Fatima," Emma marveled. "They seem not to care for the heat. I can understand it in Fatima, for she comes of a hot country, but Horatia is truly English. How does she bear it?"

"Ah, she wears only a child's thin smock and her slippers. We grown women must wear shift and gown and all, for propriety's sake."

"Oh, I'm so sick of propriety!" Emma snapped. "Damn all propriety! It kept me and Nelson apart, and keeps us sweating under miserable cloth, and shores up the Tories that sneer so at the lot of us. I can scarcely wait for the old King to die and the Prince to take the crown, and his faction to sweep away all these wretched cobwebs of propriety!"

Mrs. Cadogan started to answer, then gasped and dropped her fan and clutched at her left shoulder.

"Here, mother," said Emma picking up the fan. "Why, what ails you? You look as pale as milk."

For answer, Mrs. Cadogan grasped Emma's wrist in an iron grip. "Oh Emmy, what's to become of ye?" she panted. "Ye've got no sense—not with money, nor your health, nor society—and ye must get it quick, or fall to ruin."

"Mother, are you ill?" Emma asked, alarmed. "Let me fetch some water, and the doctor. Fatima! Oh, where has she gone?"

Mrs. Cadogan relaxed her grasp with a sigh, and Emma got up to run after her maid and daughter. She found them hidden behind the rose hedge, Fatima picking flowers for Horatia's hair. They abandoned the game quickly at Emma's insistence, and ran back to the garden bench.

There they found Mrs. Cadogan lying on her side, her open and unblinking eyes turned toward the cloudless sky.

*****

The coroner's inquest pronounced Mrs. Cadogan's death as natural, a failure of the blood-vessels of the heart, brought on by age and the summer heat. Emma was inconsolable, and James Perry was obliged to make the funeral arrangements. A service was arranged at the Merton village church, though Mrs. Cadogan's body was to be sent to Paddington and buried in the family plot, and Emma roused herself enough to send the invitations.

Perry and Goldsmid, who attended the modest service, were privately worried by the small turnout; local people came, but none of Emma's old friends appeared.

"This does not bode well for the lady's future," Perry murmured. "Not even Greville put in an appearance."

"I heard he was restrained by business," Goldsmid whispered back. "He is expanding that port, you know."

"Even so, I do wish that he lived closer," Perry confided. "As an old love, he might give her more comfort—and advice—than she is willing to accept from us."

LOVE OF GLORY

"See what you can do with him," Goldsmid sighed. "Without her mother to control her tastes, I fear Emma will eat up her fortune and die in the poorhouse."

*****

After the funeral Emma paced through Merton House alone, burdened by its emptiness. Her husband, her lover and now her mother: all were gone, and the house was quiet as a tomb. No, she couldn't bear this. "I must have company!" she cried to the silent walls. "Perhaps I should go up to London..."

Yes, she considered as she poured herself a glass of brandy, that would be best. Nelson's sisters and sister-in-law would be there for the Season; so would the old artistic crowd she had once known so well, and the current artists who had visited Merton recently. In that merry whirl she would find some gaiety, some diversion, of the kind she had known a scant five years ago.

At least she would not be so terribly alone.

Chapter 19
Dishonor

London this late in the Season was not what Emma had expected. Having given up the Clarges Street house she was obliged to ask old London friends to let her visit, and the few who were willing would invite her for no more than two weeks apiece. There were few invitations to balls or dinners. Her dresses no longer fit and had to be let out. Burdened with a sense of slow abandonment, Emma went to every party to which she could get an invitation. Nobody asked her to perform her old pieces, very few of even her old friends asked her to dance, and the only place she felt truly welcome anymore was at the card-tables. She played All-Fours, Commerce and Speculation to all hours, and with growing recklessness. Finally she awakened one morning at the end of the Season to find almost everyone dispersed to the countryside, her hosts politely but impatiently asking her to leave, and herself with no money. Sobered, she packed up her entourage and went back to Merton.

Her first visitor upon her return was Abraham Goldsmid, who seemed perturbed at her appearance. After the usual

LOVE OF GLORY

pleasantries, he sat down with her over the tea and biscuits and got to the matter at hand.

"Emma, you should have stayed away from the gambling tables," he told her bluntly. "You've bitten deeply into your funds, and unless you can find some new source of income, there will be no more."

"But what can I do?" Emma almost wailed, quashing an urge to get up and fetch the brandy. "No artists have asked me to sit for them, no opera company has asked me to sing, and the house hasn't enough acreage to farm."

"You can," Goldsmid considered, glancing at the decorated walls, "sell some of these furnishings."

"Oh, no!" Emma gasped. "These—all these—are tributes to my Nelson. I cannot give them up."

"In that case..." He hesitated, almost embarrassed. "You could stoop to trade. Turn the house into a hotel, and charge visitors by the day, or month, or longer."

"I cannot! To board strangers, in Nelson's house—Besides, I know nothing of managing such a...an establishment. And how should I entice paying guests?"

"True, the place is an hour from London. Yet there are ways, my dear. Trade upon Nelson's fame—now, while his glory is fresh—and invite visitors to come view his house as his monument, his museum indeed. Charge admission from the day-viewers, and charge for meals. I know you have a decent cook, and the fish and birds from that canal and pond would cost you nothing. I do admit that I have a bit of a head for business, and I could provide you with an honest manager. I could also advertise the venture for you. Will you have my help, Emma?"

"Oh, let me think." Emma rested her face in her hands, imagining Nelson's home turned into a common inn with herself as a cross between docent and entertainer. "Let me think on it, I beg you," she groaned.

LESLIE FISH

"I understand that the choice is hard," Goldsmid said kindly, "but the alternative is a slow march into ruin. I pray you take my advice, my dear."

Emma remained where she was for long moments after Goldsmid departed, pondering her circumstances. Selling her treasures was unthinkable, but making an inn of the house was intolerable. Surely there had to be another way, if only she could think of it.

At least the decision did not have to be made right away.

Holding that thought, Emma got up and fetched the brandy.

*****

She avoided making a decision until Christmas, when James Perry invited her to his country house for the holidays. She accepted the invitation and attended, but not even the gaiety of the season, and the presence of other children for Horatia to play with, could lift her spirits very far. Emma had begun to think often of death, and to consider that she was only waiting out her time until the beckoning angel would reunite her with Nelson. Besides, every glance in the mirror reminded her of mortality; she had grown fat, she had to admit, and there was a streak of grey in her hair that she hadn't bothered to repair with dye. She could scarcely be recognized as the beauty who had charmed great artists, and lords, and even royalty. Preoccupied, she barely noticed as Perry, smiling secretively, led her into the drawing-room and left her there with its sole occupant.

"Greetings, Emma," said a familiar voice.

"Sir Charles?" She was startled to recognize him, for Greville too had aged. His hair was entirely grey, and there were deep lines in his face. "I'm pleased to see you at last," she murmured faintly, taking a chair.

"And I you." He studied her with his old keen look. "I see the past year has treated you no better than it has me."

LOVE OF GLORY

"You were always blunt, Charles," Emma replied without heat, glancing around for any sight of a brandy decanter.

"Then let me continue to be so. Emma, you know that your gambling spree in London was disastrous to your purse."

"So everyone tells me," she replied sourly, her eyes lighting upon a decanter of wine. "Ah, would you indulge me?" she asked, pointing.

"You've indulged yourself more than sufficiently," he sighed, but nonetheless got up and fetched the decanter and two glasses, filled them both and pushed one in front of Emma. "When you were up in London, why didn't you ask to stay at my house in Paddington Green?"

"You being a bachelor, it would hardly have been proper..."

"Oh come, Emma. When did you ever concern yourself with propriety?"

"Since it cost me the crown pension," she admitted, and took a sip of the wine.

Greville gave a short laugh and lifted his glass to her in salute. "I daresay you also feared that I, with my ever penny-pinching ways, would have dragged you forcibly away from the gambling tables. As your nearest relative, by marriage, I could have done so, you know."

Emma laughed in turn at the thought of the rail-thin Sir Charles hauling her admitted bulk anywhere. "I appreciate your concern, Charles..." Another thought was surfacing. "Could it be, after all these years, that you still feel some affection for me?"

Greville blinked. "I was ever your friend, Emma," he said carefully.

"You were more than that, once." She leaned toward him, flicking back her hair in an old gesture that he was sure to recognize. "Could it be that you might wish to resume our old arrangement?"

"No," he said firmly, settling back in his chair. "Our arrangement ended, most finally, when I sent you to Sir William."

Emma blinked, remembering those days. "Had you truly tired of me, Charles? 'Twas you who got me my training in the art of being a lady; did you do it only to make me a fit gift to Will'um? Had you planned to be rid of me, even then?"

"Not precisely," said Greville, looking away. The hint of a blush colored his cheekbones. "There was the little matter of my courting Lady Middleton..."

"A wealthy heiress of 18, as I recall," Emma probed. "Of course you needed to get me out of the way. Did you love her, Charles?"

"No." Greville looked down at his hands. "I had purely mercenary intentions, I assure you. I had plans for the port of Milford Haven, even then."

A bizarre picture was forming. "...But then, you...sold me to Sir William, in exchange for being made his heir, and receiving your 'portion' in advance..."

"With which I built Milford port, and made it successful," Greville hastened to say.

"So you did not need to court your heiress after all?"

"Just so."

"But...by the time you had made Milford profitable, I was already married to Sir William."

"I confess, I had not expected that."

"Yet... You stayed unmarried all these years, Charles. Why is that?"

Greville tugged irritably at his collar, and Emma could have sworn he was sweating. "I...never met a woman I truly fancied."

"Oh." Emma thought she understood. "Did I do that to you, Charles? Have you truly waited all these years...for me?"

His reaction surprised her. "Dammit, no!" he snapped, pounding his fist on his knee. "And damn Perry's machinations,

LOVE OF GLORY

bringing me here in hopes of reigniting an old flame. I cannot do it, Emma."

"Why not?" Emma asked, holding out her arms. "I never ceased loving you, Charles, even though you abandoned me."

"Because..." Greville was definitely sweating now. "Oh, hell! I have kept your secrets, Emma; now I implore you to keep mine."

"Gladly," she promised. "But tell me why we cannot be together now? There is no legal impediment, and if you fear my reputation—"

Greville barked a short laugh. "I have more to conceal from Propriety than you do, Emma. I... This is what I beg you to keep secret. I am...not a man for women."

It took a moment for Emma to realize what he meant, and then she couldn't believe it. "But...but you did love me. I know you did! You embraced me for nearly four years..."

"That was the most I could manage, ever." He sagged in his chair and looked up at the ceiling. "I daresay I would have done less with Henrietta Middleton."

"Why...?" Emma floundered.

"Ah, Emma... When I first saw you, dancing in that transparent Greek shift at Harry Featherstonhaugh's estate, I saw that you were—to be quite blunt—the most beautiful woman in England. Your beauty stirred even me."

"Oh..."

"I had known of my...indifference to women for a long time. Upon seeing you, I felt that if any woman could arouse my passions, you could. That was why I happily took you away from Sir Harry, pregnancy and all."

"I did arouse you," Emma almost whispered, "for nearly four years."

"You did that." Greville looked down at his clenched hands. "But even you could not fan the flame forever. No, not even you. I had to accept, then, my own nature."

"So you never...?"

"No, never again. I arranged for your future—and my own fortune—with my uncle. My courtship of Henrietta Middleton was but a ploy to cover my actions. Besides my wanting Sir William's money, I was...grateful to you, Emma. I still am, in many ways."

"Then...why could we not have, as they say in France, a marriage of convenience? That would protect both our reputations."

"I confess I have thought of it." Greville took up his glass and drained it. "Unfortunately, my...lover, of many years—a younger fellow whom you've not met—could not endure it. Oh, he'd be nothing but supportive, I know: but his spirit would wither, and eventually I would lose him. I cannot do it, Emma."

"I see." Emma felt as if a cloud had shadowed the sun, for the room seemed suddenly darker. "But will you still be my friend, Charles?"

"Always, my dear."

Emma could think of nothing more to say, and let her glance stray toward the windows, which revealed the sight of the sunlit grounds.

"And as your friend," Charles resumed quietly, "pray allow me to advise you. Take Goldsmid's offer, and without delay, for your purse is steadily dwindling. If you gain no further income, you shall be bankrupted by the end of next year. I should hate to see you a pauper, begging in the streets, Emma."

"No," she whispered faintly.

"Neither could I bear to see my uncle's widow shuffled off to the poorhouse," Greville went on. "Goldsmid is here, in the gun-room discussing hunting, I believe. Let me send him to you, so you can tell him you accept his plan."

"Please!" Emma cried. "Not yet! Let me have one more year—just one year—to keep Merton to myself and mourn my dead. Please, Charles."

LOVE OF GLORY

He gave her a long, thoughtful look. "Very well," he conceded. "Next Christmas, then, we shall meet here again and you will accept Goldsmid's assistance. I pray you use the time well, Emma. ...And stay away from the card tables."

He finished his glass, rose, bowed once and left.

Emma continued to stare out the window, wondering if she could simply will her heart to stop beating.

Chapter 20
The Price of Hospitality

Back at Merton, Emma slipped into days of half-dreaming. She wandered the house and grounds, remembering what she and Nelson had said and done there, returned to her writing-desk and reread his letters, then read any mail that had come in that day and wrote letters to her old friends. Outside of dinner she rarely saw Horatia, who was getting along splendidly with Fatima. Winter slid into spring with no change.

With the warm weather and opening of the Season, though, visitors began dropping in again: artists, poets, journalists, art critics. How could she refuse them? They were her last link to her old life, and their presence cheered her. And of course they must stay for dinner, and she must perform on the piano and sing, though none of them asked to see her Attitudes performed anymore. The butler shook his head at the expense of feeding so many guests.

Only once, when a quartet of young students came to visit, did she laughingly suggest turning the house into an inn for poets and artists. They laughed with her, and then commented that a great lady should never have to dirty her hands with trade. She didn't bring up the subject again.

LOVE OF GLORY

Spring slid into summer, then autumn, and the shooting season started. Now Emma's guests were more often Navy people, sailors and officers who claimed to have known Nelson. Fatima claimed, in private, that someone must have passed the word about that the Merton house was a good place for free meals. Emma didn't care; anyone who had a shred of connection to Nelson was welcome.

As winter approached and the Season ended, James Perry came to call again. He noted the group of naval officers happily drinking in the parlor, and took Emma aside privately into the drawing room. He came straight to the point as soon as the door was closed.

"Emma, this must stop."

"What, entertaining guests?" Emma puzzled. "How can I turn away old admirers and friends of Nelson?"

"You have had far more visitors than ever sailed with Nelson, and entertained them to your detriment." Perry sat down beside her and took both her hands in his. "Emma, do you never study your own household books?"

Emma blinked, realizing she'd never thought of that. "My mother used to do that," she murmured. "It never crossed my mind."

Perry heaved a profound sigh. "Your own butler came to visit me, to ask my assistance. Emma, you have all but drained your legacy; there is not enough money left to pay the household staff and feed yourself until the end of the month."

"What?" Emma couldn't believe it. "But I stayed away from the card-tables, I swear. Sir Charles told me I had two years..."

"Greville never imagined that you would be hosting half the British Navy at your own expense. I have spoken with Goldsmid, and he has a solution. His brother Benjamin shall buy the house, while you keep all its furnishings—"

"Sell Merton house?! But—but where would I go?"

"You shall remain here, as chatelaine, but his agent—a discreet fellow named Alderman Smith—will assume the management, and run the house as an exclusive inn."

Emma remembered her days as Lord Featherstonhaugh's hostess, and shivered. "Shall I entertain the guests, then?"

"Only if you wish to." Perry patted her hand. "Though I daresay you would make an excellent guide to the art treasures of the house."

Chatelaine, Emma thought. *Hostess, rather.* "At least now, no one shall ask me to dance upon tables," she said faintly. "How shall it be done?"

"If you wish, I can send Goldsmid's agent and solicitor here this very day."

"Do so, then." Emma cast a longing glance at the decanter on the sideboard. She couldn't remember at the moment whether it held wine or brandy, but either would do.

"I shall also arrange to politely oust those roisterers in your parlor," said Perry, turning toward the door. "And of course, you are invited to my house for Christmas. Pray wait here; I can see myself out."

As he left, Emma went to the decanter and poured herself a glass. The contents, she learned at first sip, were cherry brandy. She remembered having ordered it the week before. Perhaps she should drink it slowly; heaven only knew when she'd be able to afford it again.

*****

Alderman Smith proved to be a discreet indeed: a quiet little man of middle age, with brown hair and eyes and an eminently forgettable appearance. Benjamin Goldsmid's payment for the house was quite generous, and his brother Abraham promised to invest the money and manage it himself. Between the interest on the investment and the interest on Horatia's legacy, he noted, Emma could live quite comfortably—provided she wasn't extravagant.

One extravagance she insisted on was a new gown for Perry's Christmas party. Her old gowns had been expanded as much as they could be, and were still tight. Emma took care to choose a pleated Grecian design whose pleats could be let out if necessary. She felt dully amazed that grief had fattened her when she felt inwardly as if she were wasting away to nothing.

The party was as merry as last year's, but Emma felt distant from it. Even watching little Horatia dancing a quadrille with the other children scarcely made her smile. Emma herself danced not even once, but sat in the drawing room sipping mulled wine and pondering her future. That was where Greville eventually found her.

"Hello again, Emma," he said, taking a chair beside her. "I've heard that you finally agreed to let Goldsmid rescue you."

"At the cost of becoming a guest in my own home," she brooded, peering into the depths of her wineglass. "Guest, or ghost, for I will haunt the halls that once were mine."

"You are far too substantial to be a ghost," Greville smiled. "Seriously, Emma, you should take better care of yourself. You could maintain your famous beauty better, you know."

"For whom should I maintain it?" she asked bleakly. "All who loved me, all whom I loved, are lost to me. I feel I am already a ghost of myself."

"Do you care nothing for your child?" Greville asked, arching an eyebrow.

"I do, but she cares nothing for me. She always preferred her nurse, and her governess, and of course Nelson." Emma took another mouthful of wine.

"Do you intend to spend the rest of your life in mourning, then? Will you be nothing more than Nelson's common-law widow?"

"What better fate can I expect?"

Greville heaved a long sigh. "Had you chosen your course but a little differently, you might have charmed your audiences again, loved again, and perhaps even wedded again. It is not too late, you know."

"It is," said Emma, with heartfelt finality. "I have known such passion and glory... Oh, what could content me after that?"

"Then, can I wish you nothing better for the New Year than a peaceful fading into shadows and legend?"

"I can see nothing else."

"Ah, well. Know then that I shall remain your friend to the finish, dear Em." Greville dared to give her a chaste kiss on the forehead before he rose and left.

Emma watched him go, and then turned to refill her glass.

*****

As good as his word, soon after New Year of 1808 Benjamin Goldsmid quietly turned Merton House into an exclusive inn, whose visitors were largely retired naval officers. All of them claimed to have known Nelson, and could easily be persuaded to relate tales of his life. Emma could listen by the hour, but—thanks to the discreet but immovable Alderman Smith—could not reward her storytellers with drinks, food or lodging *gratis*. Neither would anyone play cards with her for money, she learned, because Smith had absolutely forbidden gambling in the house. Day-visitors, mostly artists and critics now, came frequently, and Emma would give them the grand tour of the house and grounds, but their numbers slacked off noticeably from the days when they had not been required to pay for their food and drink.

Smith had also discreetly arranged tutors for little Horatia, to keep her busy when she was not with Fatima, and so Emma had little to do with her.

LOVE OF GLORY

Except when showing the estate to visitors, Emma spent her time either writing letters to old friends or wandering the house and grounds, lost in memories—but always accompanied by a bottle of good wine.

News from the outer world dribbled in piecemeal. The Duke of Portland was now Prime Minister. Spain had allied with Britain and Portugal to oppose France, and British troops were now fighting their way across the peninsula. The crown had commissioned a heroic sculpture of Nelson atop a tall pillar to be erected in Dublin, and the Irish were annoyed about it. Benjamin Goldsmid, who never visited the house, was said to be quarreling with one or more of his sons.

Emma noticed little of it, taking more interest in her letters and their replies and the current vintages, for letters from her old friends on the Continent transported her back into the exciting and glittering world she had left when she returned to England, and fine wines numbed her to her ever-present grief. She did not go up to London for the Season, but drifted through the estate like the amiable ghost she had called herself. Her only extravagances now were her taste for good wines and liqueurs and the ordering of new gowns as the old ones grew tighter. Alderman Smith chided her about the expense, but otherwise ran the house discreetly and well.

Only in the second week of April did Emma notice that Smith was agitated and secretive. The very next day James Perry came to visit, and took her quickly into the drawing room.

"Emma, a calamity has occurred," he almost whispered. "Benjamin Goldsmid, apparently driven to distraction by his quarrel with his sons, has...done away with himself."

Emma could only blink in astonishment. For some reason, she found it difficult to remember the man's face. "And Abraham?" was all she could think. "How does he fare?"

"He is most greatly dismayed, as you might guess. At the moment he is bending every effort to protect his brother's family from the disgrace, and from legal repercussions. He has no time, nor energy, to concern himself with your situation."

"My...situation?"

"Merton House was legally Benjamin's property. There is some question as to whether the ownership shall pass to Abraham or to Benjamin's eldest son, who is of age. I know nothing of the son's attitude, but he is certainly not the friend to you that Abraham is."

That got through to Emma. "If the son inherits, shall I be cast out of my home?" she gasped.

"Abraham and I shall do all we can to prevent that." Perry gave her a measuring look. "But on the chance that the son takes it, you had best conspire with Smith to make this inn as profitable as it can be."

"What can I do?" Emma worried. "I know nothing of trade or finance..."

"Make effort to salvage your beauty," Perry said firmly. "Cease overeating and drinking, and endeavor to lose the fat you have accumulated these past few years. Find a good hairdresser to restore the color of your hair; have you noticed how much of it has gone gray? Return to your dancing, and your singing, and playing instruments. It is not so long since you were famed as a hostess and entertainer; if you can return to that state, Merton House may become a fashionable salon—and its income shall rise accordingly. Benjamin's son will not sell off a prosperous enterprise."

Emma remembered her earlier days, thought of the effort it would take to return to what she had been, and shivered. "I don't think I can do it," she said heavily. "There must be some other way. Can I not be left to enjoy my last years in peace?"

"You are not so old as that," Perry started, then caught himself. "Well, I will suggest to Abraham that he make an arrangement with his nephew. Take care of yourself, Emma."

LOVE OF GLORY

With that he rose and departed, pausing only once at the door to look back and shake his head. Emma, reaching for the decanter, didn't notice.

Soon afterward came the news that Abraham Goldsmid had inherited his brother's estate, including Merton House, and Emma was left to go on as before.

*****

The year drew to its close with no notable change at Merton House. The resident guests went out fishing and hunting, or off to parties with friends. The number of visitors from London dwindled to nothing, as did invitations to local gatherings, and Emma was left largely alone in the house. Days began to run into one another, and Emma frequently lost track of time. Often she would be startled awake by the ringing of the dinner-bell to realize that she had slept through most of the day, and in fact could not remember much of the day before.

When the invitation to Perry's Christmas party came, she politely refused. A few sprigs of holly and the traditional foods provided Christmas at Merton House for Emma and its handful of residents who had nowhere else to go. The exchanged gifts were trinkets: scarves for Emma, toys for Horatia, books for the guests and Smith, shillings in small cakes for the servants. Emma thought of earlier Christmas parties, and chose to lose herself in memories with the help of the seasonal punch and brandy.

New Year came, and Sir Charles Greville with it. He spoke long with Alderman Smith, and finally sought out Emma in the parlor.

"Greetings, Emma," he said, looking her over. "I wish I might say you look well."

"For whom should I make myself beautiful?" she replied, setting down her glass.

LESLIE FISH

"I heard from James Perry what he proposed, and what you replied." Greville settled on the nearest chair, and pointedly eyed her nearly empty decanter. "Are you determined, then, to join your lost lover by drinking yourself to death?"

"No!" said Emma, shocked. "How can you say such a thing?"

"As a student of Natural Philosophy, I am trained to draw conclusions from what I observe," he said soberly, "not to mention what your servants, friends and steward observe. From such observations, 'tis clear that in the scant three years since Nelson died, you have let yourself go to ruin. Now we both know that self-slaughter is forbidden by law, and causes disgrace and legal problems for the surviving family, as Abraham Goldsmid now has reason to know—"

"I'm so sorry for him! I had no warning of Benjamin's state of mind, for I scarcely knew the man."

"It appears he was over-fond of his sons, for his quarrel with them caused him such melancholy as he could not bear."

"Poor man. Yet how could he fall so far into despair?"

"You should know, Emma." Greville gave her a hard look. "You seem to be following the same path, though at a slower pace."

"No, surely not!" Emma insisted. "I have no reason to despair. I have my house, my friends, my daughter, and my memories of a great passion. I am perfectly content with those, I assure you."

"Perfectly? When you have no lover? I know you, my dear; you've not been without a man since you were 15. If this is how you care for yourself when you are without one, then you should repair yourself posthaste and get another."

"After Nelson, who is there?"

"You set your sights too high," Greville sighed. "I recall you were not so choosy when you took up with Featherstonhaugh."

"I was very young," Emma remembered, "I'd just been cast off by my first lover, and I was desperate for money."

"Then remember those days, and become desperate again." Greville took her arm and shook it hard. "Between extravagance and thoughtlessness, you lost your title to Merton House and became dependent—first on one Goldsmid brother, now the other—and Abraham's protection may not last long."

"Why, what do you mean?" Emma pulled away, alarmed.

"I mean that Abraham and his brother were close partners as well as loving siblings. Abraham hasn't recovered from the shock of his loss, and his business dealings have been the weaker for the lack of his brother. There is no need to trouble you with the details, but it is enough to say that his bank is no longer successful in all of its undertakings, and has steadily lost credit. Remember that your fortune is invested in his bank, and if the one falls, so will the other. Though it may sound like betrayal, I urge you to find another source of money and invest it in some other bank. If you cannot restore yourself and find another man to protect you, then you must begin selling the furnishings of the house."

"I can't!" Emma wailed, appalled. "Everything here contains a memory—I cannot sell my past!"

"Then sell your present," Greville replied grimly. "Restore yourself and go a-hunting. There are many men old enough to take a mistress—or even a wife—who is no longer young. I believe there are many also who would have you purely for the prestige of keeping Nelson's mistress."

"I will not be used in such a fashion!" Emma retorted hotly. "I will not cheapen a great man's memory so!"

"If not, then you have no choice but to sell the furnishings. I daresay no one has offered you work as an opera-singer or artist's model in the last three years, have they?"

"No..."

"Then what remains but the road to the poorhouse?"

"I shall think of something," she temporized. "I still have the skills Sir William taught me... I still speak fluent Italian, and write well in French. I can work as a translator or secretary..."

"Barely enough to keep yourself from starvation," Greville grimaced. "Consider your choices, Emma, and act accordingly."

"I shall think on it," she promised.

"Do so quickly, then." Greville sighed again. "And do pay heed to Smith, will you?"

"Alderman Smith? Certainly," Emma promised, wishing only that he would leave.

"If nothing else, he can provide you with a good appraisal," said Greville, rising. "Fare you well, Emma." He seemed as anxious to leave as she was to see him go.

Emma watched him depart, and then almost defiantly reached for the decanter.

Chapter 21
Faded Glory

Emma truly did try to heed Greville's advice. She sent for a hairdresser, and endured a long hour of bad smells and discomfort as the artful woman applied henna on her gray locks. She did try to restrict her drinking until dinner and take tea the rest of the day. She avoided sweets and buttery dishes, and ate nothing but lean meat and salads, eggs and fruit and cheeses.

Still, when she looked at herself in a mirror at the end of the month and saw no significant change, she gave up and comforted herself with sweet cakes and brandy. She quietly gave up hope of going to London for the Season.

In late spring came another shock; James Perry came to visit with the sad news that Sir Charles Greville had died suddenly, in his sleep. Emma wept inconsolably for hours, crying that everyone she had loved was dead, and that there was no future for her. Fatima did her best to comfort her, but it was Perry who drew her back to some semblance of calm by insisting that she must compose herself enough to attend Sir

LOVE OF GLORY

Charles' funeral. Fatima repaired Emma's mourning dress, and they set out in Perry's coach for London.

The funeral was held in a modest chapel near Greville's house in Paddington Green but the reception, to Emma's surprise, was held at the Royal Horticultural Society. The members, most of them elderly, stood up in turn to recite tributes to Sir Charles—primarily concerning his skill at breeding rare plants. Sir Joseph Banks spoke respectfully of Greville's success in coaxing *vanilla planifolia* to bloom for the first time under glass in Britain. Sir James Smith promised to name an entire genus of Australian plants *Grevillea* in his honor. Other guests from the Royal Society, whose names Emma couldn't remember, spoke of his remarkable collections of antiquities and rare minerals, now to be found in the British Museum.

Emma left the reception in a daze, her grief transmuted to a bewildered awe. "I never realized how much of a scientist Sir Charles was," she noted as Perry took her home. "I suppose I should have expected it, seeing how alike in mind he was to Sir William..." Another thought struck her. "Oh, what shall become of his—his companion? I never met the man..."

"Hush," said Perry, grasping her wrist firmly. "He was one of the Fellows of the Royal Society who spoke today. He has a large and respectable family, not to mention his...other friends. I beg you to speak no more of it."

"I certainly shall not," she promised, "but I can surely feel sympathy for one who loses a forbidden lover."

"Ah, you have a good heart, Emma."

They said nothing further until they reached Merton. Perry left her there with another polite suggestion that she dispose of the furnishings as best she could. Emma consoled herself with brandy for the next fortnight.

At one point she did ask Alderman Smith to appraise all the furnishings in the house, but when he brought her the list she

LESLIE FISH

noted that a portrait of Nelson was at the top—and the price was much less than she'd expected. After that she refused to read the rest, and went back to the decanter and her memories.

She dealt with Greville's warning thereafter by not thinking about it, and the year of 1809 crept past much as the previous three had done. The only change she noted was that little Horatia could now write a decent hand, and the child often—at Smith's urging, Emma suspected—wrote to her Nelson relatives.

When questioned, Smith smoothly replied: "You must know, madam, that the crown gave Nelson's family a grant of more than 90,000 pounds, and a perpetual pension of 5,000 per year, besides the title and position given to his brother. If they might be persuaded to add to Horatia's legacy, you would have use of the interest on it."

Emma found herself utterly disgusted by all this attention paid to money, and said no more on the subject. She far preferred to write and read her letters, and roam the house and grounds treasuring her memories. That, she felt, was the proper occupation for the widow she knew herself to be.

Christmas brought another invitation to James Perry's, which Smith and Fatima and even little Horatia urged her to attend. Emma reluctantly sent for the hairdresser, had her best gown refitted, and put in an appearance.

The visit fulfilled all her worst fears. Aside from her old friends—among them Abraham Goldsmid, looking shockingly aged—no one recognized her. Other than Perry himself, no one asked her to dance. At dinner she was seated next to a grey-bearded bore of an army officer and an equally old and boring journalist friend of Perry's, and they talked across her of nothing but the progress of the war. Emma was particularly annoyed that they heaped praises on General Wellington, and never so much as mentioned Nelson's victories. As soon as she decently could, Emma gathered up her entourage and escaped back to Merton.

New Year's of 1810 was a desolate affair, with the house's tenants gone off to various parties of their own. No guests appeared, not even Perry. Emma consoled herself in her accustomed fashion. Throughout the rest of the winter, the days blended together in a waking dream that lasted through the turning of the seasons.

Only with the height of autumn did change come. Emma, sitting in the garden reading letters, heard the hoofbeats of a single horse approaching and wondered who would visit without a carriage. A few moments later, James Perry strode out to the garden in his riding-clothes, looking grim.

"Emma," he said without preamble, "I bring bad news. Abraham is gone."

"Oh," Emma whispered, trying to remember how old Goldsmid had been. "I'm so sad to hear it."

"There is worse." Perry sat down on the bench beside her. "It was...not a natural death."

"What?" she gasped. "He was murdered?!"

"Only by himself." Perry slapped his riding-crop against his boot. "His bank over-extended itself on a loan, which failed. He was ruined, Emma: bankrupt. With his death, he having left only a daughter, his property passes to his eldest nephew, who is making arrangements even now to settle Abraham's debts. I persuaded him to believe that Merton House was a successful venture, turning a tidy profit, but eventually he must learn the truth."

"The truth? I thought the house was maintaining itself well."

"Not well: scarce breaking even. And Emma, your fortune was held in Goldsmid's bank and will be swallowed up in the debt. I pray you: sell the furnishings for the best price that can be had, and remove yourself to modest accommodations. Have you any relations who would take you in?"

"No," Emma admitted. "I have no one."

"I think I could shame William Nelson into accepting you." Perry smiled sourly. "Sarah always liked you, and always loved Horatia. Now that William's son is dead—"

"What?!"

"Hadn't you heard? 'Twas a fever. Horatia wrote a most touching letter, which Sarah treasured. She showed it to the Matchams, who were likewise affected. Between the child's charm and the money you could obtain from the sale—"

"I can't!" Emma burst out. "Leave Merton, leave Nelson's memorials... I can't do it!"

"Emma," Perry sighed, exasperated. "You cannot maintain this house."

"There must be a way! I can make it a profitable hotel—Smith can help—"

"I've just spoken with him. Between what remains of your annuities from both Sir William and Nelson, and the income from the tenants, the house still loses money. Sell the furnishings, sell your jewelry, and you might last another... perhaps three years here, no more. Look, you've mourned for Nelson these past four years, and it is time—well past time—to awaken and come back into the world again. I beg you, Emma: do not wait for inexorable fate to thrust you penniless out of doors. Sell what you can now, move in with the William Nelsons or the Matchams, and be safe."

"Oh, I can't think..."

"You might think more clearly," said Perry, staring pointedly at her glass, "not to mention reducing your expenses, if you would forswear expensive wines and brandies."

"I...I shall talk to Smith," Emma managed. The thought of the house's paintings, sculpture and furniture disappearing was intolerable. The thought of throwing herself on the mercy of William Nelson or the Matchams was equally unthinkable.

LOVE OF GLORY

"There must be something I can do. Only give me time to think."

"You've said that before." Perry heaved a sigh and pulled himself to his feet. "Let me see what I can do."

"Thank you, James," Emma called as he strode away. She waited for a long moment after he was gone, then got up and paced toward the house. Yes, she really must talk to Alderman Smith, she decided. He had been Abraham Goldsmid's manager; surely he could advise her.

Smith wasn't in evidence near the back rooms, so she plodded through the house to look for him. As she approached the drawing room she heard voices, one of them Perry's, and stopped to listen.

"—she won't budge," Perry was saying, "not until she has been thrown out on the street. Her friends must take charge for her."

Smith's voice replied, too softly to be made out.

"No," Perry answered reassuringly. "you may consider yourself in our employ now, though officially your title will be that of Emma's secretary."

"And my compensation?" Smith said clearly.

"We shall see to it directly," Perry replied. "Whatever monies the house brings in must go entirely to maintaining it. As to the rest, simply keep it out of young Goldsmid's hands until our plans bear fruit. And of course, keep me informed."

So, Perry will assume the burden of Smith's pay, Emma guessed, *And he will see to the management of the money for me.*

Reassured, she moved on to the parlor. There were more letters she wanted to write to her friends in Europe. She could leave money matters in Smith's and Perry's capable hands, and need trouble herself no more about them.

As the year drew to its close and the household prepared for Christmas, another invitation from Perry arrived. She was determined not to go, but Horatia howled so fiercely about missing the party that Emma finally consented to let Fatima take her. The girl returned exhausted with happiness, and Fatima hurried her straight to bed. Emma spent the next two weeks fearfully expecting another visit from Perry, but it never happened.

In spring came a letter from Perry, which Alderman Smith brought to her personally. After the usual salutations, its message was brief and to the point: "Abraham's estate has finally settled, and his last debts are paid. As anticipated, your monies were lost in the settling of the debts. Young Master Goldsmid now owns Merton House, but feels no obligation or concern for it. So long as the house pays for itself, with rentals or the other means which we have discussed, he is willing to leave it as it stands, but be warned; should you proceed into debt, he will surely sell the house and turn you out. I beg you again to follow the instructions which I gave you, as soon as might be."

Emma read no further, but crumpled up the letter and cast it into the nearest fire.

*****

The year rolled on as had the years before it. The good weather brought day-visitors to Merton and Emma duly guided them through the house and grounds, telling anecdotes of the history behind every feature. She took care, as the discreet Smith instructed her, to see that every visit ended in the large parlor where an equally discreet maid took requests for food and drink, but before the visitors were served and money could change hands she would retire to one of the private rooms to be alone with her letters and her memories.

Return letters, especially from the Continent, spoke much of the continuing war and of hopes for Wellington's eventual

LOVE OF GLORY

victory. Emma, seeing no mention of Nelson's contribution to the defeat of Napoleon, was uninterested.

Sometimes in the mornings she would assist Fatima and the tutor with Horatia's lessons, and at such times she would marvel at how the girl was turning into a pretty young woman, with Emma's coloring and a delicate feminine version of Nelson's features. Afterward she would feel moved to write to Nelson's relatives, asking them to visit and see Horatia themselves. The replies from Sarah and the Matchams were kindly and apologetic, but they regretted that they could not visit this season.

Once Emma received a scathing letter from William Nelson, ordering her not to write to him anymore, that left her upset for days. It was mollified by another letter, a few days later, in which Sarah Nelson firmly told Emma to write directly to her instead, and gave an address—different from William's. The Matchams, contrarily, asked for a portrait of Horatia, which Emma promptly commissioned. Smith muttered about the expense, but commented that it was "for a good cause."

Horatia stubbornly refused to call Emma "mother," insisting that her name was Thompson, and her baptismal certificate proved it. She did, however, boast of the fact that Nelson was her father. Emma briefly wondered what the neighboring children, or possibly the servants, had told the child about her parentage. For the second Christmas in a row, Emma sent Horatia to Perry's celebration while staying home herself.

1812 dawned quietly, leaving Emma alone with her house, her letters and her memories. Horatia was growing like a weed, approaching young womanhood, and it became an expense to keep her in clothes.

Only once did anyone speak to Emma on the troubling subject of money, and that was Alderman Smith, who came to her in the library as she was finishing another letter. She noticed that he was carrying the list of appraisals of the house furnishings, and frowned.

"Madam," he said, very gently, "if you could please indicate to me which of these are least valued in your memories, I believe we could put them to good use."

"None of them!" Emma snapped. "They are all sacred to Nelson's memory."

"Dare I ask, then," Smith ventured, "which pieces of your jewelry you would part with?"

"Certainly not! I am not so impoverished that I must part with my personal possessions!"

"Begging your pardon, madam, but, in fact, you are."

"What?!"

Smith's face grew sad as a hound's. "The cost of maintaining the house in any fashion fit to keep even such tenants as we now have, has exceeded the rents. We are in debt, and I fear we must discharge it quickly, for young Master Goldsmid will not tolerate a debt to linger. He will surely sell the house, and everything remaining in it, to clear the debt—and he may indeed charge some of it to yourself. I beg you, madam, to reconsider."

"Later," Emma murmured, waving him away. "I shall decide later, and tell you my decision. Don't trouble me until then."

"As you wish, madam," said Smith, withdrawing.

Emma reached for the decanter.

Later, lightheaded but fortified with brandy, Emma paced through the house and grounds, trying to think of what she might sell. If she dismissed the groundskeeper and let the gardens and canal go to wilderness, the tenants would leave. What other income did she have now? It was hard to remember anything but Greville's warning that she had used up both Sir William's and Nelson's legacy on that gambling spree in London. If she began selling the furnishings wouldn't the tenants, seeing the omen of poverty, also depart? If she sold her jewelry, what would she have left? And—she braced herself for the thought—if she left Merton, where would she go? William Nelson had made his position quite clear, despite what Sarah might think. The Matchams? They loved Horatia, but had never been close friends to herself.

For one wild instant Emma thought of selling all the furnishings, taking her jewelry and running off to Sicily, to throw herself on the mercy of Queen Carolina. Surely her old friend would take her in as a lady-in-waiting...

A moment later Emma caught sight of herself in a mirror, and froze. She didn't recognize that fat, slovenly old woman. *Good God*, she wondered dizzily, *How did I let myself come to this? Carolina wouldn't know me...*

No, it was better that she communicate with her old friends only by letters, letting them remember her as she had been when they last saw her. And no, she would not importune them for money. She still had her pride; she was a peer's widow, and the beloved of the greatest hero of the age, and she would not beg.

...Still, perhaps some of the furnishings might be sold, the ones not usually on view to the tenants... But which ones?

She fumbled her way to bed still pondering the question. By morning she'd reached no decision.

*****

Emma still hadn't settled the question when Christmas came, and again she sent Horatia and Fatima off to answer Perry's invitation while she stayed home. The presents exchanged within the house were few and small, with one exception: a competent portrait of Nelson—though, she could tell, not done from life—from an anonymous benefactor. An hour's thought told her what to do with it. She went down the corridor to the music-room, which hardly anyone visited nowadays, and found a painted-from-life portrait of Nelson, almost exactly the same size as the inferior version. She exchanged the paintings quickly, took the original to the library and set it behind the writing-desk, then summoned Smith.

"That one," she said, pointing. "You may sell that one. I hope that will settle the house's debts."

"I fear not, madam," said Smith, carefully taking up the painting, "But it will make some dent into them. Let me see what can be done."

"I pray that you will do well," said Emma, collapsing into the nearest chair. *More?* she wondered dizzily, as Smith padded quietly away. *How can I bear to do this again?*

Besides, where would she get another painting to exchange?

Her ruminations were cut short by Horatia's return, the girl chattering happily about the food and music and dancing, and Fatima exhorting her about how she must change her dress. Struck by a sudden pang of affection, Emma made effort to help the girl put on another frock. She thought of inviting Horatia into the music room and singing some carols for her, but then remembered that she hadn't practiced her singing in longer than she could recall. Her voice would surely be as rusty as a crow's.

How much, she wondered briefly, could she get by selling the instruments?

*****

Shortly after New Year, Perry visited again and Emma— knowing she couldn't avoid seeing him—had him brought to the drawing room. His expression was not encouraging.

"I'm pleased that you've begun to take my advice, Emma," he said, once the amenities were done, "But I fear it comes too little, and too late. Young Goldsmid is determined to sell the house."

LOVE OF GLORY

"No," Emma whispered, refusing to imagine it.

"Worse, he is—as I feared—planning to recover what he can from yourself."

"From me? How does he expect...?"

"Emma," Perry said sternly, leaning forward, "He will confiscate the furnishings—and your jewelry, such as he can find. If that isn't enough, he will have you consigned to debtor's prison. You cannot continue to avoid your danger, my dear old friend."

"What should I do?" Emma couldn't think.

"Allow your friends to help you. Take Horatia—and your jewelry—and go upon vacation somewhere inexpensive. Pray sign this letter"—he held out a paper to her—"charging myself and others, including Smith, to remove and dispose of whatever of your property remains in the house. In this manner, you need not suffer witnessing the departure of your treasures, and you can save the more portable of them. By the time you return, we should have found suitable accommodations, where you and Horatia can live comfortably."

"Suitable?" Emma shivered.

"Better than debtor's prison." Perry pushed forward the paper, took a pen and dipped it in the inkwell, and held it out. "Sign, Emma. Please."

Almost as if she were watching someone else perform the action, Emma took the pen and scrawled her name at the bottom of the paper. Perry blotted the ink, folded the letter and stuffed it into his vest. "Your old friends will not leave you to starve," he promised, taking his hat and gloves.

Emma watched him go, trying to remember where she had heard that last phrase before.

Chapter 22
Reprieve in France

With Smith's help, Emma decided upon a bold voyage to Calais. The weather would surely be warmer there, and with Napoleon having suffered so many military and political misfortunes, there was little danger that foreign visitors to the port city would be troubled. Alderman Smith had arranged for lodgings in a modest but respectable *pension* in the British quarter, and had sent her off with enough money to keep her entourage comfortable for a month. He had also armed her with a letter of introduction to the British Legate there. Emma took a suitable number of clothes, Horatia and Fatima, her collection of Nelson's letters, and her jewelry. After some consideration, she pinned a little bag into her chemise and kept her jewelry there rather than in a cumbersome box.

Once arrived and settled into their lodgings, Emma received an invitation to dine with the Legate. She had Fatima buy henna in the local market and arrange her hair, chose the best of her gowns, rented a small but stylish carriage for the evening, and went to the dinner with mixed expectations.

The Legate was an elderly man, but quite well-dressed and witty. The dinner party consisted of only eight besides himself,

LOVE OF GLORY

all of them local merchants and their wives, most of them English. As the only single female, Emma sat at the Legate's right hand and received a due portion of his attention. He did not mention Emma's past, nor ask her to sing or play an instrument after dinner, but kept the conversation running briskly. Most of the talk, understandably, was of politics and their effect upon trade. Amid the lively banter, Emma could almost imagine she was back on that charmed voyage down the Danube. She was grimly pleased to learn that Napoleon's star was waning. It occurred to her that her life had spanned the time from a little before the French revolution through Napoleon's career, and she might live to see his end.

"Oh, if only Nelson had lived to see it!" she burst out passionately. "If only he could have seen..." Overcome, she could say no more.

"No doubt his shade watches, and exults," said the Legate smoothly, lifting his glass. "To Nelson, then."

"To Nelson," echoed the rest of the guests.

Almost painfully grateful, Emma sipped her wine. She noted with approval that it was an excellent vintage. One could not be so crass as to enquire at a formal dinner about the prices of wines, but she guessed that she would not strip her purse while here in Calais.

As the party was leaving and Emma was waiting for her cloak, she saw one of the guests take the Legate aside and ask in French: "Who was that woman, the one who was so admiring of Nelson?"

"Don't you know?" the Legate replied in the same tongue. "She is Lady Hamilton, who was Nelson's famous mistress until he died."

"Is it possible?" marveled the guest. "I had heard that Nelson's mistress was a famous beauty, and Nelson died but seven years ago."

Seven years! Emma thought, jolted. Had it truly been so long? Where had the time gone?

"Ah, time and grief are cruel to all of us," the Legate replied. "It is undeniable that she loved him beyond measure, and has not known what to do with herself since losing him."

"Ah, *pauvre petite*," sympathized the guest. "*Il n'y a rien plus triste qu'une maîtresse abandonnée.*"

At that moment the maid brought Emma's wrap, and she had no further excuse to linger in the hallway. As she made her way to her carriage, Emma considered that at least she would have sympathizers, if not friends, here in Calais.

For the rest of the month Emma went about the British enclave of Calais leaving calling cards, with the address of the *pension* written in. This necessitated not touching wine until late afternoon, but Emma found herself feeling much improved in humor. Perhaps, she considered, it was the result of the fresh sea air.

Horatia, delighted to practice her French, explored—with Fatima in tow—everywhere that a young girl not yet formally presented to society could. She attended the local fairs and markets, sneaked into the open-air dances, chatted with the young local girls and flirted with her fan at the young local boys.

Eventually Emma's purse was emptied, and it was time to return to England. The weather chilled, as did her mood, while Emma and her little entourage crossed the channel and rode back to Merton town. Instinct warned her not to go directly to the house, but to stop at Perry's first.

James Perry himself came to greet her, and hurried her into the parlor while the butler took Horatia and Fatima off to the kitchen.

"It is well that you stopped here, Emma," he told her. "Young Goldsmid has indeed seized the house and everything within it."

LOVE OF GLORY

Emma felt as if a knife had been driven through her heart. "Everything?" she asked faintly.

"Everything that we had not removed, even unto the bed-linens. We had our solicitor arguing for hours, but Goldsmid has obtained a writ against you for what he cannot regain from the sale of the house and furnishings. I hope you kept your jewelry safe?"

"I did," she whispered.

"Excellent. I sent a letter to you in Calais, requesting you to stay there, but clearly you departed before it arrived. If at all possible, return there as quickly as you may. I suspect the constables are searching through the town for you, and will doubtless widen their search soon enough."

"Oh my God, to have to flee like a fugitive..." Emma couldn't believe it. "Why is young Goldsmid so set against me?"

"He has social ambitions," sighed Perry. "A cousin of his has been recommended for a title, and nothing will do but that young Goldsmid should have one too. To that end, he must obtain not only money but land. He must also walk in the proper political circles, for which reason he has become a Tory—and therefore a proper bastion of respectability."

Emma saw it all. "And therefore a partisan of Fanny Nelson!"

"And William Nelson," Perry added, "whose reputation would suffer greatly, were it known that 'twas you who persuaded Horatio to deal in politics so as to win William his title and excellent living."

"Let alone that it was his wife Sarah who persuaded me," Emma finished. "A fine fool he'd appear, did his haughty friends know he owed his position to the conniving of two women."

"All this you should have seen seven years ago. Likewise, you should have foreseen that your funds were limited, and lived more cunningly. Emma, I know you loved Nelson well—"

"No woman ever loved more truly, or deeply!"

"But you should not have forgotten your situation, nor let your grief blind you for seven years. Now your only hope is to flee back to Calais. Wait until dark, then take Horatia and ride back to the port, and take the first ship crossing."

"I have no money!"

"I can give you enough for passage, and will send for Smith to come and drive for you. When you reach Calais, pawn the least of your jewels and live upon that until Smith can send you more. If you—"

"More? What more?"

"Have you forgotten the other part of Nelson's legacy? Horatia is an heiress, and you have use of the interest on her money until she marries. Her legacy was not in Goldsmid's bank, and was unaffected by his fall."

"Oh... Yes, I had forgotten."

"So has everyone else who was not at the reading of Nelson's will. Young Goldsmid doesn't know of it yet, and even when he does learn it, he cannot seize the money from the bank; he can only take it from you, Emma. Therefore, keep out of his grasp. Leave tonight, and return to Calais as fast as you can."

"I will. Can you at least give us supper before we fly?"

"Certainly, but you and Horatia and Fatima must eat privately, in the music room, lest anyone see you and report to the constables."

Chapter 23
Arrest

They almost succeeded.

Alderman Smith appeared at dusk, disappeared into the library with Perry for half an hour, and emerged looking grim. He went to the music room to collect Emma and her little entourage, and then took them out the back door to the stables. They loaded quickly into a light calash, Emma and Fatima holding the drowsy Horatia between them on the seat, with the trunks on the floorboards. Smith pulled up the canvas cover as far as he could, lighted the lamps and mounted to the driver's seat.

"Best cover your faces against the night chill, my ladies," he cautioned as he wrapped a muffler around his own face and turned the horse toward the narrow road behind Perry's house. Once they passed through the narrow back gate and reached the road, he flicked the horse to a brisk trot and the carriage made good time.

"Cover our faces, indeed," Emma whispered, drawing a scarf around the drowsy Horatia's nose and mouth. "With any luck, no one will see or hear us passing. Or if any do, they perhaps will only think us to be a respectable merchant's family returning from a dance." For some reason, the threat of danger and the thrill of the chase—even with herself as quarry—reminded Emma forcibly of her hectic days in Italy, and she felt more alive than she had in years.

"I need a veil, *Domna*," Fatima whispered back. "I was the only African in all of Merton, and surely the local constables will remember that."

Emma fumbled in the topmost trunk until she found a suitable scarf, then shoved everything back in and closed the lid while Fatima adjusted the impromptu veil. The carriage rattled on, the sound of its wheels seeming dangerously loud in the thickening darkness.

The carriage turned onto the eastward road, and Emma began to believe they would make their escape handily. Then a light shone ahead.

"Hold!" sounded an authoritative voice. "Halt, in the King's name."

Smith stifled an oath as he drew rein and complied. With a sinking heart Emma saw two men in local constables' badges blocking the road ahead. A third man sat in a dogcart behind them, and Emma feared she recognized him. It was the retired Captain Dalwood, who had lately been one of her tenants, and he too bore the badge and cudgel of a volunteer constable.

"Who are you, and what is your business, sir?" one of the two men on foot demanded.

Smith tugged his forelock with just the proper degree of obsequiousness. "'Tis the widow Thompson and her maid, sir," he replied, "Coming home from dinner, if ye please."

Emma remembered that Horatia insisted on calling herself Thompson. This was a good ploy on the chance that the girl might waken.

It wasn't enough. "Thompson, is it?" the gouty old captain pricked up his ears. "I recall a wee girl of that name, always running about the estate. Bring the torch close, and we will have a better look at these two."

"Careful, sir!" Smith wailed, flinching away from the approaching torch—and incidentally flicking the reins on the horse's back. The horse started forward, but one of the constables grabbed the reins just under the bridle and held the beast still.

Emma squinted in the close firelight. "If you please, my good man," she tried, raising her voice to what she hoped was an unrecognizable squeak. "we are already late coming home, and my brother shall be worried."

The old captain drew as close as he could without colliding the carriages, and peered past the flickering torch. "Aha!" he shouted, "I recognize those eyes! 'Tis her, and no mistake. Take her, me lads!"

The constable holding the reins led the horse around, back toward Merton town. The other fell in at one side of the carriage, shaking his cudgel threateningly lest the women try to jump out and run away. Captain Dalwood paced his dogcart next to them on the other side.

"Trying to run from your debts, were you?" he sneered. "Aye, and gave no warning to us left behind! First we knew of it was when Perry stripped the house, and then the new owner and his men came to turn us out on our backsides, and a fine scene that was, with the servants crying and all. Not a word of warning, my fine lady! Not a word!"

"I knew nothing of it myself," Emma insisted, crossing her fingers under her cloak. "I was away, visiting friends."

"Well, I daresay you'll be visiting your friend the magistrate soon enough," jeered Dalwood. "I believe he'll be your host this night. 'Widow Thompson', indeed! Did you think I hadn't caught many a deserter in my day, and knew all their scurvy tricks?"

LOVE OF GLORY

Emma didn't answer, being preoccupied with plotting. So she was to be taken to the town magistrate; that was much better than being taken in a larger city. Merton town had no prison to speak of: just some rooms converted to cells in the old mansion that served as the town courthouse. She couldn't remember if the town magistrate had a wife or not; certainly she'd never insulted the man, or any of his friends or family. Smith, no doubt, would be freed to return to Perry and tell him what had happened. She had friends still, and they'd surely help her.

*****

The town magistrate wasn't home, but his wife was. A fussy, motherly little woman, she was taken aback at the thought of Lady Hamilton being dragged in by the constables like a common thief. After giving the two foot-constables both edges of her tongue, with an extra dose to Captain Dalwood for ingratitude, she insisted that Emma and her maid and daughter be ensconced in the guest rooms of her house until her husband should return and try the matter.

The constables, after thorough assurance that Lady Hamilton would not escape, left hurriedly. Alderman Smith and the carriage took off for Perry house at a good clip. Horatia threw a weeping temper-tantrum at the disgrace of being sent to debtors' prison, wailing that it was all Emma's fault. Fatima philosophically unpacked the trunk and arranged for baths, laundry and supper. Emma, seeing that the magistrate's wife was near to bursting with curiosity, put off her own exhaustion to gossip with her over late tea.

"Let others sneer at my 'extravagance'," Emma finished. "I but tried to keep my beloved Nelson's house as a memorial to him."

"Well, there was that late season in London when you gambled recklessly...so they say," the magistrate's wife chided, revealing what she'd heard of local rumors.

"I did that but the once, to drown my sorrow," Emma admitted. "I've not been back to London since, but have stayed and kept my house."

"Ah, my dear," the little woman clucked, "you should have sold it all after that first year's mourning was finished, seeing how little you were left—and how shabbily the crown treated you, ignoring Nelson's wishes and all."

"I know it," Emma moaned, dabbing at her eyes. "I simply could not bear to leave that house where we had been so happy."

"Indeed, 'one who loved not wisely, but too well.' Ah, the things we do for love! ...Well, we will see how well I can persuade my husband. Meanwhile, I beg you, do not think of this as a sponging house but consider that you stay here as my guest."

"I thank you greatly."

Later, as Fatima helped her strip off her clothes for bed, Emma carefully unpinned her jewelry-bag from her petticoat and fastened it inside her shift instead. It was concealed well enough, she ruefully admitted, under the fold of her sagging belly. Once she was safe, she swore, she would tend more carefully to her health and lose that excess flesh. For now, it was ironically useful.

Next morning the magistrate arrived, heard the whole story in detail from his wife, and called the concerned parties to court that afternoon. Perry and the solicitor he'd hired for Emma met her at the courthouse door and accompanied her inside. She'd taken care to dress the part of the grieving widow, with what clothes she had, and she noted that the magistrate gave her a respectful look.

LOVE OF GLORY

Young Goldsmid himself was not in attendance, though his solicitor was, and the case turned into a prolonged duel of lawyers. Alderman Smith put in an appearance as a witness, and produced the documents which proved that Benjamin Goldsmid had indeed bought only the house and grounds, not the furnishings nor Emma's personal property. Unfortunately, he had no choice but to also confirm evidence that the house had drained money for the last seven years. Captain Dalwood was satisfyingly grilled over the questions of how much he and the other tenants had paid, as versus what they'd consumed in food, drink, laundry services and the working-time of servants. That was followed by various clerks' and brokers' statements about the monies that could be realized from the sale of the house and grounds and furnishings, and the solicitors were reduced to wrangling like fishwives in the market over precise amounts. Emma caught herself drowsing, and was grateful that Horatia and Fatima had stayed in the magistrate's house. The magistrate himself was lost in the tangle. Emma roused in time to hear him pronounce that Emma would remain in custody—his custody, he assured everyone—until the house and furnishings were finally sold and the amount beyond the debt was determined.

Perry took Emma's arm, helped her to rise, and accompanied her back to the magistrate's house. "We've accomplished this much," he told her quietly. "Goldsmid must sell the house and grounds first—which I have no doubt that he will do as quickly as possible—while we, as per that document you signed, will sell the furnishings and deliver the money to him. The amount of the debt is high, but not as exorbitant as he wished. The problem is a juggling of money versus time; the young fool will sell the house quickly, getting less than optimum price for it. Our plan is to take the time to obtain the best prices for the furnishings, but that may be...several months, I fear."

"If my debtor's prison is to be house arrest at the magistrate's, I can endure it," Emma smiled faintly. "At least I do not have to bear the expense of lodgings."

"I can arrange to speak with you again, as soon as the house is sold. Meanwhile, I suggest you continue writing to your old friends, and see if you can find a safe place to live once you have been freed."

"I've already decided. We shall return to Calais, as originally planned."

With that, Emma entered the door of her so-called prison.

*****

The magistrate and his wife found Emma charming company, and treated her more like a guest than an inmate. They let her daughter and maid go outside whenever they wished, and even allowed Emma to leave the house on occasional carriage rides, though always accompanied by sturdy footmen armed with badges and cudgels. They invited her to such parties as were held at home, and asked her advice on decorations and entertainments. They listened, fascinated, as she related tales of her adventurous life in Europe, and asked for details about the various courts of the Empire. They were quite eager to post her numerous letters, and were delighted when she chose to read the replies to them aloud.

Other snippets of news that cheered her concerned the growing power of the Prince as the Regency progressed, and a single illustration in a women's magazine which showed Fanny Nelson at a royal reception. If the years had been cruel to Emma's beauty, they been worse to Fanny; the woman was as ugly as a toad.

The only annoyance in her placid existence was Horatia, who was furious at having to live in the magistrate's house, and escaped at every chance. Fatima was run ragged keeping up

LOVE OF GLORY

with her. She also wrote angry letters to her Nelson relatives, beseeching them to come take her off her "godmother's" hands. The Matchams were agreeable, but now-Earl William Nelson forbade it. Horatia tearfully blamed Emma, claiming that she was so "disgraceful" that no "decent" family would have anything to do with her. Emma's calm reply that the magistrate certainly counted as "decent" only sent the girl into sulks. All Emma could do was promise that soon this ordeal would be over, and they would return to Calais.

"But when?" Horatia wailed. "When?!"

*****

In June Perry came to visit, and the magistrate's wife politely left them closeted in the drawing room.

"The house is sold," he reported. "As we expected, the price was insufficient to cover the debt. We had already removed the furnishings to a respectable auction house in London, and are selling them piece by piece to obtain the best price. As a result, the debt to Goldsmid is three-quarters gone. Yet, if we continue in this fashion, it may be as much as another six months before the last is cleared. If you wished to hasten the process, you could pawn your jewelry…" He gave her a questioning look.

"Oh no," Emma smiled. "I must save that to live on when we reach Calais. The travails of this last year have taught me some prudence, James."

"I'm delighted to hear it," Perry smiled back, then frowned slightly. "I must tell you, there are other creditors barking at your heels."

"Oh, what now?"

"Smaller debts, I assure you: dressmakers, mostly. Goldsmid insisted that those were your personal debts, and none of his concern. You will have to deal with them eventually."

"Perhaps I can reserve some of my jewels for that."

"Well, let's first see what the furnishings bring." Perry patted her hand reassuringly. "Be certain, your friends have not abandoned you."

Emma caught a hint in that. "How do you mean, James?" she asked.

"Ah, well," he blushed. "Who do you think has been buying your treasures at the auctions?"

"Ah, I see. Will you bring me a list of their names, and which objects they bought, so that I can write and personally thank them?"

"I will. And now I must return to business, which is lively enough, seeing that the Tories are trying to bring me to court on various charges, but never fear; I've defeated them handily before, and will do so again." He kissed her hand formally. "So I take leave of you here in Durance Vile, and shall visit again when I can bring more news."

She saw him out and waved farewell as he stepped into his carriage. Turning back, she saw Horatia grimacing from a window. Annoyed at the girl, Emma tramped back into the house and searched through it until she caught up to Horatia in the parlor.

"What did you mean by making ill faces at Mr. Perry?" she demanded, shaking the girl's arm. "Don't you know what a friend he has been to both of us?"

"Oh, I know all about your 'friends'," Horatia sneered. "Perry's well known for printing a radical paper, that approves of such sins as you lured my father into. Do you plan to seduce him, too, or have you done so already?"

Emma raised a hand, furious, then remembered that she had never struck Nelson's daughter and never intended to. "You fool girl," she snapped instead, giving the girl a good shake. "Can't you tell an honest friend when you see one? And what

LOVE OF GLORY

makes you think that anyone could ever replace Nelson in my heart?"

Horatia opened her mouth, but then had the sense to shut it again. Emma let her go, and the girl fell back onto a chair.

"And have you come to worship 'propriety' so well that you would become a Tory yourself, just to spite me?" Emma demanded. "If so, then you've hitched your wagon to a dying horse, daughter."

"Stop saying that!" Horatia howled. "You are not my mother! You're not! You're not! You're not!"

Emma sighed, seeing that there was no use in trying to talk sense to the girl. "When you've sobered from your tantrum," she said calmly, "you must eventually look in a mirror. Look sometime at any portrait of me in my youth, as well as of Nelson, and you will see the truth for yourself."

"No! No! No!" Horatia sobbed.

Seeing that there was nothing to be done, Emma turned and walked out of the room. Fatima was waiting outside, wringing her hands anxiously.

"She doesn't mean what she says, *Domna*," the maid insisted. "She's only upset at being a *prisonnierre*, for the other girls do tease her. If you wish it, I'll not let her go outside again."

"No," Emma sighed, "let her have such freedom as she can get. She is young, and needs her little adventures. Only keep her safe."

"Gladly, *Domna*." Fatima dropped a quick curtsey, and then hurried into the parlor to comfort Horatia.

Emma went back to the library to write more letters.

Chapter 24
Mother and Daughter

Christmas at the magistrate's house was a merry affair, with a feast of classic roast goose and chestnuts, games for the young children, kissing games under the mistletoe for the older children, the town's small but excellent string quartet playing, and lively dancing. Even Horatia came out of her sulk to join the kissing games and dancing, and Fatima happily shepherded the children.

For presents, Emma gave her hosts and their friends hand-copied sheet-music of various pieces that she remembered, for which they were quite grateful. She gave Horatia a satin scarf, with which the girl was clearly unimpressed. She gave Fatima a small gold brooch, at which the maid was quite affected. Presents that had arrived for Emma consisted of books, hand-knit lace gloves, and a rustic but well-made straw hat trimmed with ribbons.

Her most welcome gift was a small letter from James Perry, consisting of but four words: "Two more months.—James." Emma glanced at Horatia, who was doing her best to be coquettish and coy with a village lad, and decided to keep the news to herself.

LOVE OF GLORY

The New Year began crisp and cold, but as the days progressed they brought increasingly good news from overseas. British and Austrian troops were steadily driving back Napoleon in Europe, despite Britain having to waste troops in America. The shockingly radical new nation there had refused to rejoin Britain to fight Napoleon, possibly because Bonaparte had bribed the United States with the sale of an immense tract of land called the Louisiana Purchase. Attempts to punish the upstart Americans drained troops that could otherwise have been used in Europe. Nonetheless, Napoleon's star was in decline.

At the beginning of March, Emma ordered Fatima to pack all their belongings that weren't being immediately used, and to prepare for departure. This news couldn't be kept from Horatia, so Emma told her of Perry's promise. The girl wavered between frantic impatience to be gone, and sneering distrust of Perry. Emma also informed her hostess of the eventual departure, and gave her the gift of another piece of sheet-music.

Early in the morning of March 6th, a four-wheeled calash drew up at the magistrate's house. The driver, as Emma could see from the window, was once again Alderman Smith. She hurried to fetch Fatima and close the rest of her gear in the trunks, then went looking for Horatia—who, of course, was nowhere to be found. Eventually she sent Fatima to find the girl, and went to the parlor to meet with Smith herself.

"Lady Hamilton, I'm delighted to see you again," he said, though the dismayed look in his eyes belied his words. "Bond has been posted for your release, and if you'll please come with me now, we'll depart."

"My trunks are packed," Emma smiled. "If the porters would but fetch them...?"

A few moments of hauling and a tearful farewell to the magistrate's wife left Emma sitting in the carriage, with the canvas top pulled up, waiting for Fatima and Horatia to return.

LESLIE FISH

She passed the time and avoided fidgeting by asking Smith if he had any news from Perry. In answer, Smith handed her a large paper packet. On opening it, Emma read:

My Dear Lady Hamilton:

"The debt to young Goldsmid is completely paid, and only the bills from the lesser creditors remain. The last of the furnishings have been sold, and I include here enough money to transport you and your household safely to Calais. Beyond this, there is nothing left to give the lesser creditors; I would recommend that you settle in Calais before dealing with them, in the fashion I have previously suggested. Be aware that the next payment of interest upon Horatia's legacy shall not arrive until the 1st of next year. Enclosed upon a separate sheet are, as you asked, the names of the purchasers of your and Nelson's treasures.

Your Ever-Faithful Friend,
James Perry

Emma sighed and folded the letter. Before looking further she asked Smith: "Is there a pressing reason that Perry couldn't deliver this himself?"

"I fear so, madam." Smith gave her a rueful smile. "He is entangled in court, upon another matter. Some notable Tory or other has charged him with libel, again."

"Oh dear. I hope he'll be proven innocent."

"Almost certainly, madam, since the embarrassing facts which Mr. Perry's paper revealed concerning the gentleman are, in fact, true. The case of John Peter Zenger, though it happened in the American colonies, took place before they gained independence—and therefore set a precedent in English law, providing that true statements cannot be considered libelous."

He might have spoken further, but at that moment Fatima came hurrying up, out of breath, dragging a protesting Horatia after her. On seeing Emma waiting in the carriage, the girl realized that this was indeed the day of her liberation and ran to join her. She scrambled in without help, then paused for a moment trying to decide which seat to take: the forward-facing bench, which would put her beside Emma, or the rear-facing seat where she could sit alone. Fatima solved the dilemma by climbing into the calash and taking the rear-facing seat for herself. Horatia sat down, sulking, as far from Emma as she could get on the seat. Emma handed her a wrap without comment. Smith flicked the coach-whip, and the horses set off at a quick trot. They kept up the pace to the borders of Merton town, where Horatia leaned out far enough to make faces and spit.

"*Ma petite*," Fatima chided, "you had best mend your manners before we reach Calais. No one there shall care overmuch about your parentage, but many will care much about your *comportement*."

"I don't care," said Horatia, settling back in the seat and pulling her cloak around her. "I'm ever so grateful to see the last of that place. How soon before we reach Calais?"

Emma ignored both of them and looked further in the packet. Yes, there was a tidy bundle of five-pound notes, crown issue. There was also another paper. She unfolded it and saw that it was, as promised, a list of the buyers from the auction of the Merton house furnishings, listed in order of number and price of purchases.

The name at the top was James Perry.

Emma stared at that entry for long moments, then blinked tears from her eyes and looked further down the list. Yes, there was John Pennington's name, and no less than the Prince of

Wales, and other acquaintances from better days, including Sarah Nelson, and names that Emma recognized as British agents for various royal and noble families of Europe—including Queen Carolina and her daughter. There were lesser amounts in the names of people Emma didn't recognize, but which had addresses of various towns that she and Nelson had passed through in his triumphs. There was a large purchase, of portraits of herself and Nelson, by Lady Hale. There was even a small purchase, of a single small portrait, by Emma Carew.

My friends did remember me, Emma understood, exultant. She hadn't felt this glad in years. She took a deep breath of the sweet early-spring wind, and felt as if she could start her life over again. Yes, once in Calais she would tend to her health and try to restore something of her beauty. She would return to singing, at least enough to make her voice agreeable. She would go out in such English society as Calais afforded, renew old acquaintances and make new ones. She would see about getting Horatia into a proper school and plot to have the girl eventually presented at court.

Buoyed up by her hopes, Emma began to sing one of the Italian airs from her days in Naples. Yes, her tone was rough and badly needed exercise.

"Godmother, do stop that awful racket," Horatia whined, covering her ears.

"I'll sound sweeter with practice," Emma promised. "Meanwhile, you must endure."

She continued on, ignoring Horatia's grimaces, all the way through the countryside to the port of Dover.

By the time they arrived it was nightfall, and her voice was exercised back to a passable sweetness, though it was still coarse on the high notes. Smith drove them straight to the ferry dock, handed the women out of the calash, and began pulling down their trunks. Horatia moaned about the chill of the wind,

LOVE OF GLORY

and Fatima pulled the girl under her cloak. Emma glanced about, noting how few passengers were waiting at this hour.

And then she saw a familiar figure pull away from the small crowd and come toward her. It took a moment to recognize him.

"James!" she breathed, reaching for him. "Oh James, you got free after all. I'm so grateful!"

"Now hush," he said, taking her hands. "I'm only here to make certain you get on that ship."

Emma laughed and embraced him, and he didn't pull away. "I mean, buying the furnishings of Merton house, paying my debt..." she murmured against his neck.

"Bosh," he smiled. "Some of those pieces were chosen by Sir William's impeccable taste, and begged for proper appreciation. I couldn't let them go to some butchers' guildhall."

"So you admit that I didn't furnish Merton house badly," Emma chided.

"'Wisely, but too well'," he paraphrased. "You should have known, before you started, the cost of maintaining a museum."

"If Nelson had lived... Oh, but let us not speak of the past, James. I'm off to start anew in Calais, and I daresay Napoleon's men won't trouble me there."

"No indeed, since British troops have already passed beyond it on their way to Paris... What, hadn't you heard?"

"No! Oh James, that is wonderful news! Will'um's dream is about to come true, all that he worked for..."

"Yes," Perry sighed, "little though England appreciates your part in it. Emma, you must not return. Surely you know there are other creditors waiting for you, and political enemies as well. They'll plot against you so long as Fanny Nelson lives, or that wretched hypocrite William Nelson, I daresay. You were always happier in Europe..."

"Save for those brief years I spent with Charles..."

"Ah, those days are forever gone. Only stay in Calais, where you'll be safe. I'll write to you…"

"And I to you, and to everyone else. Oh, James—"

"Now, go on. The boat is loading, and you'll want decent seating for your little household."

Perry took her arm and firmly led her to the gangplank, then up onto the ship. Fatima and Smith were just coming toward them, and Smith reported: "Everything has been settled in Her Ladyship's cabin, sir, and the passage paid."

"Then there's no more to be done here. We must be off. Farewell, Emma."

Emma hugged him one more time, and then let him go. Perry and Smith marched away down the gangplank, not stopping to turn and wave until they reached the dock. Emma waved back, and watched until they got into the carriage and drove away. She didn't follow Fatima to her cabin at once, but stood at the rail and watched as the ship cast off and pulled away from the dock, knowing in her heart that she was seeing England for the last time.

When the last of the shore lights had faded from sight, she let Fatima lead her to the small, cramped cabin, where Horatia was grumbling about having missed supper and being ever so hungry. Fatima promised to go and fetch the girl something from the ship's galley, and hurried away. Horatia grimaced as Emma pulled off her cloak.

"Who was that man you embraced on the dock?" she asked spitefully. "Another of your lovers?"

Emma wondered if it were even worth the effort of trying to win the girl's affection. "Why, no. Didn't you recognize James Perry? We met, you must know, after I had become the companion of my last great love, your father. He was ever the friend to both of us."

"He's a notorious radical, and you're an adultruh—adult-er-ess!" Horatia stumbled over the words.

LOVE OF GLORY

"Hardly," Emma smiled toothily, "since Sir William quite approved of my affair with Nelson."

"That is not possible!" Horatia cried, knowing even as she said it that she was wrong.

"I stayed with Sir William until his death, and with Horatio afterward until he died. Had he lived, he would surely have divorced Fanny and married me."

"No, no, no!" Horatia wailed, and threw herself onto the bed in a storm of theatrical weeping.

"Deny what you like," Emma went on relentlessly as she pulled off her shoes and stockings. "If you are so determined to be the perfect, proper Tory, then artfully defend your virginity until you have safely married. Bind your husband with as many legal chains as you can, and never so much as look at another man. Then, perhaps, you'll end your days as well off as... Fanny Nelson."

Horatia howled again, and pulled a pillow over her head.

At that point Fatima returned with some tea and hot buttered scones, which were enough to lure Horatia out of hiding. "The ship's officers say we'll reach Calais near midnight," the maid duly reported. "We can hire a fiacre there to take us to the English hotel, and go to the *pension* in the morning."

"Excellent," said Emma, taking one of the scones.

Horatia promptly grabbed three of them for herself, and gave Emma a murderous look.

*****

They arrived at the *pension* the next morning, to find several calling cards waiting. Emma smiled as she took them up, recognizing Perry's manipulative hands at work. Well, she would not disappoint him.

LESLIE FISH

While Fatima settled Horatia into their rooms and unpacked their belongings, Emma sought out the landlady—a mousy little thing named Mrs. Beddoes—and greeted her warmly. She also asked for the use of the family's harpsichord so that she might practice her playing and singing, and spent the next two hours running scales and exercising her voice on solo portions of Haydn's *Nelson Mass*. Next she asked Mrs. Beddoes about proper English schools for young ladies where she might send Horatia. After that, she sent Fatima out with a letter and a large brooch to the best jeweler within walking distance. When Fatima returned with the money, Emma sent her out again to order calling cards from the nearest printer, giving the *pension* as her address.

Finally, she took stock of her clothes. There was no help for it; she must have new dresses for herself, as well as for Fatima and Horatia. The money from the brooch would cover two dresses apiece, but leave nothing over. If she used some of the money Perry had given her for Horatia's school, she would have to live very, very frugally until the interest from Horatia's legacy arrived. No, she would have to sell another piece of jewelry soon. And perhaps she could discreetly ask the Legate about persons wanting documents translated into French or Italian.

Thank heaven that good sweet wines could be bought cheaply in Calais.

Next morning Emma rented a chaise to take the three of them to a local dressmaker for fittings. With her knowledge of cloth qualities she was able to order decent gowns for all of them in a modified Grecian cut and of sturdy but relatively inexpensive materials. After that she took the protesting Horatia to the recommended school, a respectable establishment run by an elderly Anglo-French lady, and enrolled her as a day-student, which was far less expensive than boarding her.

LOVE OF GLORY

After taking Horatia and Fatima home and changing clothes, Emma went calling upon the people who had left her cards. Most of them were quite happy to receive her, shared tea and biscuits for the required quarter-hour, and commented upon how well she looked—though Emma knew that she looked well only in contrast to her earlier self. She left the Legate for last, and was rewarded with an invitation to dinner.

This time dinner was small and relatively informal, with no more than four other guests, and the talk was all of politics. The Coalition of Britain and its allies, Emma was thrilled to hear, was advancing across France and expected to reach Paris by the end of the month. Emma offered to celebrate by entertaining the guests with her singing, and the Legate cautiously allowed it. She sang portions of the *Nelson Mass*, which were received with surprised delight by the guests, and she pressed her advantage by offering to sing for the victory celebration when Paris should be taken. Afterward she quietly asked the Legate for his help obtaining employment as a translator, and he duly promised to give it. She returned home in high good humor, braced by hopes for the future.

An examination of her purse sobered her. No, she could not afford to rent even the most modest of carriages every day, but must walk whenever possible. Yes, she must dine at the *pension* every day that she wasn't invited elsewhere; meals at inns and restaurants were out of the question. She must restrict herself to no more than one bottle of local wine per day. She must either keep to this regimen or sell more of her jewelry, and she could make a good estimate of how little time the price of the gems would allow her. Emma devoutly hoped that the Legate's promise would be kept, and soon.

Next day Horatia went sullenly off to school, on foot, accompanied by Fatima. Emma spent the day paying calls upon all of her local friends whom she could reach on foot, writing and reading letters and practicing on the harpsichord. Horatia returned much improved in temper, and gossiped long with Fatima about the other students and the young men whom they had encountered during the march to and from school. Emma was delighted to receive a letter from the Legate asking her to translate some few documents for a local merchant, though she was disappointed by the proffered fee.

By the end of the week her days had fallen into a pattern of visiting, writing and translating, and she was only mildly worried at the lack of invitations to dinner. Sunday she took Fatima and Horatia to the nearby modest Church of England, and allowed the girl to flirt with the local young men on the way home. She also noted that, although Horatia had continued to write numerous letters to her Nelson relatives, so far there had been no indications that any of them would add to the girl's legacy. Still, Emma considered, her situation was greatly improved.

At the end of the month came wonderful news: the British army had just taken Paris and forced Napoleon to abdicate. The Legate would host a grand celebration in the British quarter, including a concert at which Emma was invited to perform. Delirious with joy, Emma hunted through her clothes for her best gown, decked herself in her choice jewels—including the award Queen Carolina had given her—lavished money on hiring a carriage, and took Fatima and Horatia with her to the festival.

The celebration was small compared to others that Emma had attended years ago, but it was exuberant and spectacular nonetheless. The dinner had to be held outdoors so that every Briton in the city could attend. Even Horatia was impressed. At the concert, Emma sang the selections from the *Nelson Mass* and ended with a rendition of "Rule, Britannia"—including a verse which mentioned Nelson's victories—that brought the huge audience to its feet, cheering. Exhilarated, she even took part in the dancing afterward—usually partnered with grey-bearded merchants and retired officers. When the party ended,

LOVE OF GLORY

half an hour after midnight, Emma was still exuberant despite a persistent ache in her feet. Horatia fell asleep in the carriage, and Fatima had to all but carry her to her room. It was, Emma reflected, such a triumph as she'd not had in more than a dozen years.

*****

Next morning she was woefully ill. At first she thought it was only the after-effect of too much champagne the night before, but by noon the nausea and other symptoms convinced her otherwise, and she sent to the Legate to ask his recommendation for a doctor.

The doctor, a spare man with an enormous medical bag and a nurse in tow, made the usual tests and then asked if she had ever suffered these symptoms before. Emma recalled that, yes, both she and Sir William had endured much the same during their stay in Italy. The doctor frowned and tapped his spectacles on his hand, and finally pronounced his verdict.

"I believe, madame," he said, "that you are suffering from a form of the flux common in Italy. It can remain hidden in the body for years, only to reappear in times of physical stress." He frowned briefly. "It places a great burden upon the liver, also, and in your case I believe, hmmm, that you have already stressed that organ with, ah, immoderate consumption of alcoholic beverages. You must ingest nothing but beef broth and willow-bark tea for not less than five days."

"Oh heavens, I'll starve!"

"Not at all, Madame." The doctor gave her an appraising glance and an ironic smile. "No wine, no liquors, and no solid food for five days. After that I recommend light foods, and no wine for another five days, at least. You would do well to remain on light foods and very little wine, permanently."

LESLIE FISH

"I'll be careful," Emma promised, considering that such a diet would at least be inexpensive to maintain. She cringed at the thought of never tasting sweet pastries again. Surely a little indulgence, every now and then, couldn't hurt.

It took her most of the next fortnight to recover, and ever afterward her stomach remained delicate. She made efforts to maintain her acquaintances in the British quarter, to keep up with her singing and to work at her translations, but found that she tired easily. The translations paid enough to maintain her household in the *pension* but gave her little beyond that. Emma took to studying her jewelry with a critical eye, wondering what she would have to sell next, and then swearing that no, she would hold out until the money from Horatia's legacy came.

At least Horatia seemed to be enjoying school, much though she moaned about the labor of studying, and Emma continued regular contact with her old friends through her letters. James Perry wrote briefly about how trade had improved now that Napoleon was safely exiled on Elba, and also told merry bits of gossip about London's politics. Queen Carolina rejoiced endlessly at Napoleon's downfall, but her daughter remarked that the expense and effort of the long war had drained the Holy Roman Empire to the point where there was serious doubt that it could hold together much longer. Sarah Nelson's infrequent letters spoke crossly of Lord William's growing pomposity and Tory sympathies, and his unwillingness to have anything to do with Horatia, much as Sarah and the Matchams might wish otherwise. Emma's suggestions about arranging for Horatia's presentation had set off a flurry of conflict among the Nelson relatives: the Matchams and Sarah were eager to see it done, but William and Fanny Nelson were absolutely opposed.

True to his word, the Legate often invited Emma to his dinner parties, where he asked her to sing "enheartening songs." That she did, always including at least one solo from the *Nelson Mass*. Though she was not, of course, offered anything

LOVE OF GLORY

so crass as direct payment for her performances, Emma found herself offered an increased number of documents for privately paid translations.

Horatia sneered at Emma for being a "mountebank and a paid singer," after which Emma took the girl—and Fatima—with her to all such entertainments. Though subdued and polite during such excursions—since, indeed, she could not speak in public at her age, not having been formally presented to Society as yet— at home Horatia made snide remarks about "singing for your supper." Past all pretensions to conventionality by now, Emma only laughed—and reminded the girl that in her youth she had also posed for artists, and once been asked to take employment singing at the Spanish Opera. Horatia was always incensed by such references, and retreated in blushing fury to her bedroom.

"She'll get over it, Madame," Fatima promised. "I note that she doesn't scorn the fine dinner gowns you bought her with the translations money."

"I wonder," Emma considered, "if it isn't too early to begin searching for a suitable husband for her."

"Oh yes! Too early by a year, at least," Fatima insisted. "Let us see if we can have her properly presented, first."

Emma wondered if, now that the Coalition had placed Louis XVIII on the throne of France, she could have Horatia presented in the French court. Surely she could prevail upon the Legate for his help. When she wasn't writing translations, practicing her singing or out at parties performing, Emma penned letters to everyone she knew, beseeching whatever help they could summon to insure Horatia's future.

"You've become quite the character here in Calais," Horatia complained one evening as they were dressing for a musicale. "Even my teachers giggle at *La Vielle Anglaise*, Nelson's *relict*, always ranting at how Napoleon must be kept defeated. I swear, if you could find a sword somewhere, you would yet hobble out to the lines to charge him yourself."

"If ever Napoleon returns, and his troops come into Calais, I shall do exactly that," Emma retorted, automatically checking the pouch of jewelry concealed under her petticoats. "What better death could I die than fighting the tyrant, even as Nelson did?"

Horatia had no answer to that, and they departed for the evening's entertainment. Emma outdid herself, singing to the limits of her range, ending with her version of "Rule, Britannia" that brought the audience to their feet, cheering.

"Ah, Madame," Fatima laughed as they rode homeward in a rented barouche. "We may be poor, but we are famous."

"Better so," said Emma. "Riches fade, as we have cause to know, but glory is eternal."

"It has gotten me no better dancing partners," groused Horatia. "No one wanted to dance with me but some baron's second son."

"Patience," Emma smiled. "In another year, you'll be presented to the King. Once you've come out in Society, I daresay there will be first sons willing to dance with you."

"But which king?" Horatia wailed. "Shall I never see England again?"

"Doubtless you will," Emma promised. "And have many offers to dance at the Christmas ball."

*****

The Legate outdid himself for Christmas, inviting everyone in the English quarter to the feast. French champagne and wine and English beer flowed freely, and the dishes were many and plentiful. Emma would have stuffed herself on dainties if she hadn't been obliged to sing. Only when her concert had ended, and the house orchestra began playing for the dancing, did she

LOVE OF GLORY

go to the refreshment table to load her plate. She noticed that Horatia was dancing merrily, not even caring that many of her partners were only merchants' sons, and she reflected upon what she would do with the money when the interest from Horatia's legacy should arrive. She must have a new gown for singing, and a fashionable pelisse, and of course Horatia must have new dresses likewise, and Fatima could do with more as well. Emma toasted her future in pale-gold champagne.

Only on the way home, as a cold rain began to fall, did she begin to feel unwell. Horatia, happy for once, was chatting merrily about some English baronet's third son who had 'great prospects', and didn't notice Emma fading. Once home, Fatima spent an hour settling Horatia for the night before coming to assist Emma, and by then Emma was being sick in the chamber-pot. Fatima intoned remonstrances about indulging in too much champagne while she helped Emma into bed, and went to fetch a soothing tisane.

By next morning Emma's indisposition was worse, and Fatima fetched the doctor. He examined her carefully, peered at her eyes, and pulled a long face. "It is as I told you before," he said. "The flux returns, and is placing much stress upon your liver. I shall leave directions concerning your diet, which you must follow faithfully."

He went out to have a long discussion with Fatima, while Emma sagged in the piled pillows, patted her jewelry-bag reassuringly, and sank into plans for Horatia's future.

Despite the numerous cups of beef broth and willow bark tea, Emma's condition did not improve. She was often feverish, and was generally too weak to leave her bed. New Year's and Twelfth Night passed with no improvement, and Fatima quietly wrote letters to all of Emma's friends whose addresses she knew. Even Horatia, knowing that the situation was serious, stayed home from school to help Fatima tend to the household.

LESLIE FISH

On the third Sunday after New Year's, Emma was roused by the sound of church bells, and opened heavy-lidded eyes to see her mother sitting in the corner, calmly knitting lace.

"Are you a ghost or a fever dream?" Emma asked, annoyed at how rusty her voice sounded.

"Why can I not be both?" Mrs. Cadogan replied. "A ghost would find it easier to appear to one who is halfway to heaven already."

"Am I so ill as that?" Emma asked, growing alarmed for the first time.

"Aye, indeed. Ye're no longer young, my gel, and any ailment will shake ye as a terrier worries a rat."

"Shall I live?"

"Who can say? In either case, ye must take some care for the future o' yer daughter, and yer soul. Have ye written a testament yet?"

"I hadn't thought of it," Emma admitted, reaching one weak hand to pat the bag of jewelry pinned under her chemise. "I have so little to leave, after all."

"Well, whate'er ye have, make effort to dispose of it rightly. And ye might send for the vicar, in any case, to clear yer soul. Ye've not done so for awhile, ye know."

"I'll do it," Emma whispered, "though I haven't had opportunity to gain many sins since I was last in church."

Then the sound of approaching footsteps distracted her. Fatima came in, bearing a tray with a steaming mug of willow bark tea, which she set down on the bed-table. As she stepped back, Emma saw that her mother's shade had departed. She accepted the mug, and Fatima's help with drinking from it, and said nothing about her ghostly visitor.

She did, however, ask Fatima to send for the vicar. Fatima agreed and departed quickly, not quite hiding tears. By the time the clergyman appeared Emma was feeling clear-headed, though weak as water. She endured the usual formalities with as good humor as she could manage, and then remembered to tell him that—in the event of her death—she wanted her body taken home to Paddington and buried in the cemetery there beside her mother.

The week's end brought a surprising visitor: James Perry, accompanied by Alderman Smith. Smith duly reported that the interest on Horatia's legacy had arrived, and the money was properly deposited in Emma's account at the local bank. Emma smiled and thanked him, then turned a significant look to Perry, and Smith had the good sense to depart.

"James," she began before he could speak, "I must make arrangements for Horatia's future, and Fatima's. Can you make assurances that, should I die unexpectedly, what money I have shall go to them and not to any creditors left in England?"

"I've already arranged it," Perry admitted, taking her near hand and running his thumb over the knuckles. "I settled most of the creditors before I came here."

"Ah, thank you. Yes, I'll keep my promise and not return to England, but Horatia must. She wants a proper coming out, and opportunity to find a proper husband."

"Thinking of marriage already, is she?" Perry sighed. "A most proper young miss she has made herself, from what I hear: a very Tory in composure, striving to be the opposite of you. Ah well, all children disappoint their parents in some fashion."

Emma thought of her own mother, and was obliged to agree. *If only I'd had sense, as she wished...* "And what of Fatima?" she remembered. "I daresay Horatia would hate to be parted from her..."

Perry shook his head. "She was not well received in England, and would do better to remain here. Nubian or not, an experienced maid to a famous lady could find herself a good position in France. Horatia will find loving companions enough among the Matcham children."

"I'll ask her what she wishes, then, and I'll give Horatia my collection of Nelson's letters," Emma promised. She noted that familiar hot, feverish feeling creeping up on her again, and wondered when next she'd waken from it. "Will you stay awhile in Calais, James?" she asked.

"Aye, for some few days." His voice sounded oddly roughened. "I shall visit again."

He clasped her hand for a long moment, and then quietly took his leave. Emma gazed at the clouded window, gathering her thoughts, and then reached under her chemise. It took long moments and surprising effort to pull free her bag of jewelry, longer still to make her choice, close the bag again and conceal it under the pillow. Finally she reached for the little hand-bell on the bed-table and managed to ring it.

When Fatima entered, looking oddly damp, as if she'd just washed her face, Emma bade her sit down by the bed and bend close. "Fatima," she said quietly, "if you were no longer my maid—"

"Oh, say not so, Madame!" Fatima wailed.

"But where would you go? What would you wish to do, if you could?"

Fatima wiped her eyes, hiccoughed, and thought for a while. "I would...buy a bolt of good cloth," she said, "and return to Nubia, to the capital city, and rent a shop and hire some good sewing-girls, and make dresses for the quality folk there. I know enough of the fashions in Europe and Britain that I would be the most fashionable of dressmaker in all the land. What is a modest living here in Calais would make me wealthy there."

"Ah," Emma smiled, impressed with the woman's knowledge and practicality, "and would this bring enough to make you such a dressmaker?"

She pulled her hand from under the covers and held it out, revealing what it held: a necklace of gold and pearls that Sir William had bought for her nearly twenty years past.

LOVE OF GLORY

"Oh..." Fatima whispered, fascinated by the sight. "Yes, that and more. Oh, yes. Yes, Madame, it would."

"Take it, then." Emma dropped the necklace into Fatima's astonished hands. "In fact, put it on now and conceal it beneath your shift. When next Mr. Perry visits, or Mr. Smith, I'll ask him...to arrange your passage, when it is time... Ah, meanwhile, would you bring me more medicinal tea? I confess, I am feeling feverish..."

"Yes, Madame." Fatima hastily tucked the necklace into the bosom of her dress, got up and hurried out.

Emma leaned back on the pillows again, feeling weak but remarkably unburdened.

"That was wisely done, Emma," said a familiar voice.

Emma turned her head and saw, without surprise, that Sir William was sitting in his traditional chair in the corner. That was impossible, of course; the chair had long since been sold. *Can a chair have a ghost?* she wondered, *or can a ghost create a chair?*

"I would recommend, though," Sir William went on, "that you write a letter stating that you yourself gave the necklace to Fatima, in exchange for her many years of faithful service. Otherwise, the first jeweler to whom she tries to sell it will claim it to be stolen and send her to prison, whilst keeping the gems for himself."

"Yes," Emma murmured, "I'll do that, the moment I have the strength. ...Oh, Will'um, are you angry with me? For disregarding your advice, for wasting my money..."

"You harmed none but yourself," he shrugged. "No, I'm not angry, but only grieved for your suffering."

"I'm free of it now... Sir William, am I dying?"

"You are close to it, but not yet there. You surely have time to make right what you can."

"I shall do that," Emma promised, then considered her feebleness. "Should I send for James, to witness...?"

"Ask rather for Mr. Smith, who waits in the parlor for any message you would send." Sir William cocked his head. "And I believe I hear Fatima returning with your tea."

"Ah, don't leave me, Will'um!" Emma begged, hearing the maid's footsteps approaching.

"Don't fear," the ghost smiled. "You will see me again, soon enough."

Fatima opened the door, and Sir William—and his chair—vanished like a blown-out candle flame.

Emma drank the tea until she felt stronger and more clear-headed, then asked for a pen and inkwell, paper and wax and her seal, a tray to write on, and Alderman Smith to come and be her witness. Fatima wiped her eyes, and hastened to fetch what was asked.

It took a long time, weak as she was, for Emma to write the paper for Fatima. It took longer still to write her will concerning her remaining property and Horatia. Afterward she felt terribly tired, and wished only to sleep.

She awoke some measureless time later, seeing sunlight peeping through the windows at a different angle than she recalled. *Have I slept away all the day?* she wondered. It took amazing effort simply to turn her head and see Fatima, now wearing a different dress, drowsing in a chair by the fireplace. It took more effort to call the maid's name. Fatima started awake, then smiled tearfully.

"Oh, Madame, I thought you would never wake. Pray let me bring in the others."

"Not yet," Emma managed to say. "Just Horatia."

She let her eyes drift closed, for just a moment she thought, but when she opened them she saw Horatia standing by her bed. The girl looked pale, and her eyes were red and swollen. "Godmother?" she asked fearfully.

LOVE OF GLORY

Emma sighed, giving up the struggle to make Horatia acknowledge her. "Come closer," she whispered, "I've somewhat to tell you."

Horatia did so. Emma made the prodigious effort to reach under her pillow and pull out the bag containing her jewelry. "Here," she said. "These are for you. Keep them safe. Fatima can tell you the history of each of them. She'll also tell you where to find the packet of your father's letters."

Horatia gingerly took the bag, opened it, and gaped at what she saw inside.

"Keep them close," Emma whispered. "Pin the bag inside your chemise, and let no one see it. Keep them against calamity."

"I didn't realize..." the girl whispered, staring at her. "All this time, you kept these for me?"

"Trust James Perry," Emma went on, not bothering to correct her. "He'll see to it your money is kept safe for you. I'll have him send for your cousins, who will take you back to England and care for you. Sarah, the Matchams... Once you are no longer encumbered by me, they will love you well enough... And James will make certain you want for nothing. He is an honorable man, and did well by me."

Horatia frowned for a moment, then leaned closer and asked quietly: "Godmoth... Mother, tell me. If you had your life to live over again, knowing what you now know, would you have changed...anything?"

Emma pondered the question, realizing that this was a far better confession than she had made to the vicar. "I would have been more careful about money," she admitted, "And taken better care for my health..."

"And nothing else?" Horatia insisted.

"No," Emma smiled. "I have known beauty and love and glory. I have done my part in changing the world, and... I have known a great passion. I have known and loved the finest men of this age. I would change nothing of that. Nothing."

Horatia drew back, a riot of emotions playing across her face, and finally burst into tears. "I—I'll fetch the others," she stammered, and then turned and fled.

"Can you not drink some more willow bark tea?" Fatima had appeared at her side, holding the cup for her.

Emma managed a few small sips, and then the door opened softly to admit Alderman Smith, the doctor and Perry, all wearing solemn faces. Horatia's weeping could be heard from outside in the hall. The doctor formally lifted Emma's wrist, felt at her pulse, then shook his head and went back out into the hallway, closing the door behind him. Emma managed to lift a finger and beckon Perry closer.

"Take care of Horatia," she whispered. "Send for Earl William to fetch her to England. If he'll not take her in, the Matchams surely will... Did you read the will I gave to Smith?"

"I have done," he answered, almost as quietly. "The interest on her money will go to whoever fosters her. If the Earl is too proud to take it, the Matchams will not be. In any case, she'll have it all when she marries. Have no fears for your daughter, Emma."

"Good..." Emma found it hard to draw a deep breath. "I wish to be buried beside my mother, in Paddington," she whispered.

"It will be a long journey, but I will see what can be done," Perry promised.

"Thank you... You've been a good friend, James," she managed.

"Always, my lovely Emma." He lifted her hand and held it patiently.

Reassured, she let her eyes fall closed. Yes, everything was settled, and there was no further duty she owed. She felt no

LOVE OF GLORY

pain, only a profound fatigue—and a sense of something, or someone, waiting.

In her mind's eye she could see her bedchamber and everyone in it, but that seemed to be the wrong place. She remembered Merton in its days of glory, and that seemed more fitting. She sat again in the garden, just as the roses were blooming, knowing who would come.

And yes, there he was, striding down the long flagstone path toward her. Ah, but this time his right sleeve was no longer empty, and his right eye was clear and bright. She got up and ran to him, and he met her midway down the path, took her into a strong embrace and kissed her fiercely enough to leave her breathless.

"Home to stay," he said, smiling as brightly as the sun. "At last, we have come home to stay."

"Oh, love," she panted, "swear we'll never be parted again!"

"Never," he promised, and kissed her once more.

Emma closed her eyes and sank willingly into the bright darkness.

*****

News of Emma's death spread through the British quarter of Calais with remarkable speed, and a surprising number of naval officers followed her hearse to Saint Pierre's churchyard, where the service was said. The officers, passing her grave, tossed in flowers and bits of ribbon, and many of them walked away singing snatches from the *Nelson Mass* as they departed.

The chill February wind whipped the clothes of the remaining mourners, and the sky threatened rain. Earl William Nelson fidgeted as the vicar walked away and the sextons stepped forward, impatient to be done and gone. "If we miss the mail-packet," he grumbled, "who knows how long we shall be stuck in this wretched town? I would never have thought the ferry service to be so unreliable."

"The weather has been most contrary," Perry commented neutrally. "It halted shipping for days, keeping Emma's wish for her burial from being be honored."

"Just as well," grumbled William. "Best she be buried here in Calais, lest admirers make a scene at her grave. Wherever did the sailors find flowers at this time of year?"

"I found them, and passed them around," Horatia spoke up. "There are always some sort of flower to be found in the market here." She pulled her cloak around her, looking as slender as a reed in her dark mourning dress, and surreptitiously patted the spot below her bodice where the jewelry-bag hung concealed.

"Do not expect to find any in England," the Earl huffed. "Not unless your cousins have put up a hothouse since last I visited."

"She is not to stay with you and Sarah, then?" Perry asked, sounding only mildly interested.

"Certainly not." William Nelson pursed his lips as if he'd bitten into a lime. "It wouldn't be fitting for an officer of the Church to keep a...a relative of her status in the house. She shall go to the Matchams."

"They have always liked me," Horatia murmured. "I'll be happy there."

"That is rather a pretentious headstone, don't you think?" the Earl rattled on, ignoring her. "And who ordered that lengthy quote in Latin? '*Quae Calesiae Via in Gallica vocata Et in domo...*'"

"I did," Perry replied. "Her husband would have wished it."

"Well, enough, then. We have settled with Emma in full measure. Come along, Horatia."

He waved an imperious hand at the girl, turned and strode off toward his waiting carriage. Horatia paused only a moment to cast a glance at the sextons dutifully shoveling dirt into the grave, then hurried after the Earl. Perry watched them go, saying nothing.

"It be just as well, monsieur," Fatima said quietly, "that the mademoiselle shall not live in his household. That man is cruel in his pride."

"A pride the wretched Tory does not deserve," Perry responded. "But what of you, Fatima? Will you stay in France?"

"No, Mr. Perry. I shall return to the *pension* and pack all that remains, then hire a cart south and take ship for Egypt. And I thank you again for your assistance with the necklace."

"It was only fitting. Faithfulness deserves rewards in this world."

"You too have been faithful, in your fashion," Fatima smiled.

"Ah, so was Emmaçin her fashion." Perry sighed, glanced again at the headstone, and cast a glance up at the cloud-marbled sky. "Surely that will count in her favor in the next world, if not in this."

The two watched for a moment more, then turned away and followed the others out of the churchyard.

EPILOGUE

Emma Carew faded into genteel anonymity as she wished.

Earl William Nelson lived until 1835 and died without male issue. His British titles passed to Thomas Bolton, his sister's son, and his Italian dukedom of Bronte passed to his daughter, Charlotte.

Horatia Nelson lived with her Matcham cousins until she married the Reverend Phillip Ward. She bore him ten children, and died in comfortable obscurity in 1881.

James Perry continued to publish the *Morning Chronicle*, denouncing Tory politics and fighting off charges of libel, until his death in 1821.

Of Fatima nothing was ever heard again.

The churchyard of Saint Pierre's was converted into a timber-yard in the 1830s, and Emma's tombstone soon disappeared. By the end of the 19th century, her grave could no longer be found.

Her various portraits, in oil-paint, etching and sculpture, remain in museums across Europe to this day.

-END-

ABOUT THE AUTHOR

LESLIE FISH

Leslie Fish is best known for her songs about space travel, StarTrek, and the Society for Creative Anachronism. She has been a political activist alongside of Phil Ochs, a member of the IWW, and was one of the many authors that contributed to the Merovingen Nights series of books begun by C. J. Cherryh. Leslie Fish was also the inspiration for the character Tarma in the books by Mercedes Lackey, and the two wrote numerous songs for the *Oathbound* and *Oathbreaker* storylines.

One of Leslie's greatest contributions to the interface of music and literature has been to set dozens of Rudyard Kiplings ballads and ditties to music on the recordings *Cold Iron, The Undertaker's Horse,* and *Our Fathers of Old.*

Her most recent publication is the fantasy novel *Of Elven Blood.*

Leslie Fish lives, composes, and performs in Phoenix, AZ. She breeds cats for intelligence, and is always happy to find a good home for kittens.

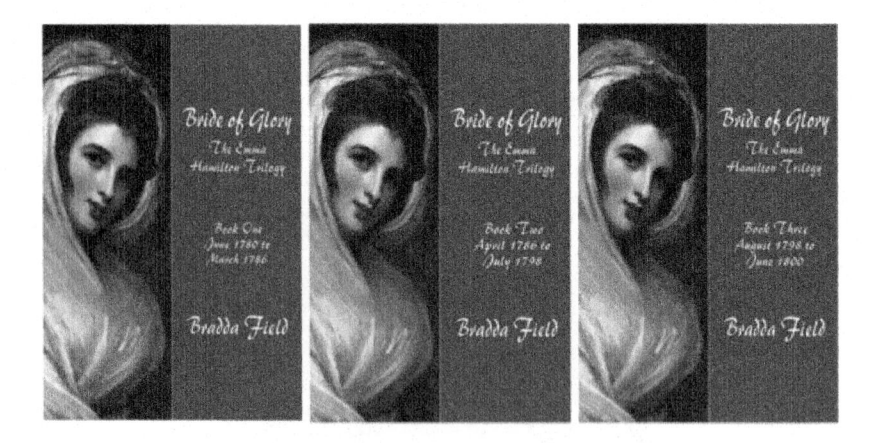

Bride of Glory
The Story of Emma Hamilton
by
Bradda Field

Bride of Glory is an extraordinarily vivid, memorable account of the Welsh country girl, Emy Lyon, who became Lady Emma Hamilton and the lover of Admiral Horatio Nelson during the Napoleonic Wars and beyond.

Don't miss all three novels!

Book 1 - June 1780 to March 1786
Book 2 - April 1786 to July 1798
Book 3 - August 1798 to June 1800

WWW.FIRESHIPPRESS.COM

All Fireship Press and Cortero Publishing books are available directly through www.FireshipPress.com, amazon.com and via leading wholesalers and bookstores throughout the U.S., Canada, and Europe.

DON'T MISS ALL OF THE EXCITING BOOKS IN THE SIR SIDNEY SMITH SERIES BY
TOM GRUNDNER

THE MIDSHIPMAN PRINCE

How do you keep a prince alive when the combined forces of three nations (and a smattering of privateers) want him dead? Worse, how do you do it when his life is in the hands of a 17 year old lieutenant, an alcoholic college professor, and a woman who has fired more naval guns than either of them? The first book in the Sir Sidney Smith nautical adventure series.

HMS DIAMOND

After surviving the horrors of the destruction of Toulon, Sir Sidney is given a critical assignment. British gold shipments are going missing. Even worse, the ships are literally disappearing in plain sight of their escorts and the vessels around them. The mystery must be solved, but to do that Sir Sidney must unravel a web of intrigue that leads all the way to the Board of Admiralty.

THE TEMPLE

Napoleon is massing ships, troops, and supplies at Toulon and a number of other ports. He is clearly planning an invasion; but an invasion of who, where, and when, no one knows. The key is a captured message, but it's encoded in a way that has never been seen before. From a dreary prison in Paris, to an opulent palace in Constantinople, to the horror of the Battle of the Nile—*The Temple* will take you on a wild ride through 18th Century history.

AND DON'T MISS THE FOURTH BOOK IN THIS THRILLING SERIES

ACRE

From Fireship Press
www.FireshipPress.com

All Fireship Press books are available directly through our website, amazon.com, via leading bookstores from coast-to-coast, and from all major distributors in the U.S., Canada, the UK, Europe, and soon Australia.

**For the Finest in
Nautical and Historical
Fiction and Nonfiction**

www.FireshipPress.com

Interesting • Informative • Authoritative

All Fireship Press books are now available
directly through www.FireshipPress.com, Amazon.com
and as electronic downloads.

CPSIA information can be obtained
at www.ICGtesting.com
Printed in the USA
LVOW04s1454260116
472355LV00018B/887/P